# CUT
## AND
# RUN

# CUT AND RUN

by

## Rupert Penny

Writing as Martin Tanner

RAMBLE HOUSE

©1941 by Rupert Penny

ISBN 13: 978-1-60543-387-5

ISBN 10: 1-60543-387-X

Cover Art: Gavin L. O'Keefe
Preparation: Fender Tucker

# CUT AND RUN

# I

IF I HADN'T STOPPED on the Portsmouth Road for half an hour that November morning, I should have missed the most exciting fortnight of my life. It might so easily not have happened, too, but an unexpected burst of sunlight tempted me, and as I am still alive I will tell the story.

My name is Arnold Dane, and at the time I shall speak of I was just twenty-eight years old. Six months previously I had been left fifty thousand pounds by a relation of my mother, and since then had wandered about Europe enjoying my freedom. I had always suspected that teaching Latin in preparatory schools wasn't the work for which I was best suited; the moment I was in a position to do so I bade farewell to Arthur Milsom, M.A., his £120 per annum in addition to board-residence and laundry, and his stultifying ideas about discipline. When I agreed to relinquish my salary he was more than pleased to see the last of me, and within a week I was in Belgium. From Antwerp I walked to Lyons, which took me the whole of June. Thence, for no particular reason, I made my way by train to Budapest, looked in at Belgrade and Tirana, crossed to Otranto from Valona, and returned at a snail's pace in the heat of the year.

I had now been back in England five weeks, and was beginning to wonder what to do with myself. All sorts of vague plans were tentatively formed in my head, examined, and thrown aside, most of them because they were too fantastic. One day I would be for buying an aeroplane, learning to fly it, and then attempting a true round-the-world flight, the full 25,000 odd miles. The next it occurred to me that I might do worse than engage a cricket professional in the hope of attaining my county side the following summer. Averagely selfish speculations, it will be perceived, and foolish too: yet never in my maddest moments did I think of arranging to be hunted for my life by—among others—a distinguished mental specialist, an American gunman, and a classically-proportioned artists' model. Fate must take the credit for that.

I had spent the week-end with friends just the other side of Haslemere, and was now on my way back to town alone in a hired car. My own had been "borrowed" by my host's sister the previous evening, Sunday, and badly damaged, which explains how I came to be driving an old-fashioned Rolls-Royce. It was the best the local garage could do, and—as events proved—a satisfactory best.

The sunlight, I repeat, induced me to draw up just the London side of Ripley, where the Portsmouth Road is bounded on both sides by open moorland. I got out, stretched my legs, looked round, and noticed away to the right a pond, reed-grown and lifeless. Now, ever since I chased butterflies as a child I've always liked the smell of reeds in marshland, and I resolved suddenly to find out if after a lapse of years the scent had changed.

I was gone about twenty-five minutes, I suppose, or rather more. Upon my return I climbed into the car again, pressed the self-starter, and heard the engine stir into obedient activity. Then I became aware that my feet were not only muddy but really damp. (I should say, perhaps, that other people frequently tell me I am absent-minded, and I agree that in general I am, if less so than they imagine.) For a moment I thought about changing my shoes, but decided not to: I had only the haziest recollection of where to find the keys of my case. The renewal of a childhood memory—the reeds, or perhaps it was the marsh, smelt just the same—had unaccountably made me thoroughly pleased with life, and I declared my decision aloud.

"I don't care twopence about wet feet," I informed the windscreen. "I'm grown up, aren't I?"

The only answer I detected was the well-bred purr of the engine, and it was all I looked for.

I began the remainder of the journey home at a leisurely rate, but a mile or two further on I halted again. In front of me, but on the opposite side of the road, had been another car drawn up, a blue Chrysler saloon, and three people standing by it. Two were men, and the third a girl in a fur coat and a close-fitting brown hat. They had glanced up from their conversation at my approach, and one of the men stepped forward with his hand upraised as I went by.

I pulled up a little way past him and waited, expecting to be asked for petrol, and quite willing to fetch him some if he behaved nicely. At a nearer view he proved to be an elderly man of medium height, dressed in a black coat with an astrakhan collar and a wide-brimmed black hat which caused his face to be deeply shadowed. His features were not easy to make out, and that I noticed them in fair detail means, I think, that I must have gazed at him with considerable rudeness.

"I apologize for troubling you, sir," he started, in a soft cultured voice, "but the fact is that I'm in rather a difficulty."

'No' I thought, 'no petrol for you. I don't like the shape of your nose, the yellowish colour of your cat's-eyes, nor the length of your front teeth. I wish I hadn't stopped—you'll spoil my mood if I see very much of you, my man.'

"The position is," he went on, as I said nothing, "that I've had the misfortune to lose my ward. She's a dear girl, but subject to loss of memory upon occasion, and when that happens she's liable to do the most erratic things. Last night, for instance, she crept out of the house in her sleeping attire, and I'm really desperately anxious about her. The police have been informed, but they don't somehow take the same interest in the matter as myself. I wonder"—here pausing to regard me with a cold scrutiny which went ill with his garrulous way of talking—"yes, I wonder if you would happen to have seen her? A young lady with red hair, probably arrayed in blue pyjamas and bedroom slippers."

"I'm sorry, but I certainly haven't seen anyone like that about," I told him curtly.

"Oh dear, I'm disappointed—I was hoping you might have done."

He nodded solemnly to himself, delicately scratched the end of his nose with a gloved hand, and gave me another speculative look.

"May I be unconventional?" he asked with unexpected vigour. "May I suggest that you allow me a glance inside your car? I do hope you understand?"

"Of course," I said, though in truth I was annoyed. Why should he think I was harbouring his halfwitted, half-apparelled ward?

"You'd better come round the other side," I added. "That door doesn't open."

Saying nothing, but again nodding his broad black hat, he began to move round the front of the Rolls with small shuffling steps: and at that moment the apparently impossible took place.

The car had at some time been fitted with a glass partition dividing front and rear, and a speaking-tube arranged between, one end just behind the driver's head. As the soft-tongued stranger rounded the silver bonnet, and I slightly turned my face to follow his progress, an agonized voice spoke into my left ear.

"Please don't let him in!" it implored in a distorted whisper. *"Please!"*

For a fraction of a second there leapt into my mind a sentence from Milsom's *First History Primer:* 'The maiden Joan of Arc became daily more troubled by the Voices, which were all about her in the air, she said, twittering like little birds'. I had stopped thinking about that before black-coat's body was more than half way towards me, though, and tackling the problem. Would I let him in or wouldn't I? If the entreaty not to do so were imaginary, then presumably I had gone mad, since I knew I wasn't drunk; but if it was real—though I didn't see how it could be, having forgotten all about the speaking-tube—then I was being asked for help by someone who sounded urgently in need of it, and had only a moment to make my decision.

Had the stranger been less displeasing to me as a person, I'm sure I should never have been quick enough; but I definitely didn't like him, and almost before I realized what I was doing the gear-lever slipped into place, my hand released the brake, and the Rolls lurched forward. I caught one glimpse of startled eyes and open mouth, and then he was yards away.

"And now drive like hell!" came the voice down the tube. "You've got about a minute's start while he turns, but he can do eighty."

I nodded agreement as the car gathered speed, and began to feel the conversation was one-sided. I could be spoken to but I couldn't answer, and to remedy this I put one hand behind me, sliding back the glass panel which shut off my unseen passenger. This immediately provoked a response.

"Do go faster!" commanded the girl, her sex now recognizable in her tones. "Burn the road up."

"Why, are they after us already?" I enquired: it seemed an apposite question.

"Not yet, but they soon will be if you don't hurry."

"All right, all right!" I said. "I'm doing my poor best. If you happen to be real, will you please pull my hair so I'll know? Not too hard."

"Certainly—satisfied?"

"Yes, thanks. And who is it we're running away from?"

"Dr. Paul," came the unhelpful answer. "Lord, I can see them! Are you flat out?"

"Absolutely—sixty-nine steady."

As a matter of fact, I was rather proud of this: the owner had assured me that he was the only person alive who could get more than sixty-three out of the old car.

"Damn—not enough! They're creeping up—what can we do?"

"Sixty-nine," I replied. "I'm doing it, though I'm sure I don't know why. Is it important to get away?"

At this the girl laughed, but a little unsteadily, I thought.

"Was there a small man in a slouch hat and glasses?" she asked in turn.

"Yes," I agreed: the description fitted the person to whom the man she called Dr. Paul had been talking by the blue Chrysler.

"Well, his name's Nick, and when they get close enough he'll shoot your tyres in. Then you'll know it's important. Have you got a gun with you?"

"No—sorry. How far are they?"

(By now, gradually, I was entering into the spirit of the thing. This talk of guns and shot tyres made it seem that we really were being chased. Previously I had not quite believed it, in spite of the rushing roadside and the weight of the car against my hands on every curve.)

"Can't see—they're round a corner. No, here they come. About three hundred yards—you're keeping the distance. I say, you know how to drive!"

"Don't be too sure," I answered. "I never set eyes on this bus till this morning, and I was brought up on a two-seater Morris."

Nevertheless, I wasn't displeased with my performance so far. We had roared through Esher without mishap, taking not the least account of built-up areas and speed-limits, but not long after I was set a momentary poser by two carts going in opposite directions and a parked lorry. I managed things to my own satisfaction if not to theirs, to judge by the snatch of shouting which reached my ears as the girl finished, but I lost a certain amount of my lead.

"I'm afraid I can't keep this up," I said. "We'll be getting into the Kingston traffic soon, though, and he'd never dare shoot then, would he?"

The reply was an urgent yell to swerve: I did so instantly, and then came a venomous crack which sounded very like a rifle. Instinctively I ducked, but in the midst of the action realized that it would do me no good: what I had to guard against was the effect of a bullet through one of the back wheels, not through my head. I found myself gripping the wheel as if it were a life-belt, and I needed nobody to tell me that my forehead was moist.

"Missed!" exclaimed my passenger triumphantly, and then gave a gasp. At the same moment, it seemed to me, there was another report, followed immediately by a tinny thud.

"That wasn't you he hit, was it?" I asked.

"No—petrol tank, I think. I only wish I'd got a gun too—I'd show them something. God, mind that bus!"

Again I swerved as a double-decker appeared suddenly from a side turning, rounded it with an inch to spare and a squeal of protesting rubber, and breathed again. There would have been a nasty mess if I had hit the thing.

"Oh, good!" exclaimed the voice behind a second later. "It's got in their way now—he can't shoot for a bit. Keep going and we may be all right, but we're losing a lot of petrol. Does it matter?"

"Not yet," I answered. "There's six gallons to play with, according to the gauge."

"Still, don't take the by-pass—get into Kingston. If we're far enough ahead at the market square we can probably slip them. I say, this is rather fun—do you mind?"

"Not yet," I repeated, regretfully braking to negotiate the roundabout at the beginning of the by-pass. In doing this I lost a few precious seconds, and then whirled onwards beneath a bridge, past a recreation-ground on the left, and soon along by the reservoirs. My ears were strained for the sound of another shot, but none came, and what attention my eyes could spare from the road ahead was directed to the possible presence of policemen. I saw none, but that didn't entirely reassure me, especially as we were still touching fifty when we swept by the river and began the entrance to the town itself.

"You're doing all right!" I was told. "They're a long way off—you'll easily get round. Now, follow my directions, and don't make any mistakes."

For five minutes I submitted myself to her orders, and at the end of that time she declared that I could slow to normal pace.

"There's a garage on the left about two hundred yards away. Drive straight in and dump the car, and then we'll make for the station—I know a short cut. At least, you needn't come, but you'll have to lend me some money. Will you, please? I haven't got a penny."

"I could let you have one," I admitted. "Maybe more if you look honest, but I haven't seen you at all yet. That's the worst of these outside driving-mirrors—they don't satisfy one's curiosity. Tell me, have you got red hair?"

"Yes, only I call it auburn."

"And blue pyjamas?"

"Yes, but they don't show. I'm quite respectable, really, except that I haven't any shoes."

"Good lord! Aren't your feet sore?"

"Very. They're still bleeding a bit."

Something in what she said, either the words or the tone, made me fully comprehend at last that this business was deadly serious, for her if not for me. I suddenly felt glad that I had not refused to help, whoever she might be and whatever the cause and nature of her trouble.

## II

**I** STOPPED AT THE GARAGE indicated by my passenger and she got out, saying it would be better for her not to be seen. I took the opportunity to glance at her for the first time myself, though, and was agreeably surprised. Quite what I had been expecting is doubtful, but I needn't have worried: the stowaway was entirely presentable, even in obviously ill-fitting clothes. Short rather than tall, with cropped auburn hair, deep blue eyes, and a cheerful smile, she struck me as being definitely attractive. I judged that she was about eighteen, though there I was wrong.

"Don't sit still staring," she said, after a moment. "You'll have plenty of time for that presently—get rid of the car."

"Yes ma'am," I agreed, and did so, giving a false name. I asserted, untruthfully, that I had just come from Epsom, and would return for the Rolls later in the day. The story might conceivably put Dr. Paul off the scent, I thought, if he should chance to make enquiries. I see now that the ruse was utterly childish, but I didn't yet grasp the kind of man I was up against.

"And what next?" I asked outside, suitcase in hand. "It's about time I knew your name, too—mine's Arnold Dane."

"Mine's Rhona French," was the answer. "And I'm sorry if you think I'm bossy," she went on, with a friendly smile, "but I understand the mess I'm in, and you don't—yet. I've got to get clear of Kingston, and the sooner the better. Will you lend me some money? Do I look honest enough?"

I shook my head very solemnly.

"You aren't leaving me out now," I told her, "I refuse to spend the rest of my life wondering why I was once shot at on a Monday morning. Look here, I've got a furnished flat in town—would that be any good? It's quite private. At least—that is—"

Again she smiled.

"Don't flounder," she said gently. "I know what you mean. Where is it?"

"Netting Hill Gate."

"Yes, that would do—if you really don't mind? I ought to warn you that you may get on the wrong side of the police as well as Dr. Paul, though."

"Oh, hang trifles!" I replied airily. "Unless they were all asleep just now, I'm that already. But what about your feet?"

She nodded, glancing down at them: bare and stained and very small.

"I'll have to get some shoes, won't I? Do you think you could possibly buy me a pair? Size three, and as cheap as you like—I'll look after your case. And I wish I'd something to cover this up with," she added, surveying her bright red woollen jumper. It not only clashed abominably with her hair but was clearly far too small for her, and the brown tweed skirt she wore as clearly far too large.

"Yes, I've seen outfits I like better," I agreed. "I'll do my best if you tell me which way to go."

In the circumstances I think I succeeded rather well, though not without some embarrassment. I purchased a pair of brown shoes, a macintosh, guessing at the size, and some stockings. As well I invested in a beret, because it seemed a good idea to cover her conspicuous head, and on chance I bought a bag of buns and some fruit.

"Thank you *very* much," said Rhona when I got back, and found her to my relief still in about the same place. Secretly I had been a little afraid that she might have vanished, or that I would encounter Dr. Paul and his cold stare. Hurriedly she donned the macintosh and hat, and then the shoes, but the stockings she pushed into a pocket.

"Oughtn't you to put them on?" I suggested.

"Not now. There's a nosy woman in a window over the road, and she's seen far too much already. And anyway, I couldn't keep them up unless you remembered to buy some garters as well."

"Good lord no!" I exclaimed. "It was bad enough getting the stockings. I pretended they were for my sister who'd fallen in the river, and the cretin tried to sell me a bathing costume."

"It was very kind of you," she said, laughing: "but I'm not properly dressed, you see."

"I don't see," I returned.

"Then believe me—I know. Now we must get to the station."

In silence we walked quickly for seven or eight minutes, Rhona seeming familiar with the locality, and then came in sight of our goal. The girl paused for a moment, looking up and down the streets; there were several people about, but they all appeared harmless, far too intent upon their own business to bother about ours.

"There may be some of the enemy inside, of course," she told me. "We'll have to risk it. Oh lord, get back!"

I did so, following her, and in next to no time we were hidden from view in a narrow alley-way beside a shop. Fortunately the gate had been partly open, and I hoped that nobody had noticed our unceremonious dash to cover.

"He saw us!" whispered Rhona, as we crouched beside a very smelly dustbin. "Nick—the one who shoots. Keep still."

She needn't have warned me about that: I was scarcely breathing, and in terror that someone would come from behind and demand the reason for our presence in a loud voice. A moment later, from in front, we heard the sound of a man's footsteps: he was running, and past the top of the gate I saw go by a head in a slouch hat.

"I think we can just do it," she murmured. "It's only a few yards to the corner—quick!"

She took my hand and made for the pavement, surprising one or two passers-by. Thence we galloped for the station, I trying to keep up and at the same time fumble in my pocket for money.

"I hope to goodness there's a train soon!" she gasped, safely inside the entrance. "Get two tickets to Waterloo—I'll watch."

Our luck held: an electric train was just pulling in. As far as I could tell we were unobserved as we found seats in an otherwise empty compartment, and I sighed with sincere relief when the platform began to slide away from us. I wasn't used to such an energetic mode of life.

As I was opening my mouth, Rhona spoke first.

"Don't ask any questions yet, please—we must decide what we're going to do. Where do you think we'd better get out?"

"I haven't the least idea. Does it matter?"

"Very much, I expect. They'll be at Waterloo for certain."

"But how on earth can they be?" I objected. "Hang it, whoever these people are they haven't got second sight."

"But they know how to use the telephone," she pointed out sweetly. "Dr. Paul wouldn't have dropped Nick unless he thought we'd stop in Kingston. Nick will realize he missed us, and ring up to cover the line."

"Really? Ring up whom?"

"I'm not sure, but he told me once that he could get hold of twenty men in London at almost a minute's notice. Maybe he was just boasting—and maybe he wasn't."

"I see. It sounds rather fantastic, but one may as well believe the worst, especially after being fired at in broad daylight on the Portsmouth Road. What was he using, by the way—a rifle?"

"Yes—we were too far for a pistol. Look, we've reached Maiden already. How about Vauxhall?"

"As you say—I suppose Clapham Junction and Waterloo will be the chief danger-spots? And how much did Nick see of you, incidentally?"

"Only a glimpse."

"Then dump the mac and hat, and perhaps you won't be recognized. Unless you were noticed in the car."

"I think Dr. Paul must have spotted me while he was talking to you. I was on the floor trying to pretend I was a rug, but I dare say I moved or something. Still, it's Nick we're up against at present."

"And there's your hair, too, if you take the beret off. Can you do anything about it?"

"Dye the wretched stuff, the first chance I get. What have you got in your case? May I look?"

I opened it for her inspection, and at once she picked out my evening scarf.

"I can do something with this," she declared. "It's a good big one. If I spoil it I'll buy you another."

"But I thought you hadn't any money?" I said.

"Not yet, but I will have if I manage to escape: enough to give you a clean scarf every day for the rest of your life."

While she was speaking she was busy with mine, which I admit was soiled; in about three minutes, incredibly, she had transformed it into something which would pass for a hat.

"Can you put the mac in your case?" she asked. "It would be a pity to throw it away after you've only just bought it. And look, I can wear that pullover—I'm sure I can."

At the end of another three minutes she had made herself as neat as possible, and was happily eating my buns.

"You're worth knowing," she told me. "You must be a very thoughtful sort of person, because I *am* hungry—starving. All I've had since midnight is one small loaf which I stole from a baker's van, and I never knew bread could taste so nice. But I'll tell you all about that later—if you want to hear."

"Of course I do. Hullo, here's Clapham Junction—we'd better get ready. I hope there *isn't* anyone at Vauxhall, but I'm beginning to think we ought to have got out much earlier—Norbiton or somewhere. It would have given the twenty men farther to go in less time—we must be more careful in future. And if we *are* being met, I suppose it's ten to one you won't recognize him, or them?"

"Confound it, I hadn't thought of that! Of course I shan't—I'm a fool. Look here, we'd better separate when we get out. I'll go first, and you can do something if anybody tries to collar me."

"Thanks," I said: "that sounds easy. No ideas about what to expect?"

"None, I'm afraid—they've never chased me before."

"Oh well, time will show. Here, you'll want your ticket—and good luck. You may want that too."

At first I thought we were going to get away with it: the platform beside which the train drew up seemed to contain no suspicious characters. But, to my dismay, as soon as Rhona passed the ticket-collector I saw two men in dark coats and trilby hats move quietly towards her. They might have been clerks on their way to lunch, by their appearance at twenty yards, or possibly plain-clothes policemen: but I knew the moment I set eyes on them that as far as concerned us they were foes.

I hung back for a moment watching, and was very much puzzled about what to do. The taller of the men raised his hat perfunctorily, and said something; the girl tossed her head in defiance, and at that the second man stepped round her other side and took her arm. She shook his grasp off with an angry gesture, and one or two people paused to look. On the slightest provocation there would be a gaping crowd, I thought, and little hope of getting clear. Something must be done, and quickly, but I couldn't for the life of me imagine what.

And then, from the corner of my eye, and not a second too soon, I spotted a policeman also watching, and I believed I saw a way out. Hardly stopping to think I ran forward, pushed the smaller man away, and faced the girl with the most irate expression I could assume.

"Oh no you don't!" I barked. "I haven't the pleasure of your friends' acquaintance, but you'd better say goodbye, because you're coming with me."

"Here, just a minute!" interrupted the taller of the strangers. "Who the hell d'you think you are?"

"I'm this lady's husband" I said decisively, and saw them stare, Rhona perhaps most of all.

" 'Ere, what's the trouble?" came a heavy voice, and the policeman approached with self-important slowness.

"Nothing at all, Officer," I rejoined. "My wife happens to have run away from me, and I've come to fetch her back."

"Your wife, eh?"

"Stuff and nonsense!" claimed the shorter enemy.

"Coo I say! Did you hear that?" murmured someone in the crowd.

"Yes, it's true," said Rhona, in possession of her wits at last. "Yes, it's quite true. Oh Bertie darling, I'm so glad you're here!"

Then, without warning, she flung herself into my arms, and I found myself being very publicly kissed.

"And who might you be?" enquired the policeman of the other two, now standing by with rather puzzled expressions on their unhandsome faces. At a nearer view they couldn't possibly have been mistaken for clerks: they were just plain thugs.

"As a matter of fact," said the taller who had a faint moustache, "we're her brothers, and what this fellow says is all lies. He's no more her husband you are."

"Huh! Sort of a family meeting, like. Well, better come along to the station, the lot of you—we can't have a scene like this here. Come along, Miss—Mum. And you, sir."

"What the devil for?" I demanded indignantly. "We've done nothing—we merely want to go home. It's these two ruffians here who've caused the scene."

(This was a downright falsehood, of course: but what was one more?)

"What for? 'Cos I say so, that's what for," was the answer; and, looking at him more attentively, it began to strike me that I hadn't chosen my policemen well. He was a surly brute, big and bristling, and he seemed to have made up his mind.

"But I want to go back with Bertie!" wailed Rhona.

"Can't help that—no arguing."

"Go on, let 'em alone," advised an anonymous sympathiser in the throng.

"Blasted bluebottle!" said someone else, and gave vent to a buzzing noise.

And then I noticed something which gave me a considerable shock, succeeded by new hope. The number on the policeman's uniform was prefixed by the letter 'F', and I couldn't imagine why a member of the Hammersmith division should be on duty at Vauxhall Station.

"Very well," I agreed meekly, and turned to Rhona.

"Don't worry, darling—everything will be all right. Just give me another kiss, and tell me you're glad to see me again."

"Of course I am," she declared, and held up her face.

"Get ready to run!" I whispered—hardly more than breathed it—as I touched her lips. Then I released her, and looked for my opportunity.

Miraculously, it was there for the taking. The crowd which had encircled us was dispersing under the supposed policeman's gruff orders, and the thugs were preparing to move off beside their quarry. Their backs were momentarily towards me: in one swift rush I dived at them, and brought the trilby hats together with a solid bang.

Somebody yelled, and the policeman raised his fist. I got in first, though, a right hook that sent him sprawling on his back. Quickly I turned, saw Rhona disappearing round a corner, and followed in spite of would-be obstructers. Anyone who got in my way was pushed roughly out of it, including the collector who had been patiently waiting to claim my ticket: I had no intention of remaining in that station a second longer than I needed.

We agreed afterwards that neither of us had ever run so fast in our respective lives. How we did it I still don't quite know, but in under half a minute we were panting in a taxi and bound for Charing Cross. There we changed vehicles, doubled about a bit by way of Chancery Lane and Holborn, and at half past one were safe indoors.

Safe, that is, for the time being: for I suddenly realized that at some time during our scuffles I had left my suitcase behind, and in it, unfortunately, was my passport.

## III

"YOU'RE SURE IT WAS IN THERE?"

"Positive. That means they know my name."

"But not your address—unless you're in the telephone book?"

"No, I'm only a sub-tenant here. I took the place furnished, so I come under the chap who let it to me: W.A. Kendrick, in case you ever want to ring up."

"Thanks—does that mean you're turning me out?"

"Of course not—but you still might want to phone. No, we ought to be pretty secure for a bit, on second thoughts. Anyway, there'll be time for you to do some explaining—I'm very curious to know what all the fuss is about."

Rhona nodded, her face grave. We had both of us bathed and eaten, and I had changed, but she still wore her same odd outfit: my flat was a strictly bachelor establishment.

"Yes, I owe you an explanation," she agreed: "and a lot of thanks. You've been simply splendid right from the word go, but now I'm afraid that when I've told you the truth you *will* turn me out."

"I promise I won't."

"Don't be too rash—it's a nasty business. By the way, you're quite sure that policeman wasn't real?"

"Oh, he was solid enough—look at my knuckles. He just didn't happen to be a policeman, that's all. I noticed something else when I hit him—it's queer how you spot things at the most unlikely times. The number on his helmet was 77, but his tunic said 97, which was a bit of carelessness on someone's part. Would it be Dr. Paul?"

"No, hardly—he was one of Nick's crowd, I should think. But why did he ask the other two who they were? He'd know, wouldn't he?"

"Yes, but he had to play his role before the crowd."

"Oh, of course—silly of me. Well, I'd better make a start some time, and I'll clear out quietly if you say so. The fact is that at the moment I'm an escaped lunatic."

Now there's no denying that this hit me right in the wind, and I don't pretend I did anything but open my eyes and mouth and just gawk.

"Well, if you say so . . ." I murmured.

"I do—and you can't imagine how much I hate it. You see, I'm not mad. Oh, I know all lunatics think they're sane, but this time it's true! I can't prove it, of course, and everything's against me—"

"But I'll believe you, all the same," I assured her. "Have a cigarette and tell me about it—I'll help if I can."

"Thank you. I need help badly, as you've probably guessed, and I've no one else to ask. It's rather a long story, but I'll give you the facts as clearly as I can.

"My father and mother both died soon after I was born, and I was brought up by my grandmother. We lived in Canterbury, and nothing much happened to me till I was sixteen. My father didn't leave a lot of money—he was a composer—but enough for school and so on.

"Well, just after my sixteenth birthday things started to go wrong. First my grandmother died, and my mother's brother became my guardian. He'd quarrelled with her when she married, and I didn't even know he existed till the solicitors introduced us. He was a queer man—he's dead now, too—and immensely rich. He'd made a fortune out of stocks and things, and he lived in a big house near Kingston, which is why I know the place so well.

"It was during the time I was living with him that I first met Dr. Paul. In case you've never heard of him he's a distinguished mental specialist, and he runs a private mental hospital just outside Esher. He and my uncle were fairly close friends, and I had to be nice to him, but I can honestly say I loathed the man right from the very beginning. There's something about him which always makes my skin want to itch, and he's got horrible eyes.

"Unfortunately I saw quite a lot of him, one way and another, and soon I decided that he wasn't only nasty but crooked too. It seemed to me that he was only friends with my uncle because he thought it would pay him to be—though I don't think Uncle noticed anything wrong. He was an extremely unsuspicious sort of person.

"Well, that went on till last April. It wasn't at all an exciting life, because I wasn't allowed to go out much or make any friends, especially during the last two years. I had to stay at home and pretend to be grown up till I really was, and afterwards I simply went on staying at home. Things were just about as dull as that. And then, quite suddenly, my uncle died, on April 30th of this year. It was supposed to be something to do with a weak heart, but I'm not so sure. I've always believed he was poisoned."

"By Dr. Paul?" I put in.

"Yes, by Dr. Paul. I haven't a scrap of evidence, so perhaps I oughtn't to say anything, but that's the way I feel. For one thing, Uncle always made a point of having himself overhauled every few months, and I know his own doctor was very much surprised.

"Now, my uncle had several peculiarities. For instance, he always designed and printed his own Christmas cards, and he refused to eat or drink anything made with milk. Things like that don't matter, of course, but three of his peculiarities come into my story.

"First, he didn't believe in girls marrying till they were at least twenty-one—nor men till they were thirty, incidentally. I know lots of people hold similar views, but not so strongly. It really used to worry him to read about eighteen wedding twenty with the magistrate's consent: he got purple in the face and grunted.

"Secondly, he hated Mohammedans, though I never found out why.

"Thirdly, he thought that all lunatics ought to be shot: that was the only way to stamp out lunacy, he said. Even if you cured them, you could never be dead sure they wouldn't relapse, and you couldn't stop them producing what he called potentially diseased stock. That was the one subject that he and Dr. Paul ever argued about.

"I'm giving you these details, by the way, so that you'll be able to appreciate the conditions of his will. Apart from a few small legacies, one to the doctor of £1000, he left the whole of his money in trust for me when I came of age, provided (a) that I was unmarried and not a mother, (b) that I wasn't a Mohammedan, and (c) that I wasn't a certified lunatic. If any of those three conditions had been broken, I was to receive two thousand guineas in cash and not a penny more."

"And what *was* the fortune?" I asked.

"Seven hundred and eighty thousand clear of death duties."

"Over three-quarters of a million! That's what I'd call worth staying single for."

"Yes, and I've never wanted to be a Mohammedan. And it'll be a bit more than that by now, of course, with the accumulated interest. But you haven't heard the destination of the money if I did marry or do the other things. It was all to go to Dr. Paul, who was meanwhile appointed my guardian."

"Aha!" I exclaimed. "Let me be bright. He couldn't make you change your religion, if any, nor take a husband you didn't fancy: but he could—and apparently did—get you shoved in bedlam."

She smiled and nodded.

"Yes, that's exactly what happened. Of course he wasn't able to certify me himself, because it's illegal, so he got two other doctors to do it: crooks, both of them, but good enough for the job."

"But just a minute: why should it be illegal for Dr. Paul to certify anyone?"

"Oh, not anyone—only me, because he was my guardian."

"Oh, I see. Yes, it's all rather clever when you come to work it out, and of course the will played right into his hands. Did he have anything to do with framing the terms?"

"I shouldn't be surprised—it was dated only a month or so before my uncle's death. But it was genuine enough—there's not the slightest doubt about that. I mean, it wouldn't be any good contesting it."

She broke off, frowned for a moment, and then stared at me very straight, her blue eyes trying to read my thoughts.

"Look here, tell me something," she said. "Do you believe the story I've just told you, or are you putting it down to my ravings? Please be honest."

"Strange as it may seem, I believe you," I answered. "I didn't care much for Dr. Paul the moment I saw him, and I don't think I should be too keen on the rest of them. Who's this Nick person?"

"A sort of bodyguard. I don't know his real name: he's an American, and he's just called Nick. Thank you for believing me."

"And are there any other important ones? Who was the girl in the fur coat?"

"Her name's Gloria Delrosa—so she says. She used to be a model, and she's got a lovely face and figure, but as a matter of fact she isn't nearly so nice as she looks."

"What part does she play?"

"She was my special attendant—naturally I was shut up in Dr. Paul's private asylum where I couldn't make a nuisance of myself. I was certified on May 20th, and I stayed there six months to the day. It's November 21st now, and I escaped at quarter to twelve last night."

"In blue pyjamas and bedroom slippers."

"Yes—I had no choice. I'd been planning it all for ages. Everything depended on who was on duty and who wasn't, and whether a particular door had been left open or shut, and if I could hit Gloria hard enough to knock her out. I'm glad to say I did."

"Then why not pinch her clothes?"

"There simply wasn't time. I had to clear out just as I was, and I can tell you I nearly froze. I ran for miles, till the slippers fell to bits, and I don't quite know where I did go. Eventually I found myself near Cobham just as it was getting light: like an idiot I'd described most of the usual circle, and I could have sat down and howled. I was starving hungry, and half naked, and I didn't know what to do or where to aim for. To make it really jolly, too, I'd no money and no food, and nothing to bribe people with to give me any, and no weapons."

"Except your face," I put in, at which she grinned cheerfully.

"To frighten them with?"

"No—as a sign of your honesty."

"Oh, thank you—such a pretty speech! But of course you're grown up, and must have had lots of practice."

"Grown up?" I repeated uncertainly.

She nodded, and then attempted an imitation bass.

" 'I don't care twopence about wet feet!' " she said solemnly.

"Good lord, did you hear that?"

"Obviously. Well, I solved some of my troubles by being lucky enough to find a garden where this jumper and skirt had been left on a line. They were simply sopping, but I couldn't help that: I pinched them without hesitating, and also that loaf of bread I told you about. And then I saw you stop your car and get out, and you know the rest."

"Except what you're going to do next."

"Yes: I can't stop worrying about it. Have I got to keep on running away from Dr. Paul for the rest of my life, d'you think? Because if so I won't even get my two thousand guineas. And that reminds me: can I ask you to lend me some money? I haven't got a stitch on except what you see and the pyjamas"—and she lifted her jumper at the waist to disclose a patch of blue silk.

"Of course," I said. "And I'd better tell you something about me, I suppose"—which I did. "And now, how much do you want?" I asked. "Will a fiver be all right to get on with?"

"Heavens, yes! A pound would probably do. I'll only need undies and a cheap dress and one or two odds and ends like the garters you forgot."

"Well, you know best, but if you're sensible you'll get something warm: and I think that for the present you'd be wise to stay here."

"Here? With you?"

"Yes. You'll be quite safe—in every way."

"Oh, I know that. But don't you mind what people think?"

"Not a bit: especially as nobody will know. This is what they call a self-contained flat, and the one underneath is empty, and the family on the ground floor are away in Scotland. We shall have the place to ourselves."

"But who looks after you?"

"I do," I said. "I should have thought you'd guessed that. You see, I haven't been back in England long, as I told you, and I rather wanted to be on my own to think things out. I loathe hotels and boarding-houses, and so I decided to shift for myself. Most days I eat out, and a woman comes in for an hour every morning to make the bed and dust the mantelpiece and do the washing-up. We can always dispense with her, if you'll do it instead."

"Of course I will. Have you got two beds, though?"

"One and a half—the thing you're sitting on is alleged to let down and make up, or whatever divans do. I'll have that, and you can use the real one. There are loads of blankets and things, and we ought to be pretty comfortable. Anyway, it'll do for the time being, while we think out the next move. Will you find it bearable?"

She nodded for answer, and then to my utter amazement burst into tears. For a moment I was startled, but apparently I needn't have been: she was only behaving like that because she was happy, she assured me between gulps, not because the immediate prospect made her miserable.

## IV

**B**EFORE THE SHOPS SHUT THAT EVENING Rhona went out to buy what clothes she most urgently needed. On my advice she also made certain other purchases, with which we later employed ourselves for some hours.

First there was a hair dye, and by its aid we soon transformed her auburn crop to an even shiny black. This, together with a new style of dressing, made what was to me a surprising difference in her appearance. Next she carefully followed the directions on a bottle of artificial sunburn lotion; intensified—under protest—the natural colour of her lips, thinned out her own eyebrows and applied new ones, and finally screwed on a pair of rather ornate marcasite ear-rings. I surveyed the result—she was wearing a dark-green woollen frock and more suitable shoes than those I had bought for her—and I had little doubt that she would pass unrecognized by anyone except Dr. Paul and his two chief assistants, and possibly by them too. I felt myself that I was sitting opposite a complete stranger: a person more unknown to me than the real Rhona had ever been, short though our acquaintance was.

You will please understand that I had not fallen in love with the girl at first sight, or done anything approaching that foolishness. She was pleasant to look at, admittedly, when she was herself; she was plucky, in need of help, and sincerely though not ostentatiously grateful to me: of all these things I was aware, but my heart still kept its old routine. In any case—the admission will have to be made sooner or later, and may as well come now—I hadn't entirely forgotten the label round her neck. As far as the outside world knew she was an escaped lunatic, and even the most willing mind could hardly have swallowed her story whole and needed no time to digest it.

Nine-tenths of me felt morally certain that she was as sane as myself: but the other tenth, at intervals, would remind me that there might be room for doubt. Was not her story, suggested this tenth part, just such as a lunatic might easily concoct? Were not the mentally unbalanced notoriously liable to suffer from persecution mania? And was it not long odds nowadays that anybody who had been certified by two qualified medicos stood in genuine need of treatment and restraint?

But I had myself encountered at least some evidence that her version could be true, the rest of me rejoined. The subtly unpleasant Dr. Paul was not to be summarily dismissed as a mere nothing; nor the false policeman and the two toughs in trilby hats; nor the shooting at the Rolls—that least of all. Again, her present manner and behaviour were wholly in her favour, and would not my eyes, accustomed to dealing with normality, be likely to detect instantly any departure from the normal? I had experienced a far keener sense of the bizarre during my few moments' talk with Dr. Paul than in the hours I had spent in Rhona's company. I had, I told myself, at once concluded instinctively that here was a man to be guarded against, because one's dealings with a thousand others might scarcely help at all in handling him. His face said one thing and his tongue said another: his cold suspicious stare was accompanied by a gentle flow of semi-whimsicality which jarred the ear. And, finally, were crooked doctors unheard of? Of course not, any more than were crooked business-men and crooked politicians.

So much for my private debate: but, whether Rhona were mad or sane, I had promised to do my best for her, and I intended to keep my word. I was interested in her story, more than inclined to believe it, and quite determined to see what would be the outcome of her present predicament. Certain risks might attach to my taking up her cause, but I was ready to run them: not in any spirit of bravado, or so that I could have the satisfaction of regarding myself in secret as a hero, but because they seemed to be an inevitable part of the affair. I could do nothing for her without to some extent putting myself in her own position with regard to Dr. Paul, and it was to her credit that she pointed this out herself.

"It's all very well, you know," she remarked, pausing in the adjustment of an eye-brow. "I look like anybody but me, but you're still you, and they've seen your face, and I don't suppose they love you. Oughtn't we to do something about it?"

"What can we do?" I asked. "Ear-rings wouldn't suit me, and my hair's quite ordinary, and anyway I dare say I shall find it very useful to be myself at times. My bank probably wouldn't cash my cheques, for instance, if I walked in as one of the Marx brothers."

"No, there's always that side of it," she agreed.

"And anyway, I don't think I've got a particularly striking sort of face—certainly not one that people would recognize from a description."

"But there's always your passport, don't forget."

I laughed at that.

"More hindrance than help, as far as the photograph's concerned. It's four years old, for one thing, and for another it was never very like me, thank heaven."

"In fact, the usual passport photo?"

"Exactly: done somewhere in the Strand for three and sixpence while you wait—if you've got the patience."

"What else was there in the suitcase? Can you remember?"

"I think so. There was your mac and beret, my evening things, pyjamas, shaving tackle, socks and shoes and so on, a gold cigarette case I'm rather sorry about losing, a pipe or two, and a copy of *Ulysses*."

"To prove you're grown up? But seriously: there weren't any letters?"

"No, I'm sure there weren't."

"No driving licence? Wallet? Cheque-book? Visiting-cards?"

"Nothing like that."

"Good—then I don't see how they can trace you here. All the same, I shouldn't bet about it, because Dr. Paul's pretty smart. I wonder what he'll do."

"Can't say. Have the police really been told about your escape, do you think?"

"Oh yes. You see, as far as anybody knows I'm a genuine lunatic, and he'd be in a false position if he didn't report. I don't suppose for a minute that he'll mention you, though, or that business this morning. By the way, I meant to ask about the car. You didn't give your own name, of course?"

"If the 'Of course', why the query?" I countered. "I said I was a Mr. Latimer, if it helps. And that reminds me: I must write to the owner tonight to tell him where it is, and send him a cheque for the damage. I'd better put off my charwoman, too—we don't want her rolling up at ten o'clock tomorrow morning. And now let me ask you a question. When *is* your twenty-first birthday?"

"Very soon—December 6th."

"Is it now? That's a fortnight and a day. Are you sure? I mean, if I'd been guessing I should have stuck a couple of years on."

"Thank you for nothing. I should hate to think I looked like a kid of eighteen."

"You don't, at the moment—far from it. You look about twenty-five, and rather hard and worldly: responsible for at least two suicides, and mixed up in several divorces. But you were young enough this morning."

"And after being up all night!"

"Yes, I was forgetting. You must be dog-tired."

"Not really—not yet. There's been too much else to think about, but I shall sleep all right once I get to bed. Look here, have you a gun anywhere, just in case we get into trouble again?"

For a moment the tenth part of my mind became actively suspicious, until she smiled.

"As a matter of fact, yes, though it isn't licensed."

"Oh, don't worry about that. I very much doubt if Nick's is, but it wouldn't stop him using it. Can you?"

"Can I what?"

"Use yours?"

"Moderately well: it's an old-fashioned revolver, and extremely simple. I don't shoot pips out of aces or things like that, of course, but if I tried to hit anyone I fancy I might manage to frighten him."

"Then I think you ought to keep it handy."

"Carry it about with me, do you mean?"

"Yes—why not?"

"All right, but I shall feel terribly like a criminal."

At this her face—that strange assumed mask—became very sober.

"You probably are one already," she told me. "It can't possibly be legal to help a lunatic escape."

"No? Then I'll put the thing in my pocket and play the part properly. If I can find it, that is."

After some search we discovered it, and also the requisite ammunition. I was rather proud of the feat, since I usually give myself a clear day to turn out anything I haven't seen for some weeks.

"And one other point," said Rhona, gravely. "You must please keep a strict account of every penny you spend for me. If I ever can I'll pay you back, and if I can't then at any rate you'll know how much to sue me for."

"Very well," I consented: "provided you don't get uppish about it. For instance, I'm not going to put down things like 'To two rashers of bacon at thirteen rashers for 1/5'. You can pay for that by washing the plates up afterwards."

"All right—only I'll probably want three rashers! What do you propose we do tomorrow?"

"Lie low, mostly: but I shall be going out in the morning. For one thing I must lay in some spare cash—we may need it. Also, I've an idea that I may be able to get some useful advice. One of my few real friends is a barrister, and if there's anything we can do legally to put matters right, he's the man to know about it. At all events I can gather some clear notion of just how you stand. If you daren't show your face ever any more, real or disguised, then you'll have to give up your two thousand guineas and emigrate."

Rhona shook her head emphatically.

"On what I could scrounge from you?" she asked, her voice unexpectedly stern. "I'm damned if I will. While there's half a chance of getting what I'm entitled to, I'm going to fight for it, and a bit longer as well. Your friend's all right? I mean, he won't feel he ought to call a policeman?"

"He's as trustworthy as I am," I said. "If that means anything."

"I'm sorry—I shouldn't have asked. I must be getting a bit jumpy."

"That's all right: and we'll fight like a couple of tigers. As far as I can see, if only we keep you out of the way till tomorrow fortnight, and somehow arrange for you to be de-certified as well, then we win hands down. There wouldn't be any point in Dr. Paul's chasing you then, would there? Once you've got the money he's out of the game: or isn't he? It doesn't revert to him if you die?"

"No fear! Once it's mine I can do what I like with it—bank the lot, or give it away, or even spend it all on nice clean silk scarves."

"I see. Well, Malcolm and I will see if we can't fix things somehow between us. I refuse to believe you're absolutely cornered—there simply must be a way out."

Rhona nodded.

"That's how I feel," she agreed. "Or what I keep trying to persuade myself. In any case, I'm a lot better off than I was a week ago, shut up in that asylum with no friends and not really very much chance of escape. I was lucky to get away, and I only hope to goodness I go on being lucky. At the moment I think I shall"— and she smiled at me in the most friendly manner possible.

## V

WE WERE BOTH UP EARLY the next day, Tuesday November 22nd, Rhona in high spirits and refreshed after a sound sleep. During breakfast, which she cooked extraordinarily well, we discussed our plans. It was decided that she should stay indoors in the morning while I went out to see Malcolm Imery, the barrister I'd told her about the previous night. She was to answer the door to no one: it seemed a sensible precaution to take, although we had little reason to think that our enemies would know our whereabouts.

Before I set out we went shopping again, purchasing a good store of food and returning laden with packages. This was doubtless very optimistic of us, but I don't see how we could possibly have foretold what the result of the next few hours would be.

I found Imery at his chambers near the Law Courts, fortunately with nothing much to do, and before long I was putting before him a hypothetical case very like Rhona's own. Once or twice I thought he looked sharply at me, but he made no comment, however strongly he suspected the truth of my story about inventing a plot for a thriller. Imery is a good chap, and doesn't ask questions at awkward times.

"Well," he said, when I had finished by requesting some free and useful advice, "I can tell you one thing, Arnold. If your escaped lunatic evades capture for a fortnight, then she automatically ceases to be a lunatic."

"Really?" I murmured, trying to hide my excitement as I worked out fourteen days from midnight on Sunday. It came to midnight on December 4th, twenty-four hours before Rhona attained her majority. For the first time the game looked like going our way: surely it would be possible to keep her safe till then?

"Yes, really," Imery went on. "She can be as mad as a hatter in actual fact, of course, but before anyone's allowed to shut her up again she must be recertified."

"And what exactly constitutes capture?" I asked, as casually as possible. "By whom can it be effected?"

"By the person in whose charge she was, or his employees, or by anyone else authorized by him in writing to apprehend her."

"But not by an ordinary policeman?"

"Oh yes, of course: she'd come under the heading of a lunatic wandering at large. But not by just anybody without some definite authority, either general as in the case of the policeman, or particular as the superintendent of her particular asylum, or his representative. As for precisely what a recapture would consist of, I'm afraid I can't say, but I should rather think that something more was necessary than a mere temporary arrest. In this case you said she's supposed to have escaped from a private mental home, didn't you? Then, leaving the police out of it, you can probably assume that before she's genuinely recaptured she must be not only in the care of someone licensed to look after lunatics, but also in a place where it's permissible to keep them. That's only my own opinion, though."

"Then if she was staying with friends, and the asylum johnny burst in on them, what would happen?"

"Well, she'd have to go along with him."

"And if she wouldn't?"

"If he'd got any sense he'd call a copper."

"And suppose that while he was taking her back she managed to give him the slip: could she count the time she'd already had clear, or would she have to start her fortnight all over again?"

Imery smiled, and shrugged.

"I'd hate to guess," he told me. "There's no precedent to go by, or if there is, then I certainly don't know it."

"I see. Well, very many thanks—you've helped a lot."

"Have I? That's good. By the way, did you see a newspaper this morning?"

Something in his tone put me immediately on my guard. I glanced at him warily, to find his keen grey eyes avoiding mine.

"No, I didn't," I said. "Why?"

"Well, there's something that might interest you. Get a *Telegraph,* and look at the middle page. Then if you'd care for any more—any more advice, let me know."

I had now an unpleasant feeling down my back, as if bad news were about to catch up with me.

"Do you happen to have a copy here?" I queried.

He stared at me for a moment, and then nodded; but while I read it he gazed out of the window at the murky London haze.

## LUNATIC AT LIBERTY IN SURREY

### MIDNIGHT ESCAPE

It is learnt that late on Sunday night Rhona French, aged 20, one of the patients, escaped from Holmwood, Dr. Herman Paul's private mental hospital near Esher. The attendant in charge at the time was found unconscious, and it is believed that she had been stunned by Miss French.

The escape was made in night attire, and in an interview today Dr. Paul expressed his confidence that the missing girl will soon be located. 'There is no cause for alarm' he said. 'Miss French is not at all dangerous. Her chief trouble is that she fancies she is being persecuted by the staff here, and myself. This is of course no uncommon thing with the mentally unbalanced. It is a distressing affair, and I sincerely hope that no harm will befall her, particularly as I happen to be her legal guardian.'

Dr. Herman Paul, it will be remembered, is ' the author of several standard works on the treatment of mental disease. The missing girl has red hair, and when last seen was wearing blue pyjamas. She is of medium build, has blue eyes, and stands about five feet in height.

I was glad to see there was no mention of the money, but things were quite bad enough without that.

"Why did you think I'd be interested?" I asked Imery. For half a minute he remained silent; then he turned towards me, his lean face smiling slightly.

"If you must have it, because I happen to remember the terms of the will."

"Ah!" I said, a little foolishly. "Sorry about spinning you fairy tales."

"Not at all—the less I know the better, officially speaking. Do you reckon you can last a fortnight, Arnold?"

"I don't know, but I'm going to have a thundering good shot. Look here, is there any harm in your knowing, as long as I don't ask you to help? I'd like to tell you."

"Thanks—I admit I'm curious. It doesn't seem much of a bargain for you, though."

"Nonsense—you've done your share already."

For perhaps an hour we talked hard, examining the position from every aspect. When at last I rose to go, he held out his hand.

"Good luck!" he said. "You'll need plenty. You're in a tricky situation, and so's the girl, but it's a game worth playing. By the way"—feeling in his pocket: "this might be useful."

He held out a small rusty key, which I took wonderingly.

"Do you remember the caravan at Thames Ditton? You stayed there with me for a week the summer before last. It's called *Avalon,* and that'll let you in. Know how to get there?"

"Yes, rather—many thanks. You see, you are helping after all."

"Very indirectly, but it might come in handy as an earth if the chase grows too hot. And if you're in a real jam you'd better ring me, either here or at home. I expect I'd throw discretion to blazes."

"I will if we can't do without you," I promised: "and thanks again."

On my way back to the flat I thought over the information I had just been given, and decided that on the whole it favoured us. Rhona would be glad to hear that she must remain in hiding for only a fortnight. She need no longer dread having to spend the rest of her life running away from Dr. Paul and the lunacy commissioners, to say nothing of the police. The one thing which worried me was the uncertainty about what constituted a recapture. It seemed wisest to take the most rigorous steps against anything that could possibly be termed one: but quite how, until danger actually threatened, I was by no means clear.

Such were my thoughts during the tube journey home, and on the short walk to No. 29 Bainbridge Gardens. When I opened the front door I had no idea that anything was wrong; but as I turned to close it I became aware of a small pock-marked man in a raincoat and slouch hat. He was leaning negligently against the wall in the corner: upon his nose glittered a pair of rimless spectacles, and in his right hand was a black automatic with an excessively long barrel.

"Up!" he said, indicating with a jerk of his head that I should raise my hands, and because I could think of nothing more sensible to do at the moment, I obeyed. If this were the American gunman Nick, as I felt sure it was, I should stand little chance of making a false move without getting a bullet in me. The house had at present no other tenants, as I have mentioned, and although he might be expected to hesitate about shooting because of passers-by in the street outside, something in his air of self-assurance made me prefer not to take the risk. He looked a very determined little man, with bright brown eyes behind his glasses, thin colourless lips, and a pale scar running from his left nostril to his ear.

Nevertheless, in spite of my momentary compliance I wasn't intending to let him have things all his own way. At the first opportunity I was going to do something: I promised myself that.

"What next?" I asked, for something to say.

"Upstairs when I've relieved you of that bulge," he answered, and took my gun from my inside pocket. With expert hands he made sure that I was carrying only the one, and then again jerked his head at me.

"Climb!" he ordered laconically, and we did so, he very close behind me and the automatic pressed into the small of my back. As we approached the door which separated my flat from the stairs I heard voices, and once inside I wasn't long in discovering to whom they belonged. In the back room were three persons: Rhona lying on the divan, tied at wrist and ankle and gagged, a tall and unusually beautiful girl in a fur coat, and Dr. Paul.

For a second there was silence, and then the doctor spoke.

"Give Mr. Dane a chair, Nick—after all, it's his home. There, that's better. This is Miss Delrosa, by the way—please don't trouble to get up."

The tall girl gave me a disinterested nod but said nothing, and I had the impression that she might be a little afraid of her employer.

"And now," he went on, "we can have a pleasant chat."

"What about tying him up too, Doc?" interrupted the gunman. "He's good an' hefty—he might be awkward."

"No, I don't think so. I'm sure he understands how much wiser he'll be if he isn't awkward—don't you, Mr. Dane? Nick shoots very straight, and his pistol makes surprisingly little noise with that silencer attached—hardly more than the cracking of a walnut."

"I'm in your hands entirely," I said. "May I ask what you propose to do?"

"Certainly, certainly—that was what I thought we might discuss. By the way, Gloria, pull the curtains to, please. We don't want to be overlooked, and it's amazing how inquisitive some people are."

Swiftly the girl moved to the window behind him, and I noticed for the first time that the electric light was already on.

"Thank you," remarked the doctor gently, and turned his attention to me again.

"First I ought to express my gratitude for your valuable assistance, Mr. Dane. In tracing my ward, I mean"—indicating Rhona with a sly sidelong glance.

"*My* assistance?" I queried, studying his face intently: I wanted to find out what gave me so strong an impression of evil about the man. Nothing in the features themselves, I decided: his broad high forehead was unexceptionable, his nose straight if perhaps a trifle too long, and his chin markedly cleft. What hair he had was grey, but his brows remained startlingly black. Leave out the eyes, and it was an arresting but not repulsive face: they were what worried me, I told myself. I found their amber clearness fascinating, and it was only with an effort of will that I managed to look away, so closely did they seem to hold my own.

I realized that I was more than a little afraid of Dr. Paul, and the realization displeased me.

"Yes, your valuable assistance," he agreed, in reply to my question. "If you hadn't so obligingly left your suitcase with my friend's friends"—here peeping for a moment at Nick, sitting expressionless and alert to my left—"if you hadn't done that, I really believe we might have had some small difficulty in tracing you. Nothing of any proportions, though, of course. I believe the organization is very thorough—eh, Nick?"

"So-so," grunted the gunman.

"Except for your careless amateur policeman," I suggested. "He ought to have had the same number on helmet and uniform, you know. But just how did you find us, Doctor?"

"Through your evening clothes," he explained, after he had finished chuckling at my criticism of his friend's friends. "What could be simpler than to call upon your excellent tailor? To persuade him that his handiwork had been left behind by a guest whose address I had mislaid? Your name was inside the inner breast pocket, of course."

"Yes, very ingenious," I murmured, and meant it: I had overlooked the fact, and was beginning to grasp another, that there were no cobwebs on Dr. Paul.

"And now could we come back to my previous question about what happens next?" I continued. "I confess I should like to know."

As I spoke I looked at Rhona—not for the first time, I may say—and was given a fleeting smile. Or so I fancied, but since only her eyes and the top half of her nose could be seen, it was difficult to be sure.

"And—quite by the way—is it absolutely essential to truss Miss French up like a Christmas chicken?"

The doctor nodded vigorously.

"I'm afraid so—yes, I'm afraid so. She's an athletic young lady—eh, Gloria? I think she will be best as she is. And now let's come down to facts, Mr. Dane. My immediate plan is to escort my patient back to *Holmwood*—the name of my sanitorium. Despite what you have been doubtless told, she definitely stands in need of specialized care and attention. I should also remind you that at the moment she is a certified lunatic. You knew that?"

"Yes, I knew that."

"And yet you were apparently willing to let her loose upon society, with her delusions and her irrationality and her manifest inability to cope with normal everyday life? You must be a strange young man, Mr. Dane."

"I wouldn't put it quite so strongly," I demurred, in no way taken in by his remarks. "The truth of the matter is that she didn't strike me as being peculiar—certainly not more so than Nick here, for instance."

"Me?" said the watchdog through his chewing-gum. "Meaning what?"

"Well, I was brought up to believe that no right-minded person ever wore brown shoes, spats, a soft collar, and a bow-tie all at once."

At this, unexpectedly, the girl Gloria emitted a dainty chime of laughter. It occurred to me that she and Nick weren't on the best of terms, and I put the suggestion away in my head for possible future use.

"You're observant," declared Dr. Paul, leisurely cutting the end from a small black cigar.

"I don't offer you one," he added, as he saw me looking, "because I don't think you'd like it if I did. There is a certain proportion of hashish admixed with the tobacco—I find it stimulating. But have a cigarette, by all means."

I thanked him and lit one, Nick watching me all the time: I could feel his brown eyes follow every movement.

"Yes, as I was saying, you're observant," pursued the doctor. "The affair with the policeman shows that. It may perhaps then not have escaped your notice that to me, at present, you constitute an unwelcome encumbrance. A millstone, one might almost term you."

"In which case, I hope I have the appropriate effect," I remarked.

He creased his mouth into a smile at my feeble sally, but his yellow eyes were unamused.

"I doubt it. I merely used the word millstone because it seems that I must take you with me, however unwillingly. For various very good reasons it won't be convenient to have you at liberty making a nuisance of yourself: not, anyway, for a week or so."

I was on the point of correcting him, but refrained. It would be better not to let him know how exactly I appreciated the time-factor with regard to Rhona and the will. And then a horrible thought flashed into my mind.

"You're not proposing to get *me* certified as well, are you?" I demanded point-blank, and I dare say I was quite pale. I had seen a vision of myself helplessly immured for ever, a prisoner in a small room walled with felt and smelling faintly of antiseptic, my hands bound in fingerless mittens and my feet chained.

"You anticipate my very suggestion!" he told me with a smile. "It will be quite the best way out if it can be arranged—and I don't doubt it can. As I pointed out before, you must be a very strange young man, and I have dealt with saner people than you on a professional basis."

"Just tell me one thing," I requested savagely. "Are there *any* lunatics in your asylum?"

He received my jibe with perfect coolness; and in fact, as I afterwards discovered, it was extremely hard to make Dr. Paul lose his temper. He could be stern, but he was rarely irate. In general he maintained his pose as a puckish elderly gentleman: yet one good look at his eyes was enough to convince anybody that he wasn't really like that—harmless, almost gentle, inclined towards friendly banter. Somewhere in the corner of the imagination was space for a possible picture of him as a force guiding a whip about the body of a screaming child.

"I hope you will have the opportunity to judge for yourself," was all he said, and the very lack of emphasis sounded deadly. I glanced quickly at the others. Rhona seemed greatly troubled, and I think was trying to speak, but her gag prevented her. The girl Gloria looked bored, though once or twice I had caught her regarding me in a curiously speculative way. Her face now was empty again: the painted bow of her full lips, the symmetrical arches of her plucked brows, the delicate colouring of the cheeks, might have belonged to a well-made wax dummy. On her chin, though, I could just detect a bruise beneath her make-up: where Rhona had hit her, I supposed.

Nick, in his own fashion, was similarly disinterested, but the pistol in his hand remained quite steady and his spectacled eyes were vigilant. I shifted my foot slightly, to test him, and I saw his whole body momentarily grow taut. It would take a clever man to bamboozle him, I felt.

"By the way," I said, addressing Dr. Paul, "you might clear up another point for me, if you'd be so kind. Since you're obviously prepared for me to be shot if I start any funny business, why not do it straight away? Or can't you stomach murder?"

"Oh, I don't object to it in principle," he replied easily, as though I had merely asked his views on Sunday games. "Put it that I kill only as a last resort. Sudden deaths are tricky things, you know, and corpses need a lot of explaining away. No, I'd rather keep you alive if possible: but mark this, Mr. Dane,"—and his voice became as icy and deliberate as an announcer's—"if I have no choice, I shall not hesitate."

"I see. And does that hold good for Miss French too?"

"Oh no—oh dear me no! That would spoil everything—it's absolutely imperative that she survives. Did you omit to tell your new friend that, my dear? A trifle negligent, I think. You see, Mr. Dane, my actions are entirely guided by the explicit terms of her late uncle's will, about which you've doubtless heard. In the event of Rhona's dying prior to her twenty-first birthday, the whole of his fortune goes to various charities. Probably most deserving ones, and I expect her immediate decease would benefit a great many more people than she could ever hope to do herself should she inherit. The trouble is, from my point of view, that I'm not one of them.

"Believe me, Miss French is as safe in my hands as if she were the whole royal family."

"Until she's twenty-one," I said. "And then what's her market-value?"

"Two thousand guineas," came the prompt reply. "And whatever she would fetch as herself. You see, once I have possession of the money there's simply nothing she can do about it which will worry me."

"You don't mind being exposed?"

The doctor smiled blandly.

"Exposure—what is it?" he asked with a shrug. "At worst, a fresh start somewhere else—and what better send-off than the best part of a million pounds? And in any event, who'd take the word of a certified lunatic against mine?"

I nodded gloomily: it was clear that our ideas of safety didn't tally.

"And myself?" I murmured.

"At the moment I can't prophesy. It will depend largely upon how you behave, but I don't advise you to be too sanguine. And now, Nick, we'd better prepare for our return. Give Gloria your pistol, and then go down and fetch Mappin and the car—you're more likely to know where to find them than she is."

"Okay," said the gunman, passing the automatic across in such a manner that I stayed covered. "Will you need Mappin up here?"

"Yes, it would be as well. Have him pull up at the corner, and be quick—it's getting on for one o'clock."

## VI

I THINK WE BOTH KNEW instinctively that if we hoped to escape, now was our only opportunity. As the sound of Nick's footsteps died away I glanced at Rhona, still lying on the divan. She seemed to nod, as though agreeing with my unspoken thought. Meanwhile Gloria stood a yard away, the pistol in her gloved hand pointing full at me, and Dr. Paul was fumbling in his overcoat. A moment later he placed on the table between us a small box, and from it took a hypodermic needle; then he looked up with a smile which to my mind made him appear even more sinister.

"A necessary precaution!" he observed. "It wouldn't do for the neighbours to see you struggling on the doorstep—oh no, that wouldn't do at all. There's no need to be alarmed—it won't hurt you. Just a momentary prick of pain and it'll be all over."

"For keeps?" I asked.

"Why, of course not: six or seven hours, no more. It's quite harmless—don't be afraid."

As can be imagined, my brain was working at top speed: yet what could I do in face of that unwavering pistol ready to spit death at me? What could Rhona do, tied as she was and helpless on her back? And what use could there be in appealing to Dr. Paul? One might as well plead with Bradman not to be too boisterous with weak bowling.

It seemed all pretty ominous, until I remembered something I had read once, a trick performed by the handsome hero of a thriller in rather the same position as my own. There might be a faint chance that it was worth trying to emulate him, and accordingly I did so.

To begin with I smiled at the doctor—the smile, I meant it to be, of the man who realizes he is beaten and is prepared to take his beating good-temperedly; and then I did my best to appear suddenly distracted by something at the window behind him. Fortunately the curtains weren't quite drawn, and I stared with definite interest over his right shoulder.

And then I waited, hardly daring to believe that my ruse could ever succeed and with my ears strained for the noise of Nick's return. What Rhona must be thinking I couldn't imagine: all I prayed was that she wouldn't spoil things by diverting Dr. Paul's attention.

The thing worked—or the first part of it. After regarding me carefully for a few seconds, as I felt rather than saw, the doctor slowly turned his head to discover what I was gazing at. And now for the second part, I thought, and hastily stole a look at Gloria. Again I was lucky: seeing her employer direct his eyes towards the window at his rear, for just the fraction of a second she too glanced away.

For only the fraction of a second, I say: but it was long enough, and I blessed Rhona's quick wits. Somehow screwing her feet up she made an abrupt lunge, and the soles of her shoes caught the unsuspecting girl at the base of the spine. There was force behind the unorthodox blow: its recipient went staggering forward with a sharp cry, and at the same instant I too acted. I leapt from my chair, hurled the table overboard, caught Gloria with my left hand round the nape of the neck, and with the other sloshed the doctor as hard as I could.

At least, I think that's the order of events, but they took place so speedily that it seemed only a matter of moments before we were on top, one of our enemies being unconscious and the other in my grip. Yet, even so, I had time to reflect that that was the second vicious punch I had delivered in about twenty-four hours. The pistol, I was thankful to notice, had gone clattering harmlessly to the floor.

This was clearly no time for chivalry, gentility, or what-not. My right hand was now free, having done its job of work on Dr. Paul's cleft chin, and as Gloria began to bellow I clapped it over her mouth, taking what care I could to make sure she didn't bite. A few strategic twists and she was lying on her face, her nose tight against a cushion and I sitting on her back. Her legs threshed the air furiously, but did nothing except expose their lengthy silk-clad beauty. Feeling in my waistcoat I pulled out a penknife; in a moment Rhona was free, and at once kneeling beside me making sure that Gloria should be put similarly out of commission. Our victim managed to get only one word out before she was gagged, and that word isn't repeatable in print.

Speed was now essential: we could expect no more than a minute or so to ourselves. I bade Rhona go into the front room and watch for Nick and his companion, while I went hurriedly round collecting what personal belongings I valued and knew where to find. After that I returned to our unwelcome visitors, searched the doctor, and appropriated his keys: it seemed a move likely to embarrass him.

And then I had a really brilliant idea. Lying near him on the carpet, scattered when I had upset the table, was the box he had produced and its contents: not one hypodermic needle but two, both fully charged. Almost without thinking I picked them up.

I won't go into details, but within another minute the needles were empty. Having only the vaguest idea of how to use them I probably didn't do the job properly, but I did it. The doctor received his dose in the arm, but the girl's was difficult to get at— she was wearing a close-fitting dress under her fur coat. However, since I had abandoned manners for the time being, a minor point like that didn't trouble me. Her skirt was already over her knees, so I lifted it higher, sinking the needle in the plump white flesh of her thigh above the top of her stocking. She struggled a bit, but ineffectually, and was very soon unconscious.

When I had thus settled the pair of them to my satisfaction I dashed into the kitchen, and from the shelf above the sink took down a large bottle of ammonia. What my charwoman employed it for I had never known, but now it was going to come in useful. I quickly poured out two cupfuls, and just as I had finished I heard what I had been expecting: a warning cry from Rhona.

"All right, I'm ready," I answered.

As I have said, the flat was self-contained, shut off from the staircase by a door whose top two panels were of frosted glass. Behind this we now crouched, each with a cup poised.

"You take the first one," I whispered, "and I'll have a go at the second. And for goodness' sake throw as straight as you kick."

She did. Nearer came the mounting footsteps, shadows appeared against the glass, the handle turned, and in walked a tall man I hadn't seen before: Mappin, I presumed he was. Immediately on his heels followed Nick, and I fancy they received their welcomes about simultaneously. The howls they began to let out merged into the unpleasant sound of choking, but we didn't stay to listen. Dropping our empty cups we raced downstairs and out into the street, though more circumspectly: and there before us was an unattended bright-blue car. I recognized it in a flash: it was the Chrysler by which we had been chased the previous morning. We looked at one another, and then without a word got in.

"But there's no key!" cried Rhona, and was scrambling out again when I suggested that she wait. And once more my luck was in: Dr. Paul's bunch possessed one which fitted, and soon we were progressing decorously along Notting-Hill High-Street in the direction of Lancaster Gate.

"Where shall we go?" I asked politely.

"Not too far," she advised. "It won't be safe to hang on to this bus long, will it? They're sure to notify the police it's been stolen, and the colour's very conspicuous."

"Yes, you're probably right," I agreed, though regretfully. "It's a pity—I wouldn't have minded a day in the country. Still, safety first and all that. Shall we dump the thing in the Park?"

"Yes, that's a good idea—not many bobbies about there. And then we can decide what to do."

I finally came to rest near the Serpentine, in the most deserted spot I could find. There were very few people near, and none of them seemed to take the slightest notice when I walked round to the bonnet and opened it.

"What are you going to do?" enquired Rhona interestedly. "Muck it up?"

"Just about," I answered, as with my penknife I cut the plug leads, effectively ruined the magneto, and as a crowning touch managed to remove an important part of the carburettor. That done, and with a passing realization that I was rapidly becoming a thorough-paced criminal, I set off beside Rhona towards Knightsbridge. Once out of the Park we caught a bus, and thirty minutes later were eating in a small restaurant near Victoria. The time was a quarter to two.

Up till now we hadn't discussed the situation at all, being too busy pretending we were just two ordinary people with nothing to fear and no one after us. Over the coffee I made a start by telling my companion what I had done to Dr. Paul and Gloria, and she applauded the feat. I also mentioned my talk with Imery, explaining how she had only to remain hidden for a fortnight to be free from the stigma of lunacy, and in a position to inherit her fortune as well.

"I say, that's marvellous!" she exclaimed. "The dates fit in perfectly, though where in the world I'd have been without you I simply can't imagine. But we've just *got* to dodge Dr. Paul now, you know. I mean, he'll hate you like hell for what you did this morning, and Gloria won't be in love with you, either.

"She's got nice legs, don't you think?" she added mischievously.

"First rate," I answered gravely: "what I saw of them."

We then settled down to the problem of what to do and where to go.

"At all events, we've plenty of money," I said presently. "I drew out £50 this morning."

As I spoke I felt for the roll of bank-notes in my inside pocket, to show her: and received a greater shock, I believe, than when I had turned to close the front door of the flat and found myself covered with a pistol. The money was gone.

We stared at each other in dismay: things weren't going so well for us after all.

"I must have dropped the stuff somewhere!" I muttered miserably at last. "Isn't it the absolute limit?"

Rhona said nothing for a moment.

"How could you possibly drop anything out of a deep inside pocket like that?" she asked a moment later. "It sounds more like a thief to me."

"Nick!" I exclaimed. "When he searched me to see if I'd got a second gun."

"That's it—I didn't know about that. He could take a rattle out of a baby's mouth and it wouldn't notice—I mean a dummy. Curse the little swine! How much does that leave us with?"

We examined ourselves rapidly. Of the five pounds I had given her, Rhona still retained twelve shillings and twopence; I had two pound-notes and a few coppers.

"Cheque-book?" she queried briefly.

"Yes—but I won't dare go to the bank again, will I? It's only round the corner from the flat."

"No, but you can write and ask them to register you something. That'll mean waiting, though—you wouldn't get it before Thursday, and it's only Tuesday today."

"Maybe I could borrow some," I suggested. "From Imery, the chap I saw this morning. He's about the only person I could touch, though, and I've nothing really worth pawning."

Forthwith we went out, and from a call-box on the station I tried to ring up Malcolm. The result was another blow to our hopes: he had set off for Leicester an hour ago, I was told, in answer to a telegram about a dying relative.

"That's bad luck," I said. "It'll have to be the bank after all."

"Yes," agreed Rhona: "and meanwhile, where do we go? On two pounds five between the two of us? We oughtn't to have had such an expensive lunch! And we haven't a scrap of luggage either, which puts hotels and boarding-houses right out of the question."

"Well, there's always the caravan," I remarked; and saw by her wondering expression that I must have forgotten to tell her about it.

"Then that's settled!" she smiled a few minutes later. "You've got a nice habit of pulling out an ace when it's wanted."

Before we left town I wrote what I considered a satisfactory letter to my bank. I enclosed a cheque for the same amount as I had already withdrawn once that day, £50, and asked for it to be sent to John Clive, c/o the G.P.O., Thames Ditton.

"But why the false name?" enquired Rhona, when I told her what I had done.

"To be honest, I don't quite know, except that I feel I'd better start being careful. It's the sort of habit that may help, by the look of things so far."

"And what will the bank think?"

"I don't give a hoot. Anyway, the manager married a sort of cousin of mine."

"Another ace!" she said with a laugh. "Oh, but couldn't you have rung him up and borrowed instead?"

I shook my head emphatically.

"He's the last person in the world to help," I explained. "He never borrows anything himself, and he never lends to other people. In fact, as far as caution goes I shall take him for my pattern."

Next we did some shopping, and then made our way to Vauxhall. Today it was back to its normal dullness, with no hint that anything exciting had ever happened there, and by five o'clock we were safe in the caravan. Our purchases consisted of stockings, handkerchiefs, and a cheap powder compact for Rhona; more handkerchiefs for myself, as well as socks and shaving things and tobacco; and, for the two of us, food and cigarettes and matches and a quart of milk. We were left with just under eighteen shillings in cash and a feeling of relative security which was worth a great deal more.

# VII

**N**OBODY COULD EVER PRETEND that Malcolm Imery's caravan offers much comfort to one person, far less to two. Inside it measures about ten feet by seven by six high, and the roof consequently just fails to clear my head. The whole concern is situated on the bank of the Mole, a tributary of the Thames: it stands about thirty yards from the narrow ribbon of muddy water, and between lies a grassy slope laid out roughly as a garden. Neighbouring it are other caravans, some with proper wheels and some with false ones: the theory is, if I remember aright, that owners of movable dwellings avoid payment of rates, and wheels denote mobility. In the case of *Avalon* they were real but untruthful, because firmly attached to the river side of the alleged vehicle was a veranda resting on brick supports.

By the look of things we were going to be the only residents in the immediate locality. This fact wasn't surprising in view of the time of year, and we were both glad. We could do without a lot of snooping busybodies round us, wagging heads and tongues about the impropriety of our association.

There was in truth, I had better say at once, nothing whatever improper about it. The interior of the caravan had been fitted with two built-in bunks, one below the other, and upon these we slept, doing such undressing as we felt inclined for in the dark. I can fairly assert that during the time we spent there I saw nothing I shouldn't have done: unless you count the occasion when Rhona slipped on the step down from the veranda and went sprawling head over heels on the damp turf; and that was in broad daylight.

Our two chief troubles turned out to be lighting and cooking. Both were provided by oil, and neither lamp nor stove proved very satisfactory. We could get a kettle of hot water in about three-quarters of an hour from scratch, and we could just see to read, but that's all. We ate our solid food cold the first evening, and felt hungry enough not to mind, especially as we weren't too badly off for warmth. There were two oil heaters, effective if smelly; but we could always go outside for fresh air when necessary.

After a high tea of ham and sardines and cake we sat down to talk, our conversation being mainly about what we should do on Thursday morning after I had collected the money from the post-office. It was Rhona's opinion that we should be as well off in the caravan as anywhere, and I was inclined to agree. All the same, we discussed other possibilities.

"It boils down to this," I said at last. "Do we leave London or don't we?"

"Not for choice," she answered. "For one thing it's supposed to be the easiest place to hide in, and for another, you may be able to get Imery's help if anything *does* go wrong. We both know our way about, too."

"Including here?" I asked.

"Oh yes—Greater London, you know. As a matter of fact, I'm quite at home in Thames Ditton."

"Good: but there *are* one or two points against staying, aren't there? Nick's gang and the police, for instance—lots of bluebottles in London, and real ones at that."

"Yes, but also lots more people for them to look after than outside. There aren't any strangers in London except for a few obvious freaks, but we'd stick out a mile if we went to the seaside or tried to bury ourselves in the country in November."

"But only as far as the local inhabitants were concerned," I objected. "How on earth is Dr. Paul to find out that a couple of unknowns turned up in Margate or Malvern or Manchester?"

"But it isn't only Dr. Paul," she reminded me: "it's the police as well, as you said yourself just now. You know, I think one of us ought to creep out presently and get an evening paper, to see if there's anything in it about this morning."

"Yes, I suppose so—I'll go in a minute. Even if we do stop here, though, you'll have to disguise yourself all over again, won't you? They know everything about your present appearance. It's a pity, because I was just getting used to it. Oh, and while I remember, there's something I've been meaning to ask for hours. How did Dr. Paul and the rest of them get into the flat? You surely didn't open the door to them?"

"Of course I didn't! I promised I wouldn't, and when I say I won't, I don't. I haven't the least idea how they managed it. There was a faint noise outside on the stairs, and a second later Nick had his gun pointed at me. You didn't leave the key in the door?"—maliciously.

"I did not: yet nobody could have picked the lock in daylight, with people passing all the time."

"Therefore they had a key just the same. The question is, whose?"

"Why, the house-agents', of course!" I answered, the truth suddenly striking me. "He got the address from my tailor, scouted round, spotted there was an empty flat, read the notice pasted on the window, and rushed straight round for an order to view. He's a cunning brute—I hope I don't see any more of him."

About eight o'clock I duly went along to more populated regions and bought copies of the evening papers. It was threepence wasted, however, because there was nothing in any of them about us, and I'm afraid that's all we were interested in at the moment. At least, as far as my own case goes that isn't strictly true: I was interested also in getting to know Rhona better, and when I clambered into my bunk that night I felt that I had certainly picked the right sort of girl to help. She struck me as being shrewd, good-natured, thoroughly reliable, and entirely sane. Nevertheless, if I am to be quite honest I must admit that once or twice when I looked at her an uncomfortable thought invaded my mind. Here was I sitting opposite a certified lunatic with as little concern as if she had been a deaconess: but suppose she suddenly began to roll her eyes and gibber?

Before going to sleep it was my intention to do half an hour's thinking, about the position in general and my own in particular; but somehow the next thing I became conscious of was Rhona prodding me persistently with one hand while she balanced a steaming cup of tea in the other.

"If you're alive, for heaven's sake show it!" she was saying. "Otherwise I won't bother—I've been doing this for five minutes and my arm aches."

"It's my clear conscience," I explained, as I rubbed my eyes.

"Then you must have a very bad memory. Think of all the things you've done lately—throwing ammonia at people, and stealing cars, and sticking hypodermic needles into ladies' hindquarters, and—"

"That's slander," I said. "It was her thigh—no more, no less."

"And that makes it perfectly all right, of course. But don't go trying it on me, that's all."

"I won't promise," I retorted. "Wait till I find a long pin."

After breakfast I again went out for newspapers, and this time the money was well spent—too well for our liking. In fact, not to minimize the matter, we received yet another most unpleasant shock. Four dailies gave us a small paragraph, one a quarter of a column, and one—not the least sensational—allotted us half the front page. To make things worse, part of this space was taken up by our photographs: bad ones, admittedly, mine being from my passport and Rhona's, she said, from a snap made when she had toothache, but there was sufficient resemblance of feature to cause us grave anxiety. As well, the descriptions were remarkably clear: our respective heights and builds and colourings were dwelt upon in detail, and our clothes accurately put down. The story of the car theft obtained due prominence, as also the fact that the missing vehicle had been discovered 'brutally tampered with' in Hyde Park: but for some reason the ammonia wasn't mentioned. The part which made us frown most, though, was the following.

> Furthermore, it is alleged that Dane seriously assaulted Dr. Paul and Miss Delrosa after knocking them insensible, injecting into them with a hypodermic needle an unknown and virulent drug. Late last night Dr. Paul was stated to be comfortable at the hospital where he is being treated, but Miss Delrosa's condition is more serious, and she has not yet regained consciousness.

"Corks!" I exclaimed, aghast. "I never thought of that, you know."

"Thought of what?" asked Rhona, ploughing her hand through her sleek black hair and glaring at me with unintentional sternness.

"I mean, like a fool I took it for granted that what Paul said was true—that the stuff in those needles would only send them to sleep for a bit. It never occurred to me till now that it might really have been a poison. Suppose the wretched creature goes and dies? Then where shall we be?"

"Heaven knows—it's pretty vile, isn't it? And all my fault—you must be simply loathing the sight of me. This time on Monday you were an honest citizen, and now look what they're saying about you. But don't worry. If anything like that does happen I'll swear blind I stuck the thing into her. They wouldn't hang me—I'm daft."

"Nonsense," I demurred, though more than grateful for the thought behind the suggestion. "Anyway, she isn't dead yet, and I dare say they're piling it on. Perhaps they think we'll get frightened and give ourselves up: but we blooming well won't."

"Not you," she agreed: "but mightn't it be best for me to?"

As she said this she looked at me very solemnly, her blue eyes full of concern. I suspected that it wasn't by any means all on her own account, either, or she would never have dreamt of chucking her hand in.

"Hey, no more of that drivel!" I told her, quite sharply. "We're in this together, and don't you forget it."

Now that would have made a fine opening for an embarrassing display of gratitude, or even of flattery, and a less sincere person might have taken advantage of it: but not Rhona, I was glad to see.

"All right—thanks," was all she said, and then smiled suddenly. More to herself than to me, though, I thought, as if she had just had good tidings.

"What I'm specially worrying about is your appearance," I went on. "They've got your description too pat—not only your present one but what you look like normally. It doesn't matter about me, because there's a cupboard full of Imery's togs under your bunk and I dare say some of them will fit, but that won't help you."

"Yes, that's one trouble; and the money may be another."

"Why?"

"Well, surely the police will manage to find out where you bank, won't they? And be on to the manager? Maybe you'll find a dozen of them waiting for you outside the post-office tomorrow."

"Lord, you're certainly being cheerful!" I remarked. "Still, I don't think Harold would give me away."

"Harold being the neither-borrower-nor-lender bloke?"

"The same. Yes, I agree things don't smell so fresh at the moment, but I shall have to go along tomorrow all the same. We can't do without money, you know. Let's look through the cupboard."

We did so, and decided that a fairly new grey suit might fit me reasonably well. There was also an old raincoat, apparently cast out by one of Imery's girl friends, and this Rhona could get on easily. When it was buttoned up it hid her brown coat and skirt and yellowish jumper—part of her purchases with the fiver I had lent her on Monday evening. As well she had a longer matching coat and a green hat, but these were both taboo because of the newspapers.

"We've just seventeen shillings and a penny left," I remarked presently, "and we ought to keep half a crown in reserve. What can you possibly get for fourteen and six that'll make you look different? Or what can I get for you, rather? You still daren't be seen out of doors with that gipsy face and telltale hair."

"Oh, I don't know. I could try washing, couldn't I? And lots of people have black hair. If I take off the ear-rings, and do something about the eyebrows, I think I ought to be safe enough. Then I could go out shopping, and maybe get some more hair dye. What colour shall I go this time?"

"Grey, I should think!" I said, and laughed. "But what can you possibly get in the way of clothes? If you weren't so—well, so obviously feminine, I might perhaps rake round for a secondhand schoolboy's-suit, but as things are I'm afraid it wouldn't be much good."

"Not at that price," she agreed.

"Not at any price," I declared. "You're no schoolboy."

She frowned, and sat thoughtful.

"Ah, but—" she began, and then stopped with another private sort of smile.

"I wonder?" she then said cryptically, and went out to the nearby pump which constituted our water-supply: the stuff in the Mole wasn't at its best. For the next hour she was fully occupied in washing off her sunburn lotion and somewhat lightening her hair. At the end of that time she presented an appearance which differed considerably from either of her recorded descriptions.

"That's splendid," I said. "You'll almost do like that with the mac on, won't you?"

"Well, I'd rather go out shopping, if we can afford the money—then I'll feel really safe. You see, it's always possible we mayn't get anything from the bank tomorrow, and then we shall have to go on the roads or start begging."

She was away for another hour, which I passed in some anxiety, and then returned with a fair-sized parcel.

"Two and a penny change," she remarked, handing it to me. "And now please walk round the garden, and promise not to peep through the windows. Oh, you've put on Imery's suit. Yes, it doesn't look too bad—but just wait till you see me!"

And, a short while later, I did indeed receive a surprise. Upon direct invitation I opened the caravan door to face what was apparently a leggy schoolgirl of fifteen in a navy gym tunic, white blouse, long black stockings, and black shoes.

"And I match underneath, what's more!" she told me proudly. "How do I look? I feel about nine."

I duly congratulated her, but queried the shoes. For answer she showed me a small tin of polish and a brush, and I realized that they were the same ones in which she had gone out.

"That's the best of cheap suede," she remarked happily: "brown one minute, black the next. We've still got four and sevenpence with the half-crown you put by, too, and—if you can bear them—sausages for lunch."

"I don't believe it," I said. "It's not possible, on the money."

"Who said it was? Actually I asked for ducks' eggs, after making reasonably sure they hadn't any, and then sent the man to find out if they could order me some, and the result is sausages for lunch."

"Then I don't think it matters much whether the £50 turns up tomorrow or not," I told her. "I shall just stay in bed while you scrounge a week's supply of everything."

## VIII

There's nothing of any great interest to record about the rest of that day. It began to rain in the early afternoon, and continued steadily until long after dark. For a while we talked, mostly of the future and what it might hold in store, and later we settled down to a book each.

If that sounds unromantic it can't be helped. By some kind of tacit agreement we were letting our friendship ripen as slowly as was possible in the circumstances, and anyway we had—we hoped—the best part of another fortnight together before us. As far as immediate plans went we could do little until we knew if my bank would send the money, and we had already exchanged enough information about our respective past histories to be going on with. Therefore we attacked Malcolm Imery's scanty store of books, Rhona choosing *The Food of the Gods* and I making myself comfortable with an omnibus volume of Sherlock Holmes stories. Nevertheless, we didn't ignore one another completely. Now and again we would look up and smile, and for my part I found the anxiety of the last two days slipping gently into the back of my mind.

On Thursday morning it was fine again, if only temporarily by the look of the sky, and I set off for the post-office about ten o'clock. I went alone because there seemed simply no point in Rhona's accompanying me. If—inconceivably—things went wrong, and Dr. Paul should be tranquilly awaiting my arrival, she would be far better off elsewhere; if things went right, I should return within half an hour.

"Be quick, and be careful," was her parting word, and I promised I would fulfil both injunctions. Looking back now, I wonder I had the nerve to provoke fate so openly.

'There's nothing to worry about,' I told myself as I walked along the damp pavement. 'It's England, and daylight, and none of these people know you, and that passport photo was never much of a likeness. And after all, you haven't done anything very terrible:

help an escaped lunatic who's as sane as yourself and mildly assault in succession one bogus policeman, one elderly mental specialist, one pretty girl, one unknown stranger, and one Chrysler car. Pull yourself together—worse things happen on boat-race night.'

'But maybe it isn't all quite so idyllic as that' retorted another part of me. 'Don't forget the police are after you—the real police, properly dressed. Don't forget there's a good ten days to go before the girl's legally safe. And above all, don't forget that Gloria Thingummy *may have died.* Then where would you be? Still assuring yourself there's nothing to worry about, or wondering how to convince a jury it was manslaughter and not murder?'

Thus I argued within me as I pursued my way: but at least, I considered, I was safe from Dr. Paul. Whatever the man's character and powers he was certainly no magician, and it seemed to me that no one less could possibly be aware, first that I was within a hundred miles of Thames Ditton, and second that I proposed to visit the post-office there for the purpose of obtaining £50 in the name of John Clive.

Then a nasty thought struck me. How was I to prove to the postal officials that I *was* Clive? I had no used envelopes, no driving licence, nothing at all which would establish the identity. This was only to be expected, of course, since in reality it didn't exist, but I could hardly offer that fact as an explanation if I were asked awkward questions. The problem made me halt in my tracks for quite a minute; but I wasn't going to be baulked by so small a detail. I turned into the first bookshop I saw and bought a copy in the *Penguin Library* of *Deep Waters,* by W.W. Jacobs. It seemed an apt title. I then entered a cheap cafe, secluded myself in a corner with a cup of vile tea, and after much cogitation evolved the following inscription, which I copied into the title-page of the book:

'*To my friend, John Clive, with thanks for a most pleasant week-end. Sincerely yours, W. W. Jacobs.*'

(If the distinguished author in question ever hears about this misuse of his name, I can only say in excuse that the forgery has long since been destroyed, and that he is at liberty to do the same at my expense as often as he pleases.)

After I had put away my fountain-pen I fingered the leaves to take off the newness and slipped the book into my pocket. Then I emerged on to the pavement just in time to save the life of Jervis Brown.

It wasn't a spectacular performance: merely the usual business of an absent-minded man about to step under the wheels of an omnibus, and perhaps I exaggerate. However, that was what he said I'd done when we were both safe again. He was a pallid undersized little creature of forty or so, and his weak grey eyes almost had tears in them as he began to thank me. For some reason he removed his bowler hat before he started speaking; the action was so natural, so nearly automatic, that I could hardly believe it was done for my benefit, yet I could think of no other solution until it occurred to me that it might be some kind of signal. I glanced wildly round, and decided that I must get away from the gathering crowd.

". . . saved my life, that's what you did," came his thin voice, but I cut him short.

"Piffle!" I said. "The bus would probably have bounced over you anyway. Look here, I'm in a frightful hurry—good morning."

But he wasn't to be disposed of so easily. He extended an arm and took hold of mine, peering up at me intensely. I stared at him very squarely, told myself that nobody who looked so simple could possibly be dangerous, and began to move away, he following me because we were still linked.

"Oh but—but I haven't thanked you properly yet," he protested. "Why"—with a giggle which might have been due to nervousness, "why, I don't even know your name, sir."

"Clive," I told him. "Let's dodge all these people."

We hurried down a side street, thrusting our way past gaping women and congratulatory men, and presently found ourselves alone outside the entrance to a goods-yard. Then we paused to regard one another, and for no special reason I started to laugh. The situation struck me as vaguely humorous.

For a moment he stared, and then his white hairless face creased into an answering smile.

"It was very good of you, sir," he began again, timidly—"really very good. I'm not much of a hand at this sort of thing, but you saved my life, not a doubt about it, and I only wish I knew how to thank you properly."

"Don't try," I said. "Just forget anything happened—and keep your eyes open next time you cross the road. Good-bye."

I held out my hand and after a little hesitation he took it, at the same moment removing his bowler hat once more. He jerked my arm up and down more forcibly that I should have expected, and then in the midst of an upward movement let go of me as if I had become suddenly red hot.

"I know," he observed mysteriously. "Just a sec."

Back went the hat, and he searched his inner pocket, after some trouble producing a grubby card.

"Here, take this, sir," he begged. "If you've ever got a job in my line I'll do it gladly and no charge, and you shall have the best of everything—silver fittings and the very finest horses in London. Truthfully, sir, I mean it. Just telephone and I'll drop all else. Clive you said your name is, didn't you?"

"Yes, John Clive."

"Right, I won't forget. Any time, day or night—and heaven bless you."

And, again surprising me, he turned suddenly and bustled off without a backward glance.

For some seconds I gazed after him in wonder. Silver fittings and the finest horses? It sounded like something to do with the Lord Mayor's Show. I directed my attention to his card, which so far I had had no time to read: then I laughed till it hurt, because this was what it said.

---

**JERVIS BROWN**
*Undertaker and Funeral Furnisher*

| | |
|---|---|
| 16 South St, | Reverence |
| Thames Ditton. | Taste and |
| Tel. 404 | Refinement. |

Deferred Terms

---

When I had recovered I continued my way to the post-office, staring round cautiously as I re-entered the main street. In spite of exercising the utmost vigilance I saw no one who looked in any way suspicious: it seemed that as far as the passers-by were concerned I lacked all interest. For a moment I had the curious feeling that I was invisible: that if I were to stand in front of the approaching woman in the red hat, she would waddle through me unawares.

I obtained possession of my money in much the manner I had hoped for. The assistant at the counter repeated my false name in a listless drawl, walked across to a set of pigeon-holes, after a short search pulled out a registered envelope, glanced at me shrewdly once, gave me a form to sign, and handed over my property with a brief smile. The *Penguin* in my pocket grew noticeably heavy as I passed through the swing doors, as if protesting at its inutility.

And now, again a comparatively rich man, I became immensely wary without quite knowing why. Perhaps it was that the ease with which the programme had been carried through so far made me suspect fate of trying to gull me. My senses sharpened: I looked about me anxiously, ready to read danger in the innocent way an errand boy plunged his bandaged hand into his basket, only to produce not a pistol but a bag of groceries; prepared to believe that the smartly-dressed girl stooping to leash her terrier was merely endeavouring to pretend she wasn't watching me. Yet all the time common sense told me I was being ridiculous, that the sanest thing to do would be to return casually to the caravan by the most direct route.

There was really nothing whatever to be frightened of, that I could see: no parked cars tenanted by thugs with turned-up collars and turned-down hats, no loungers waiting to find out which way I went, not even a policeman in sight. To hesitate was fantastic: yet actions dictated solely by instinct often are, in my opinion, and none the worse for that.

I began to stroll away, not quickly and not slowly. As far as possible I kept to the inside of the pavement, and most of my attention was now concentrated on persuading myself that if I veered round suddenly I should discover nothing I feared, and simply prove that I was a complete fool. But in spite of all my mental reassurances the desire to turn became too strong. I obeyed it, swinging on my heel with a jerk which might well have wrenched my ankle. And then I felt my scalp tingling, for barely five yards distant stood a thick-set man in a leather coat. One look at his brutal face and his small steady eyes told me that this time instinct had been right. I was confronted by an enemy, and I had no notion what to do.

## IX

IN CASE ANYONE SUGGESTS that I ought immediately to have taken to my heels, let it be remembered that the last thing I wanted was to draw attention to myself. Suppose my pursuer raised the traditional cry of *Stop thief!*—what then? In such circumstances it would be a fluke if I escaped scot free. Or perhaps it will be said that I should have held my ground and waited for him to make the first move: but I'm afraid I didn't think of that. Motion seemed imperative, and a second later I found myself walking straight into the shop outside which I had come to so abrupt a halt. I perceived instantly that it was a butcher's, and within the same breath I was ordering a pound of fillet steak and insisting that it be English meat.

The shopman moved away to satisfy my demands, and I ventured a sidelong look towards the door. Again I experienced the tingling sensation in my scalp, and with reason. Not only was the leather-coated ruffian actually coming in after me, but two more significant figures were loitering at the window.

I scarcely had time to notice what they were doing in detail, for Leather-Coat assumed the offensive. He contorted his ugly face into a bad imitation of a surprised grin, and smote me heavily on the back.

"Why, Charlie boy!" he exclaimed heartily. "Just fancy seeing you in this part of the world!"

What the devil was a fellow to do? Especially one who daren't risk a disturbance because the police were after him: once in their hands my hopes of helping Rhona would be negligible. I had two choices: to make a dash for it, and have half Thames Ditton chasing me over ground that it knew and I didn't, or to go quietly, as they say, and rely on my wits to set me free at some later occasion. If only I could somehow convey the £50 to Rhona, I thought bitterly! Yet that was plainly impossible. However fictitious a name I invented for the butcher, the address would be far too dangerous.

I faced the back-slapping stranger with brisk despair.

"Hullo yourself!" I returned. "I thought you were still in clink."

The remark took him by surprise, as I meant it to, and I saw the butcher's bald head lift in sudden interest.

"Who, me?" he countered. "Nah, you're mixing me up with some other fellow. Still, you always was a one for a joke."

He attempted another smile, which got stuck somewhere between eye and mouth and conveyed only the fact that his front teeth needed attention.

"Ha! ha! Me in prison!" he remarked, as if it were the funniest suggestion possible. *"Coming my way?"*

It was both threat and command, and I disliked the tone in which he spoke. He was at my elbow while I paid for the useless steak with the last of my small change, the vendor being obviously puzzled by the tenseness of the atmosphere. When I turned towards the door he took my arm, and through my overcoat I could feel his fingers grip me like a rat-trap.

"Going to be good?" he enquired in a low voice as we reached the pavement, and the other two closed in. Both were strangers to me.

"Needs must," I rejoined. "What's the lay-out?"

"That's easy," said the shorter of the others, from his bearing evidently their leader. His name I afterwards discovered to be Brett, and I will call him that to save confusion.

"First we'll collect Miss French," he went on, "and then we'll take you both to lunch with the doctor—he's expecting you."

It was a question of bluffing them now or never and I acted accordingly, because never is a long day. I stared at him as if amazed, opened my mouth to speak, hesitated, and did my best to go white, though I don't suppose for a moment that I succeeded.

"Collect Miss French!" I echoed. "Good lord, what a fool I am!"

"What d'you mean?" demanded Brett quickly. He was dressed conventionally in dark coat and bowler, a neatly rolled umbrella hung on his arm, and his sharp foxy face studied me intently. His companion was vacant-looking by comparison, and the man in the leather coat had fallen back a pace so that I was unable to gauge the effect of my words by his expression.

I ignored Brett's query.

"Still, it might be worse!" I muttered, and then raised my voice. "All right, gentlemen—if you understand the term. First we collect

Miss French: only you'll have to lead the way because I don't happen to know where she is at the moment."

"And now tell us the one about the big bad wolf!" remarked the lout beside me unoriginally. "Say, you must think we're a bunch of coots. You don't happen to know where she is! Haw! haw! Try again, brother."

"Hold your tongue, Sam!" commanded the leader with impatience. "And why don't you know where she is, Mr. Clive?" he asked quietly.

I suppose their presence should have prepared me sufficiently for the use of my false name, but I admit I felt shaken. That at least was secret, I had thought, for there had been no one near me in the post-office and Jervis Brown seemed wholly genuine. Had my cousin's husband been talking, I wondered? But hardly so or he would never have sent the money, and anyway it wasn't somehow like him.

"I'll explain if you want me to," I replied, "but can't we go into a pub or somewhere? I hate standing about on pavements, and I could do with a drink."

"Sorry—I'm a teetotaller," said the other firmly. "This is as good a place for an explanation as anywhere. Why can't you take us to Miss French?"

"Because I don't know where she is. Good heavens, man, don't you understand the language unless people spell it? Not that I would take you if I could, mind, only the question doesn't arise. We decided to part company the night before last, and I've no more idea what she's done since then than you seem to have—now."

"Now?" he demanded instantly.

"Exactly: now. You know, if you'll excuse my saying so you don't strike me as over-bright. Maybe that's because you're temperance, though."

The third man broke his silence at this, emitting a feeble snigger and obtaining in response a scowl from Brett.

"You see," I went on, as convincingly as I could, "I'm not used to a hectic life like this. I'd had quite enough by Tuesday afternoon, and I was hanged if I saw why I should be mixed up in a police case, so I quit. All the same, I can't say I've been feeling very proud of myself since. I naturally expected you people had got hold of the girl again by this time, and I was half thinking of telephoning Dr. Paul to find out. But now you tell me you don't know anything about her either, and on the whole I'm pretty glad."

Sam, just behind me, had apparently recovered from his previous snub.

"That be damned for a yarn!" he snorted: and I was very much inclined to agree with him. It sounded pitifully weak, yet for some reason Brett seemed inclined to consider it seriously.

"Where did you two part company?" he asked.

"At Victoria Station: about half past six, as near as I remember."

"And what have *you* been doing with yourself in the meantime?"

I tried not to falter: it was a question I had known would be forthcoming.

"On Tuesday night I stayed at a hotel as plain Mr. Smith," I said, "and the same last night, only at a different one, and there I was Mr. Jones. Then I came along here and bumped straight into you."

"To collect £50," interjected the man who had sniggered.

"Yes—though I can't imagine how you guessed."

"We didn't guess," was Brett's curt answer. "What made you arrange about that?"

"The girl—it was settled before we agreed to separate. It's been a confounded nuisance—otherwise I'd have been in Scotland by now."

And then an idea appeared to strike me.

"Blazes!" I exclaimed. "Now I *do* begin to see things! She's the only person who could possibly have told you I'd be here today. The little—!"

My language about Rhona was deplorable: but, as I had hoped, Brett looked a trifle more impressed.

"You're wrong," he said. "We didn't find out through her, else we wouldn't be bothering about you."

"No? That's nice to hear, anyway. I was thinking maybe Dr. Paul was a bit sore with me."

"I dare say he is, but business comes first," he observed, and stared at me critically with his long nose outpointed and his pale eyes unwinking.

"Can you give me a shred of proof you're not making all this up?" he asked, and I shrugged.

"I don't suppose so—not the sort you'd accept."

"Well, try."

"All right. I told you a moment ago that Miss French and I agreed to separate on Tuesday evening, and I also told you I haven't been so pleased with myself for turning her loose. That's the only reason I didn't make a bolt for it just now: I was reckoning you'd caught her, and I might be able to help. Otherwise I assure you I'd have given you a pretty good run for your money, and I fancy you expected me to or you wouldn't have rolled up in such force."

Brett nodded.

"Yes, that's all very nice, but I'd hardly call it proof. It would be much more to the point if you told me the names of the hotels you stayed at."

"Ah, it never occurred to me," I said, and named two of the largest though by no means the most exclusive. At once he looked towards the third man.

"Go and find out, Wilson," he ordered. "Initials?"—to me.

"J. both times, I'm afraid—I wasn't feeling very original."

Wilson departed in search of a telephone. The rest of us moved down the street, crossed, and halted presently by an unattended Packhard.

"Get in after me," said Brett, and I did so. Sam followed, and there I was nicely sandwiched. I had about as much chance of getting away as a fly has on a new and sticky paper. We then waited in silence, and for myself the time passed unpleasantly. Everything depended on the report the third man brought back. If it proved to be what I hoped, what I was gambling on, perhaps they would decide to take me along for an interview with Dr. Paul. On the other hand, if they weren't satisfied they might prefer some quiet spot in the country and the effect of a little third-degree work.

But luckily nothing like that happened. Wilson declared, not without disgust, that on Tuesday night the first hotel had harboured no fewer than nine gentlemen passing as J. Smith, and the second seven who called themselves J. Jones on the following evening: the gamble had come off.

Brett frowned for a moment at the news, and then made his decision. Almost at once we were in motion, on our way to Dr. Paul's private sanatorium, and although I closed my eyes I was very far from being asleep. I pondered my position from every angle, and could see only two bright things about it: Rhona's whereabouts were still unknown to her enemies, and nobody had yet relieved me of my hard-won £50.

# X

**B**EFORE WE GOT TO ESHER my companions blindfolded me with a scarf, rather theatrically I thought. Thereafter the road seemed nothing but corners, all taken at a high speed, and I suspected that they were purposely making it impossible for me to remember the route. For some time I was unable to see any sense in the manoeuvre, until I realized that it was a precaution against any future attempts at escape I might make. Doubtless Rhona's successful effort still rankled.

When the car eventually stopped I was helped out, not too gently, and half led half carried into a building. A few minutes later someone removed the scarf, and I was face to face with Dr. Paul in what looked to be his study.

One glance showed me that the newspapers had grossly exaggerated the effects of my injection on Tuesday. He was dressed in black coat and striped trousers, and his chin bore a patch of sticking-plaster where I had hit him: otherwise he appeared perfectly fit, and I must say the discovery relieved me. As if he read my thoughts he at once smiled, and declared that neither he nor the girl Gloria felt any serious indisposition.

"All the same, I don't fancy she's too well pleased with you," he remarked, "but perhaps that isn't altogether surprising. And now, Mr. Dane, do sit down and make yourself comfortable—while you can."

"Which means what?" I asked, and he shrugged, surveying me with those curiously yellow eyes of his.

"It's hard to say—it depends so much on you. In spite of that very ingenious story you told Brett, I can't really believe you know nothing of Rhona's whereabouts. You don't somehow strike me as a quitter, Mr. Dane. I'm afraid you haven't enough sense for that."

"But it remains true," I lied quietly. "I'd quite convinced myself she was back here in your abominable charge: else I shouldn't have dreamt of putting up such a feeble show in Thames Ditton. And that reminds me: would it be too much to enquire how in the world you traced me there? Magic is all I can think of at the moment."

He smiled again, showing his long white canines; yet looking so benevolent that for a second I could hardly credit what I had been told, and had experienced for myself, was his real character.

"That's a common failing," he observed. "I mean, the attribution of the apparently unfathomable to extra-natural causes. In general it's a form of vanity, I believe. '*I* can't see how it was done; therefore there wasn't any known way; therefore it was achieved by sorcery.' I'm not saying that's necessarily so in your case, mind, because I don't think you're serious in suggesting magic. You mayn't have much sense, but you aren't quite so silly as that."

I bowed sardonically, and he continued a moment later in the same mock-whimsical manner.

"Shall I tell you or shan't I? There seems no reason not to, and it may help to impress you with the foolishness of opposing me. Do you remember the Chinese proverb which says, If you are sure there is a tiger on the mountain, avoid the mountain? I think you might do worse than take it to heart."

I grinned without concealment.

"That wouldn't be vanity, of course?" I murmured: but he affected not to hear.

"We discovered where you banked from a careful search of your flat," he told me. "When Nick's little pick-pocketing trick came to my knowledge—he really does it to perfection, you know-—I was fairly safe in assuming that you'd soon be in need of ready cash. After that it was merely a matter of application. That you would communicate with your bank was inevitable, and in view of what the newspapers were saying you'd hardly care to approach another branch. Further, a communication—and a consequent answer—by post seemed indicated, since before you could withdraw money you would have to present a cheque. We took pains to ensure that you did not go in person, of course. One of my men—or rather, one of Nick's men—was even arrested for loitering with intent to commit a felony; but he'd been in trouble before, so that was scarcely your fault.

"Some time on Wednesday, then, your bank would be sending you money. Our task was to discover to what address."

He paused, and gave me a twinkling smile: his manner was so attentive that I might have been a valued friend.

"What would you have done in my position, Mr. Dane?" he enquired. "How would you have solved the problem?"

I shook my head, for I had no idea.

"Held up the bank, perhaps?" I hazarded; but he dismissed the suggestion with a little wave of his flexible hands.

"Too risky," he said. "No, I prefer my own method: I arranged for the temporary disablement of the clerk who posted the registered letters. Not on the way to the office, naturally, but when he was returning with the registration slips in his possession. It was really very simple: done with a hypodermic needle containing much the same substance with which you treated me. Willing hands were nearby to assist the poor youth—loosen his collar, and restrain the crowd, and of course abstract the receipts. I admit I hadn't expected you to think of using a false name, but the *poste-restante* address left little doubt of our goal. Nevertheless, it may interest you to learn that enquiries are probably still being made at a hotel in Norwich which seemed a possible alternative."

"Yes, you were very clever," I agreed, and could hardly have done less. After all, even if his scheme did strike me as somehow not quite fool-proof, he had doubtless given me only the barest outline, and my presence in the same room with him was sufficient evidence that it had worked. To some extent I felt not so much inclined to kick myself for being caught, and I made a mental resolve never again to underestimate Dr. Paul's resources. How sadly and how often I was to fail in that resolve I could not know, and looking back I am glad. I think my own particular brand of ignorant optimism was about the only attitude which could have carried things through.

There was an interval of silence, during which the doctor seemed lost in thought. I spent the time gazing about me, and making sure that we were the only two persons in the room. From somewhere near, though, I could hear muffled voices and the sounds of human movements, and I was under no delusion about my present chances of escape. I might perhaps manage to lay my companion out, but that promised to do me little eventual good: I was without the remotest idea which way I ought to go if I ever got outside. The only window in the study where we sat was curtained, draped with some kind of gauze impossible to see through.

Presently Dr. Paul looked up, and for once he forgot to smile.

"The trouble is, of course, that Brett and the others made a regrettable mess of things this morning," he informed me. "Anyone but a lunatic would have waited to see where you went after obtaining your money, not have shown his hand so prematurely. It just shows how difficult it is to find reliable agents."

"Well, you've got Brett's remedy handy," I remarked. "This place is supposed to be a lunatic asylum, isn't it?"

He nodded, and frowned a little.

"You should learn to be less facetious," he told me gravely. "There are times when your speech becomes irritating to an adult intelligence. Whatever I might do to Brett and his equally stupid companions wouldn't repair the damage. I must face the plain fact that they brought me back the wrong person: unless of course I can discover ways of turning you into the right one."

"Yes?" I prompted, anxious to learn his intentions towards me. I didn't see how he could release me—it would make my intended role of unsuspecting guide to Rhona too obvious: but I found it considerably easier to imagine how I could be forced to divulge all the information he wanted. Anybody who thinks I was then, or am now, anything of a hero is greatly mistaken. Although I tried not to show as much, I was distinctly afraid: partly about what might be done to me, and partly because I had only small faith in my powers of resistance. There was one word thumping away at the bottom of my mind like a metronome: torture. If Dr. Paul felt sure I was lying, then his simplest course would be to make me talk, and I knew in my heart that he would need to be very dull not to succeed.

Again he seemed to read my thoughts: or perhaps my fears were true, and I had merely been reading his.

"I'll be quite frank with you, Mr. Dane," he said. "At the moment I'm not absolutely positive how much or how little you know. If I could afford a day in which to study you attentively, then I've no doubt I could reach an accurate opinion, but I cannot. Miss French must be located with all speed: otherwise she may take fright at your non-appearance."

Was he trying to trap me, I wondered? I decided to find out.

"As she isn't expecting me, I don't really see she'll have much to be frightened about if I don't turn up," I said.

(And yet by now Rhona was probably in a torment of apprehension, I thought, and tried not to consider her plight in case it affected my judgment.)

The doctor nodded, ambiguously, and drowsed again in his swivel chair, his hands folded over his waistcoat and his yellow eyes shut. He reminded me of a well-fed cat on a sunny windowsill.

"Why not set me free?" I suggested a little wildly. "If I knew where she was I'd go there, and you could follow. In point of fact, as I keep repeating, I don't know, but I give you my promise that I shall be looking for her quite as hard as you will."

"Why?" he demanded, alert in an instant. "I understood that you'd decided to abandon her, Mr. Dane."

"I did," I told him steadily, "but I've thought better of it—more than ever since being brought here. I hate to think of her being in your hands."

"Really? And you believe that if I released you, and had you followed, you could not only find her but also outwit your attendants? I take that to be your meaning?"

"Right as usual, Doctor: unless you've got a few more employees I haven't met. After all, I don't think it would be too boastful to recall that the day before yesterday I outwitted you yourself."

Contrary to my expectation, he took no offence.

"You mean by staring over my shoulder at nothing? I admit the point—forgive me for not congratulating you earlier. However, I lay no claim to infallibility, though I usually win in the long run. So you'd like to be set free, confident in your ability to elude pursuit and also locate Miss French? Really, Mr. Dane, you *can* be quite funny at times!" and he actually laughed.

"I'm afraid I don't see the joke," I said.

"Don't you? I do. Let's apply a little common sense to the situation. If you don't know any more than you admit then you may as well remain here, because there's nothing you could do which I shan't be able to think of for myself. If on the other hand you're withholding information, as I'm inclined to believe, then I've no doubt I can persuade you to impart it. My chief reason for hesitating is that I'm not sure about you, as I said just now. Also, though you mayn't accept the statement, I'm a kind-hearted man. Even though you have assaulted me and my servants, and damaged my car, I should still dislike to hear you screaming unnecessarily."

"And why would I be screaming?" I asked, my stomach troubling me somewhat.

"Because the person whom I should instruct to question you is probably one of the cleverest men in Europe at making people scream if they don't answer," he told me seriously. "Not up to Asiatic standards, of course, but then I've never met a white man who is. There seems to be a strain of softness at the core of the western mentality: revulsion sets in beyond a certain point. One day when I have time—and the necessary means—I intend to investigate the question, though I can't guarantee that you'll be in a position to appreciate my results."

He regarded me with a cold appraising scrutiny.

"Have you ever had a live tooth slowly filed down to the gum, Mr. Dane?" he queried. "They say it can be excruciatingly painful."

My stomach grew even more disturbed: Dr. Paul's manner was suddenly so quietly malevolent, and with uncanny instinct he had gone straight to a weak point. If there's one thing I detest more than another at the dentist's, it's the feel of his drill. I loathe the sense of helplessness as one lies waiting with head back and mouth agape for the moment of contact, in one's ears the horrid soft whirr of the machinery and presently in one's nostrils the smell of burning bone; and always in the mind the fear that his hand will slip. The only thing that makes the ordeal bearable is belief in his intentions: that they are peaceful and curative, that he isn't out to inflict pain.

Sitting there in Dr. Paul's study I had no such support. I found the implications of his threat appalling: I shrank from the thought of being impotently delivered to the devilries of some unofficial dentist, one whose object was to make me talk or suffer. Yet, paradoxically, my outward reaction a moment later was defiant. That may have been because I was obscurely ashamed of my timidity—I can't say.

"A charming suggestion!" I remarked with a sneer. "The great mental specialist watches his victim's teeth ground down, much as a particularly nasty small boy might enjoy watching somebody else cut off a frog's legs. Well, carry on, and much good may it do you! The longer you fool around with me, as you admitted yourself just now, the more chance Miss French will have to get clear. Not because she's waiting for me, but because we none of us know where she is, and she'll be better off if you're three days behind her than if you're only two. Meanwhile, do you mind if I smoke a pipe while I can still hold it?"

He regarded me dispassionately, unaffected by my outburst.

"Smoke by all means," he agreed. "You know, you're rather a queer type, Mr. Dane. I'm not sure I've met anyone quite like you before."

"And I'm very sure I've never met anyone like you," I returned. "What exactly *is* the effect of hashish in cigars, I wonder? I must remember to look it up when I get the chance."

"*If* you get the chance," he corrected equably. "I don't think you will, though. And now be kind enough to enjoy your pipe in silence—I want to consider the situation."

By the time I had applied a match he was ready for me, however.

"I can't release you," he said, "because you'd be not only useless but possibly dangerous. On the other hand, unless you can give me positive assistance there seems little point in burdening myself with you indefinitely. What I propose to do is this. You shall have two hours of solitude to reflect upon the attitude you intend to adopt. At the end of that time I shall send for you, and if you prove obstinate I shall hand you over to the assistant I mentioned just now. Incidentally, he's a fully-qualified dental-surgeon, so you needn't be afraid he'll bungle. Or perhaps I ought to put it that he used to be qualified, until he rather foolishly took advantage of a young woman under an anaesthetic."

"But since I'm not a young woman," I remarked gravely, "I haven't even that to look forward to. And when you finally come to grasp that I really *don't* know anything."

His black brows contracted in a frown.

"If I were ever convinced of your ignorance I expect I should lose interest in you, and act accordingly."

"Certification?"

"I'm afraid not—the circumstances are different from when we discussed the matter the other day. Miss French is no longer in my abominable charge, as you term it, so what concern am I likely to have in your survival? However"—and he leant forward, tapping his desk impressively—"you can purchase your life, and also your ultimate freedom, easily enough. Tell me where to find the girl, and you shall be released a fortnight from today."

"In what condition?" I asked pointedly.

"The same that you're in now, on my word of honour."

I was tempted to answer lightly, but some sense of caution restrained me.

"I'd accept your offer if I could," I told him—"or I believe I would. As things are, you'll just have to do your worst. For all I know Miss French may be abroad by now, and I rather hope she is."

He nodded, pressed a bell in the wall behind him, and the man called Sam came in. I was blindfolded again, and within two minutes had been conducted along corridors, down one flight of stairs and up another, and through a door. When I removed the scarf from my face I found myself alone in a small room no bigger than the caravan, though loftier. Its walls were of distempered stone, its only window was barred and well above my reach, and it was lit by a naked electric bulb in the ceiling. The furniture consisted of a chair, a low table, and a sort of divan, all of the cheapest materials and poorest workmanship; the air smelt faintly of creosote, and the place was bitterly cold. On the whole I felt pretty depressed as I turned up my collar and sat down to take stock of the position.

## XI

**M**Y FIRST ACTION WAS TO LOOK AT MY WATCH. To my surprise it registered only 12.30: yet long before now Rhona would have become alarmed at my absence. I could picture her restlessly running to the door every few minutes to begin with, and then by degrees less frequently, until at last she remained brooding in her chair, a lonely figure in schoolgirl's dress. I sincerely hoped she hadn't left the caravan in order to look for me, and then reflected that for all the help I was likely to afford her she might as well go and surrender to the nearest policeman. As far as I remembered she had about two shillings in cash and a slender supply of food, and I tried not to think of what would happen to her when both were exhausted. Instead I turned my thoughts towards my own troubles, though—in defence—not selfishly. I was conscious that whether through any fault of mine or not I had badly let her down, and it obviously devolved upon me to make amends. Only how?

I had been pushed into the room with little ceremony, and the sound of the shutting door was an unpleasant clang suggesting steel. After I had risen and gone over to it my suspicions were confirmed. There was no handle on my side, and the whole fitted so closely that I could hardly have got the blade of a pen-knife into the crack even if I had had mine on me. About two-thirds of the way up was a small square opening, plainly intended for purposes of observation from without. It helped to show me the thickness of the door, some two inches, but that was all. The grille which covered it I found impossible to move, and if I had been able to file the bars away I could never have got more than my head through.

After a rapid search I became convinced that until someone chose to release me I had no hope of escape. The walls, when banged with the chair, sounded as solid as the pyramids, and the concrete floor offered no remotest hint of hidden trap-doors. What it amounted to was that I must use not force but guile. My best move would be to attract somebody's attention, and then attempt to bribe him. I still had my registered envelope, and it looked like being my only weapon.

It occurred to me then that I hadn't yet opened it, and I did so. The money contents were correct, and there was also a letter from my cousin's husband; not the usual printed affair, but a dozen lines in his own stiff script. 'I trust the situation is not so serious as would appear' was one of the phrases, and I laughed grimly. The situation was roughly a thousand times worse than that, and I now regretted bitterly that I hadn't made a bolt for freedom in Thames Ditton. I should at least have had some chance of getting away.

Probably the least important of my troubles was the intense coldness of the cell I occupied, yet such is human nature that very shortly I began to pay it more attention than anything. My overcoat seemed to produce no warmth, and Imery's suit beneath was designed only for summer wear. I looked at my watch again, and was horrified to discover that I had wasted more than ten minutes of my precious two hours. Something must be done, since inaction had little to recommend it, and I accordingly set about shouting. When no one answered I continued to shout, and at twelve minutes to one I heard footsteps in the passage outside.

I peered through the grille and immediately found myself regarding the girl Gloria, now neatly garbed in what seemed to be a nurse's uniform. It certainly suited her, but I refrained from saying so: indeed, there was little opportunity, because it was she who spoke first.

"You really mustn't yell like that, Mr. Dane!" she told me sharply, without the ghost of a smile. "You'll disturb the patients. What is it you want?"

"Heat and food, principally," I said. "And if I don't get them I shall go on making a noise till something happens."

She smiled then, a little to my surprise in view of what Dr. Paul had said about her feelings towards me.

"That would be just too bad!" she observed. "Then I should have to give you a dose of medicine—with a needle, of course."

The moment the words were out of her red mouth an idea jumped into my mind. Without hesitation I pursued it, though indirectly.

"Yes, I'm sorry about that," I averred. "I wouldn't have dreamt of assaulting you so ungallantly if there'd been any choice. Were you out for long?"

"About five hours," she answered, and I absorbed the information with interest. If things came to their worst, it might be a possible way of delaying the next stage of the proceedings.

"But I forgive you," she went on. "You see, it meant a bonus."

"Splendid!" I said. "Is that a hint? Because I'd gladly give ten bob for a blanket and a piece of bread and cheese."

She laughed, the silvery tinkle I remembered having heard in the flat, and regarded me with friendly amusement. With her golden hair just showing under her nurse's cap, and her faultless features and figure, she was by no means unattractive; in spite of what I had been told about her I was soon responding with an answering grin.

"No, I wasn't cadging for tips," she assured me. "I'll see what I can find for you, though. Anything to drink?"

"What you've got—poison excluded. At least, I'm not even sure about that. Look here, you do *seem* to be human—will you answer a straight question?"

I spoke seriously, and she studied me a moment with apparent interest before nodding.

"If I can," she added.

"Thanks. Then what I want to know is, am I really going to have my teeth filed down if I don't satisfy Dr. Paul I can't help him?"

I wasn't in a very good position for watching how she took the question—the passage was rather dark. All the same, I fancied I saw her turn pale.

"Is that what they told you?" she asked quickly. "Who?"

"The doctor."

She frowned, and hesitated a second.

"Then if you do know anything I advise you to tell him," she said. "He's quite capable of filing half your head off if you annoy him."

Her manner was less sympathetic than I could have wished, yet I felt inclined to think that she had been somehow disturbed at my news. For a short space she stood irresolutely looking at me, or at my face, rather, which must have been all she could see, and cut up into squares by the grille at that. Then without another word she turned and hurried away; I heard her footsteps fade and die, and once more I was alone.

'I wonder if she'd take a bribe?' I asked myself. 'She can't be indifferent to money, or she wouldn't be so pleased about her bonus. Yet she's sure to have a pretty good job here, as far as pay goes, and she'd be a fool to risk losing it for the sake of £50. Not even that much, either, because I must keep some spare cash.'

I pondered the problem, less because I had much hope that bribery would prove a solution than because I could see no other. Then it struck me that if I were provided with food and a blanket—though it seemed uncertain, judging from the way Gloria had gone off—then before they could be introduced into my cell the door would have to be undone.

That of course led to considerations of a sudden attack upon whoever should enter, but I may as well say that I soon discarded the idea. What chance would I have of even finding my way out of the house without being seen? My knowledge of the local geography was absolutely nil, and I had nothing fit for aggressive use unless I tore the chair to pieces. Besides, I profoundly disliked the thought of slinking round a strange building with my heart between my chattering teeth, in a wild search for the most direct route to the nearest main road. Doubtless my attitude was a cowardly one, and if I had been at all competent for my position I should have welcomed the smallest start towards freedom. The truth is, as I said before, that I'm not a hero.

Some ten minutes passed, and then, when I had almost given up hope, I heard Gloria's returning steps: no man could have walked so firmly without making twice the noise. I went to the grille, and there she was with a rug and a tray of food.

"That's decent of you," I said. "I'm very grateful."

"So you ought to be," was the reply. "There'll probably be a hell of a row if anyone finds out."

"Then why do it? Because you're sorry for me?"

"Maybe!" she answered lightly: "though it's your own damn fault for interfering."

As she spoke she produced a key from the pocket in her white apron, and despite my previous resolution to avoid violence my heart began to beat more quickly. It was just as well that I hadn't built any great hopes on the opening of the door, though, because I should have been disastrously disappointed. The key fitted an unseen lock which served only to undo the grille: my way of escape was level with my collar, and that was about as far as I could have got through it.

In succession she handed me the rug, half a loaf of brown bread, a large piece of dutch cheese, three tomatoes, a bar of plain chocolate, and tea in a sort of milk-can with a lid and handle.

When the transaction had been completed I thanked her again, and then made my first move towards the business I had in mind.

Standing where—I hoped—she could see clearly what I was doing, I produced my registered envelope. From it I took a ten-shilling note, and held it out to her.

"That was the price, wasn't it?" I remarked: but she shook her head.

"You can have it for love!" she told me pertly, and turned to go: at which I became alarmed.

"But you may just as well take it!" I protested. "It doesn't look like being much good to me."

She faced me again at that, and what she said showed that she had seen the envelope all right.

"Then why not the lot?" she suggested mockingly. "Don't be silly—put it away and eat your food. You're supposed to be hungry."

"I am," I agreed: which was true, in case I haven't mentioned it. "But I've got worse things than hunger to worry about. As far as I can see, in roughly an hour and a quarter I'm due to be tortured, and I don't fancy the prospect. Can you think of any way of avoiding it?"

"What sort of way?" she countered, staring at me with her head a little to one side and her full lips open.

"Oh, hang it!" I exclaimed. "Don't let's waste time beating about the bush. I want to get out of this confounded place: will you help me?"

It wasn't what I had intended to say at all, but from her just perceptible nod I received the impression that I might perhaps have acted wisely in being frank.

"Why should I?" she asked, her face as innocent as a child's. "You don't mean anything to me, you know. I'm sorry if they're going to hurt you, but it's really none of my business. Besides, we should never get away with it—you'd be caught and I'd be half skinned."

"I wasn't suggesting you should help me for nothing," I pointed out. "I'd make it worth your while—or try to."

"How much?" she demanded quickly, with evident interest: and for the first time I really began to believe that luck might be with me.

"I can give you £40 in cash here and now," I replied, trying to make it sound like the price of a superior gold-mine, "and I'll send you another £100 within a week."

Her answer to that proposal was a giggle.

"My dear good man, talk sense! Why, if this affair goes through all right I shall get at least £1000 from Dr. Paul."

"So you may think," I said, endeavouring to keep my head. "Personally I doubt it, from what I've seen of the gentleman: a metaphorical kick in the pants would be more his mark. Still, I understand your point of view; naturally you wouldn't be in the game if it didn't pay. With looks like yours you could walk into any musical-comedy manager's office in London and be a star in six months."

"Bilge!" she retorted. "And I know, because I've tried. Pretty faces and long legs are nine a penny, and I simply can't sing a note."

"All the better," I asserted. "The singing's always the worst part. Look here, I'll tell you what I'll do. If this business *doesn't* go through I'll see you get £2000."

"Meaning if I let you escape and Rhona inherits?"

"Yes."

"Then you *do* know where she is?"

"Not at all: but we've made an arrangement to meet two days after her twenty-first birthday."

"And why should I believe she'll pay up on your say-so? Or you either, for that matter?"

That was a facer, of course, and I decided to appear fairly honest: she was looking at me very intently.

"I'm darned if I know," I answered, shrugging. "I haven't a cheque book with me, and you probably wouldn't think much of an I.O.U., but it's all I can offer except ordinary verbal promises."

Gloria said nothing for half a minute, standing deep in thought within an arm's length of me. If I had cared to put my hand through the opening in the locked door I could have touched her.

It may be imagined with what anxiety I waited, and how I strove—I dare say unsuccessfully—to hide my rising excitement. There was still hope: she hadn't yet declined. All the same I foresaw the possibility of considerable danger even if she did consent to help me. What was to prevent her from taking my £40, guiding me to some exit from the house, at once raising the alarm, and subsequently collecting another bonus from Dr. Paul? Perhaps the undoubted fact that I couldn't have got out by myself: she might be afraid that the doctor would see through her ruse.

That thought made me halt a moment. What would the girl plan to do after I was gone, should she decide to betray her employer? I could think of nothing except for her to accompany me, and that would never suit. Pretty she might be, but I should find myself far too busy to dally with her even if I felt inclined, and I can't honestly say I did. There are other things to a girl besides looks, and so far Gloria hadn't displayed them: matters of character and disposition, I mean.

To tell the truth, I became so engrossed in my own reflections that the sound of her voice startled me.

"All right!" she whispered. "I'll help for £40 in cash and your solemn promise of £2000 if you win out. Not that you're likely to, so send me the £100 you talked about as well. Agreed?"

"Yes, I agree," I told her. "How's it to be managed?"

"I think I see a way; but you'll have to be smart, so you'd better listen carefully. As far as I know everybody's at lunch now, but I'll go and make sure. Then when I come back you'll pretend to be ill, and I shall come in to find out what's the matter, and the minute I'm inside you'll jump on me and tie me up. At least, that's what I shall say you did afterwards.

"Now this is the part you must follow closely. When you get outside this door turn left, and at the end of the passage bear right. You'll then see a glass door in front of you, leading into the garden. That's your way out, but first go into the end room on the left where the men hang their coats and take the long yellow oilskin. It belongs to one of the attendants, and he's about your size. When you've put it on—and the hat that goes with it, which you'll probably find in the pocket—then leave the house as quietly as you can. Mind you don't make a noise opening the door—it's inclined to squeak.

"The moment you're out of doors turn left, and follow the gravel path parallel to the house. But when it bears left again you must go straight on down a narrow cinder-track across the grass. In front you'll see a greenhouse, and farther on a brick wall with a little door in it. When you're through that—it isn't locked—you'll be in a wood and the road's only about five minutes' walk away.

"You'd better hide the oilskin somewhere among the trees, and when you're clear keep to the right, downhill. It's about a mile and a half to the main London road, and if you're lucky you'll get a lift or catch a bus. And remember one thing: while you're in the gardens, *walk*. You're supposed to be a man called Amos, and Amos simply never runs. D'you think you can manage it all?"

She spent another few minutes making sure I understood her directions, and then departed. By now I was more cheerful than I had been for some hours: the image of myself fastened into a dentist's-chair seemed suddenly remote and improbable. I was practically on my way to liberty, and the thought made me feel giddy, as if I had taken a long drink of sparkling wine in mistake for beer.

While I was waiting I noticed the food, and made use of the interval before Gloria's return in cramming some of it down my throat and the rest into my pockets. I also disposed of the tea, but immediately regretted the action: suppose it were drugged? A week ago such an idea would never have occurred to me, I realized, but now I was living in another and more dangerous world.

The girl came back at twenty-five minutes to two by my watch. She unlocked the door, very softly, and tiptoed in; whereupon I handed her £40 in notes. She counted them, and slipped the packet somewhere inside the neck-band of her uniform. Then, as coolly as you like, she sat down on the chair and began to take off her stockings.

"Now jump on me!" she commanded, when she was ready. "Better do it properly, else I'll look too neat. Then tie me up. Oh lord, don't dither! You weren't so shy the other day, and I don't mind—I used to be a model."

Within a short time she was as dishevelled as anyone could have wished: her apron torn, her cap over one ear, and her skirt much too high for decency. Her hands I had fastened behind her back with the stockings, and her mouth was gagged by the scarf which had previously covered my own eyes.

"That do?" I asked, and she nodded. It was time for me to embark upon the next stage of my journey to freedom.

First, as she had previously suggested, I shut the cell door. Apparently it might take the others some minutes to find a second key: the one still in the lock I pushed through the grille. Then I turned left, as I had been told, and slunk down the narrow corridor. The floor was of stone, and I had to go carefully to avoid making a noise; but I heard nothing to alarm me, and duly reached the cloakroom in about fifteen seconds. The yellow oilskin was conspicuous on its hook and I donned it hastily, though with some trepidation. The wretched thing rustled so much, and so tense were my nerves, that I imagined someone must be bound to hear me.

There was little inducement to linger. I took one startled look at my unfamiliar self in a cracked mirror on the wall and then crept out, producing with every step the kind of sound the wind makes in long dry grass. A moment later I shut the outer door behind me with the utmost caution, and at once began to see some sense in Gloria's instructions about my garb: it was now raining steadily.

At last I was in the open air, and the inclination to run was almost overpowering. I fought against it, following the gravel path till it joined the cinder-track with scarcely a glance to right or left. My feelings as I did so were indescribable: my whole back seemed to be listening for the sound of pursuit, and my feet behaved so unnaturally that they might have been borrowed like my coat.

Once on the cinders I perceived the greenhouse, a good deal further away than I had been reckoning for. Between stretched a desert of soggy vegetables—great overgrown sprouts and swollen cabbages on either side, lounging untidily in rows and seeming to watch me. The wall and its door were now plainly visible, not above a hundred yards from the house in sober fact, I suppose. To me then, in the state of apprehension which had seized me, the distance looked a mile, and every footstep became somehow a negation of movement. Once I nearly broke into a sharp trot, but Gloria's words came back to me—"Amos simply never runs"—and I refrained.

Twenty yards to go—fifteen—ten: and I still knew nothing whatever about the general aspect of the garden. My attention was directed towards one end alone: to gain the shelter of the wood, and safety, without arousing suspicion. I could have sworn I felt eyes peering at me from the rear: I could visualize faces at windows staring at me with unwinking scrutiny. That wasn't *quite* how Amos walked, was it? Surely Amos was a little taller than that? And didn't he invariably swing his left arm? Or was it his right?

I reached the door in the wall; I put my fingers on the discoloured brass handle: and then came the shout I had been dreading, the hoarse excited sound of a man's voice. It galvanized me into action. Frantically I turned the handle and pushed—but nothing happened. I pushed again, hurling my shoulder against the stout wood with desperate fury, and heard more clearly the yelling cry behind indistinguishably publishing my escape.

I must have wasted five seconds before I had the wit to see that the door opened inwards. After that it took me next to no time to dash through: but that wasn't an instant too quick, it seemed. There came a queer hissing noise, and then a dull thud against the weatherbeaten wood. Somebody had taken a pot-shot at me, and his weapon was fitted with a silencer.

## XII

I HAD AT THE MOST about ten seconds' start, I reckoned, and I tore off through the trees at the highest possible speed. There was no time to look round, and consequently none to take my bearings: with only my legs to save me I must needs keep on running.

Because I remembered Gloria saying that the road lay to the left, at first I instinctively went that way. Then it struck me that this was probably just what my pursuers expected, and in a fright I changed direction. The oilskin coat was now a definite handicap, not only impeding my movements but offering a clear target: yet if I paused to remove it I should lose some of my precious lead. On the whole I decided that I would rather be alive in Dr. Paul's hands than dead in a thicket: presently I stopped to strip the thing off, tossing it and the hat among some brambles.

Up till then I had made so much noise, or seemed to, that there had been no chance to tell if those from whom I fled were near or not. During the half a dozen seconds in which I was comparatively quiet I heard nothing of them, but just as I was about to start running again my ears caught a distant shout, and I needed no further spur. The wood was fairly thick, and seemed composed mainly of brush and young fir saplings. Here and there I encountered paths, but these I shunned as much as possible for fear they were tenanted. Sooner or later, I knew, I must come to clear ground, and what I should do then remained to be determined by the circumstances. It would probably pay me to get away, I thought. A wood makes a good hiding-place, but is also apt to prove a trap, and doubtless Dr. Paul commanded enough men to surround it pretty adequately.

I went on running, my breath growing shorter and shorter. Such violent exercise wasn't in my normal routine of life, and it found me ill-adapted to meet the physical strain. I kept going till my throat felt tight and my legs like heavy telescopes: then from sheer exhaustion I halted for the second time, unable to have taken another step if a lion had been after me. Somehow I crawled under a bush and lay there panting, greedily gulping in the damp air and at the same time trying to listen. It appeared that I had temporarily evaded pursuit, however: I heard nothing but the patter of fine rain on fallen leaves and the wheezing noise of my own respiratory system.

As soon as I had enough breath I began to think of moving again, and now with a return of caution. While I remained where I was, within reasonable limits, discovery could come about only by chance: but if I started advertising my presence I might unwittingly facilitate recapture. Also, I became increasingly uncertain of my position with regard to the asylum and the road. Reviewing my headlong progress I seemed to recall various twists and turns of which I had been only half aware at the time, but which now refused to assemble themselves into any coherent route. For all I knew to the contrary, I realized despondently, I might have followed Rhona's example and described a circle: perhaps the patch of odorous earth upon which I lay prostrate was no more than a few yards from the bullet-riddled door in the wall.

With such uncomfortable thoughts to mind I turned naturally to action. Instead of brooding I would rise and find out what was to become of me: whether I was destined for the freedom I so urgently desired, or for the dentist's-chair which I had already paid £40 to avoid. Accordingly I scrambled up, only to gurgle with alarm as a rabbit scuttled away within a stone's throw. But a moment's reflection made me believe that it was a good sign: rabbits and ruffians didn't go together, I told myself.

After about seven minutes of careful walking I came to the outskirts of the wood. During that period my confidence grew deeper, and when at length I stood half hidden among the last of the young firs, surveying a flat expanse of moorland, I seemed to feel liberty within my grasp. I watched the gorse-speckled landscape for signs of human activity, but saw none: apparently I was the only person about for miles. It was true that in the distance little tufts of smoke rose lazily from some chimney, but the one building visible was so small and far off that it looked like a white doll's-house perched upon a miniature hill.

After prolonged search I detected a road about half a mile away, running parallel to the edge of the wood and rather below me. I traced it to the left as far as I could, for I felt that London lay in that direction, and presently saw what might have been a motor-coach creeping along. The sight reminded me that my next task was to reach Thames Ditton, and discover if Rhona were still in the caravan. After that events would have to shape themselves, and I only hoped they would be more placid than those of the last few hours.

Before venturing from my hiding-place I finished off the food in my pockets: exertion had made me hungry, and I would have given a pound for a drink. Then I set off, and without incident caught up the distant road at just before half past two. The time seemed in some way significant, but it took me several moments to remember why. It was that fixed for the expiry of my two-hour respite in the cell: had I still been there I should shortly have needed to choose between betraying Rhona—or trying to bluff Dr. Paul with an untruthful account of her whereabouts—and surrendering myself to the dental activities of his assistant. To me the escape from such a predicament was worth £2140 of anybody's money, and it was to be hoped that when I regained the caravan I should meet with agreement and approval.

At 3.15, after I had walked a good three miles and got thoroughly wet, I managed to stop and board a Green-Line bus. It carried me as far as Kingston, a place of which I had no very pleasant memories. I felt little disposed to loiter there: procuring first some provisions and then a taxi, I was soon safe within a hundred yards of Imery's caravan. By now, incidentally, I had quite given up bothering about my appearance. There was still the danger that somebody would recognize me from the newspaper photograph, but it seemed microscopic When compared with those I had already experienced. On the return stages of my journey—intended to take me no further than the post-office, I recollected with a smile—I naturally kept my eyes open, but saw nothing to cause the slightest anxiety. No one did more than glance at me heedlessly, and while I was in the bus I satisfied myself that there were no cars trailing it.

I don't think I've ever seen anyone so patently glad to greet another person as Rhona was to welcome me back. As she heard my approaching footsteps she came running to the door, and the relief in her eyes was a pleasure to behold.

"Where in the world have you been?" she demanded in a rush. "Oh Arnold, I'm so glad you've come—I've been practically dying of misery! Tell me what happened—you look terribly untidy. Have you been fighting?"

"Only pretending to," I answered, thinking of my pre-arranged tussle with Gloria. "By and by I'll make your hair-dye come off listening to me, but first food—I'm starving and you ought to be dead. I'm alive and unhurt, and that'll do to be going on with. If you untie that parcel you'll find a cold chicken and rolls and butter and milk, but you'd better do it outside because I'm soaked through and I'm going to change."

By the time dusk had fallen we were side by side once more, silently stuffing; but every now and then Rhona would glance quickly up to make sure that I really was back. I must say I found her attitude most comforting: it was a long while, I realized, since anybody really cared whether I was within call or half way to the back of beyond.

After the meal was finished I lit a pipe, and then gave her an exact and probably rather laborious account of my adventures. I started by showing her my forged inscription in *Deep Waters,* which I then burnt, and went on steadily to subsequent occurrences. She received my story to begin with in a mood of mingled alarm and amusement, but by degrees I observed that her main expression was becoming a frown; when I reached the bargaining with Gloria, that is. Presently the frown grew more marked, and when the recital of my mad flight through the wood fell flat I broke off to rally her.

"Don't look so beastly glum," I said. "I know £2000 is an awful lot of money, but you'll hardly notice losing it when you inherit. And anyway, you can always repudiate the debt and leave me to muddle through Carey Street by myself."

"Good Lord, d'you think I mind about that?" she retorted. "I wouldn't have lost any sleep if you'd gone up to guineas."

"Then what's the matter? Something obviously is."

She nodded and regarded me searchingly, an absurdly attractive figure in her gym dress.

"Did we ever finally settle the question of my sanity?" she asked. "As far as you're concerned, I mean?"

"We did," I assured her. "You can consider the subject closed. What's worrying you?"

"I'm trying to explain," she said, with a smile for my belief in her. "All right, I'm sane, and I've lived in pretty close contact to Gloria for six months, remember, and I think I'm a fairly observant person."

"Well?"

"Just this, Arnold. If you'd been able to give her £2000 in cash on the spot I could understand her letting you go, but it simply isn't like her to do it for a mere £40 and the rest in promises."

"Yet it happened," I remarked, not grasping the implications of her statement.

"Oh, I know it happened!" she agreed, with a somewhat impatient nod. "I'm not doubting your word or your presence—nor the honesty of your looks. But the Gloria I lived with would never have behaved like that in a lifetime—not if you were twice as handsome as her favourite film-star and swore you'd give her a million. There's something wrong about it somewhere, to my way of thinking: it doesn't ring true."

"You mean I didn't really escape?" I suggested, becoming slightly more intelligent. "But hell, that would make me have been followed, and I tell you I wasn't. At least, I was going to tell you when I got that far."

"You're sure?"

"Dead sure—it's completely out of the question. And don't overlook the fact that I was shot at—I assure you that happened too. The bullet hit the door I'd been standing in front of a split second earlier."

"Yes, I know that seems to be against it; but then, I've seen Nick shooting for fun, and you haven't. He's simply terrific with any kind of gun—I've watched him pick the petals off a sunflower at thirty feet with an ordinary automatic. If he was using a silencer then he didn't have the rifle, and that means he was within twenty-five yards of you. He's no fool at running, either, and that yellow oilskin would make the sort of target people like him dream about. He just couldn't have missed you—and yet here you are.

"Please don't think I'm being silly, Arnold, or not glad to see you safe—I've never been gladder about anything. What it comes to is that you must have had so much luck I can't properly get used to it. And even luck doesn't explain what possessed Gloria," she added. "That part leaves me gaping. There wouldn't have been any tender passages between you that you didn't mention?"

She said this with a smile, and accepted my denial with apparent nonchalance: as though, I thought, she would readily have admitted extenuating circumstances if I *had* reported any lapse. Somehow I felt rather disappointed in her carefree demeanour.

"But I've spoilt your story," she went on, a moment later. "What happened when you stopped breathing and lay down?"

I told her in a few brief words, and at once returned to the problem she had raised. We discussed it for some minutes, she questioning me about the amount of caution I had exercised once I was out of the wood; but I remained of the same opinion.

"If they deliberately let me escape," I said, "then it could only have been in order to follow me, hoping I'd lead them to you. In which case, how do you explain away the fact that nobody who wasn't invisible could possibly have kept up with me? How *could* I have been followed?"

"Aw, don't let that bother you, pal!" came a somehow familiar voice from the doorway of the caravan. "Four cars, a dozen men, a few field-glasses—it was pretty simple. Kindly elevate the arms—you too, young woman."

We both gasped: neither of us had heard a sound, yet there in the entrance stood Nick. He had a pistol in his hand, there was a faint smile on his scarred face, and the rain-drops on the underside of his hat-brim glistened in the lamp-light.

We were up to our ears in trouble again.

# XIII

IN A DAZE I PUT UP MY ARMS as he commanded. I perceived that the pistol was adapted for comparatively silent slaughter, and I remembered what Rhona had just been telling me about his shooting ability. Another thought troubled me, too. I realized that I no longer had any particular value for Dr. Paul: I had served my turn as unsuspecting guide to the person he was really interested in. What I recalled of his conversation that morning led me to doubt if he would hesitate at a murder which suited his purpose, and there was no burking the fact that in his eyes I must be a considerable nuisance. I felt that I had better find out what was likely to come next.

"Your move, apparently," I said. "How many friends did you bring along, and what do you propose doing?"

"I don't need friends," answered the gunman with soft arrogance. "Just a sap to drive the car—he's waiting outside. And the next move is what you think—back where you came from."

He addressed Rhona rather than me, and she found the courage to laugh scornfully.

"You're a fool, Nick!" she remarked. "You'll never get away with it."

"No? And who's to stop me?"

"The police," she answered coolly, and staggered both of us; but I'm afraid I was the one who goggled.

"Police? What d'you mean?" he demanded briskly, glaring at her through his rimless glasses.

"Can't you guess? I said you were a fool. You don't really imagine we were going to sit still and just wait for you? When Mr. Dane didn't show up by midday I went to Scotland Yard and explained the whole position. They sent me back here, and as far as I know there's about forty of them closing in on this place right now."

I had grasped that she was lying, of course, but she did it with such magnificent assurance that anyone might have been deceived. Nick was clearly perturbed, and beginning to regret that he had chosen to act alone, I thought. It wasn't his expression so much as the intense immobility of his features which betrayed his state of mind, and I appreciated his difficulties. He could scarcely go outside to test the truth of Rhona's bravely uttered words, and at the same time keep us covered with his pistol: yet if she *were* in earnest, he must be thinking, then he stood every chance of being helplessly trapped. In silence I applauded the readiness of her wit, so much more alert to the occasion than my own, and kept my mouth shut for fear of ruining things. As far as possible I assumed a superior smile, and even ventured to dust a cobweb from the ceiling of the caravan with one uplifted hand.

All the same, I couldn't in my heart believe the bluff would work. The seconds were slipping by: soon they would stretch to minutes, and still no forty policemen arrive, and after that it was bound to be all up. I tried to concentrate on the problem of what to do for the best, and found the task beyond my powers. It seemed that my resources were exhausted for one day: I achieved no more than an aimless encircling stare, and as I was still smiling frozenly I dare say I looked remarkably stupid.

I realized in an oddly detached way that I was noticing irrelevant details. The draught from the door was making the lamp smoke; Rhona had apparently finished *The Food of the Gods,* since it was back in its place on the shelf; her gym tunic was too short for her. With her hands upraised the skirt ascended some way above the knee, and one black stocking-top had already a hole in it which seemed to wink at me mournfully.

The silence became oppressive, being emphasized rather than relieved by the ticking of my watch. Perhaps no one else heard the sound, but to my ears it grew reverberant and sinister, like the drum-roll at the end of the *Emperor.* And then, for the ninth or nineteenth time on that amazing day, the unexpected happened.

I can only describe what took place during the next half-minute as I pieced it together afterwards, because in the nature of things I can't look both right and left at once. Rhona—apparently—fainted, first swaying as she stood and then sagging towards the floor. Her face held a dreamy sort of look which struck even me as a bit improbable, witless though I was, and that may be why I made no move to help her. Nick started forward, however, his pistol arm outstretched and his back to the door: and round the latter on the instant appeared a hand which held what looked like a child's Christmas-stocking. There was a circular motion, and succeeding it a dull thud. Without the least murmur the gunman collapsed in a heap, the pistol miraculously not exploding.

"One for his nob!" cried Rhona gaily, and was on the floor beside the fallen man. For myself, I turned to see who it was who had thus delivered us: and in walked Malcolm Imery. At least, it would be more correct to say that he hopped in, because he had only one sock on: the other, filled with wet earth, was the weapon he had used.

"Illegal but effective!" he remarked, as I still gaped. "I've always wanted to whack somebody on the head the way they do at the pictures, to find out if it works, and I seem to have chosen a good time. It was smart of your little girl to pretend to faint," he added dryly, with a glance at Rhona's attire.

"I saw you peeping round the door," she explained: "and I'm sure I don't look as young as all that. Arnold, stop behaving as if you were petrified and introduce us."

Once I returned to my wits it took me an incredibly short space to do her bidding, make the situation plain, and enquire if there were anyone waiting for Nick outside in the road. Malcolm immediately became grave.

"Yes, there's a big black saloon with one man in it," he said. "You'd better skip from here, but that won't be difficult because I've got a car too. What does one do with the body? I'm afraid I'm not experienced."

I ought perhaps to have stated that Nick was merely unconscious, not dead: Rhona soon satisfied herself of that. She now stood up, the pistol in her hand.

"You'd better look after this," she said, holding it out to me. "It might come in handy one day, at the rate we're going."

Then she turned to Malcolm with a questioning look.

"It's your caravan, Mr. Imery," she reminded him. "Do you object to leaving him here?"

"Not a bit."

"And are you proposing to lend us your car?"

He smiled at her.

"I wouldn't be surprised," he said. "Better get your things together before the lad outside wakes up. And you could lend me a pair of socks if you like, Arnold—I see you've discovered my wardrobe."

We were ready to depart within five minutes, during which time Malcolm told us the reason for his presence.

"I didn't like what the papers were saying about you," he explained. "The moment I could get away—I've been up to Leicester, you know—I tore straight back to town. You weren't likely to be at the flat, and I guessed you might have found the key to this place useful, so I came along. That parked car outside worried me a bit—the chap at the wheel didn't look a very high-class type. I drove by and stopped round the next corner, so if we're careful we shan't be seen. All set? Then let's go."

"Just a minute," I said: I had thought of something. Kneeling by the insensible gunman I rapidly searched his pockets, and rather to my surprise soon found what I was looking for—my £50. There seemed no point in not getting my own back while I had the chance, so I took it. I also appropriated a handful of ammunition for the pistol and smashed his glasses, which were still on his nose. Neither action caused me any qualms of conscience.

Instead of approaching the road direct we cut across the garden of the adjoining caravan, and eventually reached the little side lane where Malcolm had put his car. While he helped Rhona in I stood for a moment listening; at first I could hear nothing, but then there came faintly to my ears the sound of voices. That was natural enough, perhaps, considering that it wasn't yet seven o'clock in the evening, but my thoughts at once reverted to Nick's companion. Had he grown tired of wailing, and gone to see what had happened? Or, worse, had reinforcements arrived?

I mentioned my suspicions to the others, and Rhona nodded.

"He wouldn't have tried getting us both back by himself," she declared. "After he'd followed you here I expect he telephoned for another car, and then got sick of hanging about. He never could resist trying to be clever. Will you take us for a nice ride into the country, Mr. Imery, please? Anywhere will do so long as it isn't Esher."

"Yes, we'll go," agreed Malcolm: "only I've just remembered something nasty. This lane is a *cul-de-sac,* and there isn't room to turn—I'll have to go back and risk being seen. I thought I was being rather smart slipping down here, but now I'm not so sure."

Nor was I, when we surreptitiously reversed into the main road. The voices were in evidence once more, appreciably nearer, and just as we began to go forward away from them, I heard the alarm raised for the second time since noon.

"Oh lord, here we are again!" I growled. "Step on it, Malcolm—if they get too close I shall bust your back window and take a pot at them."

"My word, you are getting tough!" he remarked, as he went rapidly through the gears. "I dare say I'll learn the ropes soon, though."

It occurred to me then that I had taken his assistance rather for granted. Admittedly Rhona had asked if he would let us use his car, but not when there was any serious question of pursuit, and I felt I ought to find out if he minded. Again she was before me, though.

"Look here, you don't *have* to get mixed up in all this," she told him, leaning forward across the back of his seat. His answer was an impatient kind of snort, followed by a request not to be so infantile as she appeared from her attire.

"Now I'm in, I'm in," he said. "You keep your eye on the enemy—are those their lights I can see in the mirror?"

They were, and very soon we had reached a speed of fifty miles an hour. That may not sound much, but in the conditions prevailing it was worth another twenty. Malcolm's car was ancient, but had been a good one in its day, and though he cared little for its outward appearance he habitually tended the engine with careful skill. It rattled till one wondered why the body didn't give up and just disintegrate, its steering was something on the stiff side, and the clutch was inclined to slip. Nevertheless he assured us now through his teeth that if the road were dry—which it emphatically wasn't—and if he were in less inhabited regions, he would be able to get within nodding distance of seventy.

"But they're using the Packhard," said Rhona depressingly, "and seventy's about what it starts at when Sam's driving."

"Is that the man in the leather coat?" I asked, and she agreed that it was.

"But he won't be able to go really fast on a surface like this," insisted Malcolm in my ear. "Look at it—like greasy glass. How're we doing?"

He shouted the question, so that it would reach Rhona above the rattlings and the whine of the wet tyres, and she replied with equal violence.

"It might be a lot worse. You've got a lead of about a hundred yards—maybe more. Where are we going?"

There was no answer for a moment, Malcolm being too busy correcting a front-wheel skid. When he did speak it was with an air of authority, and for my part I felt glad enough to let him take charge. This sudden reversal of all our hopes came too soon after my own earlier exertions for me to be at my best. The speed of events had temporarily become too much for me.

"I think we'll try Kent," he told us. "I've got an aunt who lives on top of a hill miles from anywhere. It'll be just the place to hide if we can dodge the crew behind, and if I can find the way."

"Won't your aunt mind?"

"No fear—she'll probably enjoy it. Still keeping the distance?"

"Just about—and there's only one lot after us, thank goodness! I thought at first there were two, but I expect the others stopped to look after Nick."

By now our rate had increased somewhat: the needle on the dashboard hovered just short of the sixty mark. Malcolm was beginning to get the feel of conditions, as he told me in a muttered aside.

"And you still know where you are?" I demanded anxiously.

"I'm hanged if I do."

"Nor me," added Rhona, who was peering over my shoulder. "What are you trying to do—cut across through Ewell and Reigate?"

He nodded, his lean face staring sternly before him.

"It means sticking to built-up areas rather a lot," he said, "but that's probably better than open country if they're faster than us. Especially if they're likely to shoot, and I seem to remember something of the sort. All I hope is that we don't bump into any speed-cops—that would just about settle everything."

"Well, it's up to you," I told him, "and I must say I'm darned grateful."

"So am I!" declared Rhona warmly. "You two are the nicest gentlemen friends a female lunatic ever had."

For the next half an hour the drive became something of a nightmare. When Malcolm's car was closed, as now, the windscreen was the only part which could be seen through; all the mica side-curtains were hopelessly scratched and dirty. As things went, with the rain beating steadily down and only one wiper working, I could gather but the vaguest idea of what lay ahead. When there were street-lamps they merged into a fleeting line of wet yellow blurs, and when there were none I was quite unable to distinguish the left-hand edge of the road. Our headlights weren't of the best, and once a violent outward swerve betokened a narrow escape for some drenched cyclist.

"Why the devil don't they use rear lamps?" grumbled Malcolm. "They're a positive danger to all law-breaking fugitives."

At frequent intervals Rhona would report on the distance between us and the pursuing car. I noticed that she had carried out my threat to break the small oval window at the back, and felt seriously tempted to try my luck with the pistol. I said nothing so long as we maintained our lead, but after we had been going for some twenty minutes it began to shorten.

"Curse it!" said Malcolm, when he was told. "That's because we're getting into the open, but I daren't double back or I won't know where I am. We'll just have to go faster, that's all, and heaven help us if we hit anything!"

With anxious eyes I watched the needle climb to sixty-eight, nicker a moment uncertainly, and then jump to seventy-one. The sense of speed was almost terrifying, probably because our surroundings were so obscure. We seemed to be hurtling along in a windowless box continually sprayed by water.

'If we get into a skid now we're done for!' I thought. 'Or meet a hump-back bridge, or a lorry parked on a blind corner.'

I began, foolishly, to imagine the consequences of such a collision: the screech of brakes, the appalling instant before impact, the crash of glass and twisting metal, the vast backward jolt which would break our necks or leave us skewered by wreckage. I had a morbid vision of Rhona's contorted body remaining in the back of the car while her head bounced out of an open door, and it so upset me that I tried vigorously to pull myself together.

"I'll light some cigarettes," I said aloud, and did so, sharing them round.

Five minutes later we were told that the Packhard was creeping up again, and the news decided me.

"I'm going to see if I can't blow one of their front wheels off," I informed Malcolm. "Is that all right with you?"

"So long as you aim straight!" he replied with a grim nod. "Notice anything queer about the petrol gauge?"

I stared, and then began my projected enterprise without delay: we had apparently less than half a gallon of fuel left. When Rhona understood my intentions she helped me clamber out of my seat, and lit a match while I examined the pistol dubiously. My ignorance of its mechanism must have been unmistakable, for a second later she extinguished the flame and put her hand on my arm.

"Don't be cross, Arnold," she said, "but do you mind letting me have first go?"

I looked towards her in the darkness, and felt like kicking myself for my lack of gumption.

"I'm sorry," I murmured. "If I had a grain of sense I'd have asked you to. Carry on, and good luck."

The pressure of her fingers tightened for a moment on my elbow. Then without a word she took the weapon, and I heard her fumbling with it expertly before applying herself to the window.

"About thirty yards," she whispered. "It shouldn't be too much."

"Shall I get Malcolm to slow up?" I asked, but she declined the offer.

"Just tell him to keep straight," she said. "We daren't let them get any nearer in case I miss."

I passed on the message, and then crouched down to wait: I felt sure she would prefer not to have me breathing over her at such a tense moment. Upon the correctness of her aim depended the outcome of the chase, and I was content to leave things in her care.

I was expecting an interval of perhaps a minute while she accustomed her eyes to the light, or lack of it, but I had scarcely settled myself when I heard a peculiar muffled sound, something between a click and a hiss. Within a few seconds there came two more, and I unsuccessfully strained my ears for audible results. Then Rhona was beside me again, and actually chuckling.

"Have a look!" she bade me, and when I had done so I forgot she was a girl and clapped her hard on the back. Far away in the distance, and ever instant growing fainter, was a stationary pair of illuminated pin-points: the Packhard's sidelights. We were clear of Dr. Paul again.

"The lamps to begin with, and then a guess at the wheel," she told us. "And the first two shots were good, so I think the third may have been. How much longer can we keep going?"

"Five miles, about," answered Malcolm. "But then it's only a matter of stopping for half a minute. There's a reserve tank with another gallon in, only you have to get out and switch it over by hand."

Not long afterwards he drew to a halt, jumped from his seat, and performed the necessary adjustment. There was now no sign of a following car, and we continued our journey in good humour. Malcolm and I were eloquent in admiration of Rhona's prowess with a pistol, she and I were similarly eloquent about the merits of our conveyance and the driver's command thereof, and if there was nothing for which they could praise me, I can honestly say I didn't feel the least bit jealous.

Everything seemed to be going right at last. The rain suddenly stopped, we found a lorry-drivers' cafe where we obtained hot drinks and slabs of yellow cake, and by and by the stars came out. For the second time I recounted my adventures, and Rhona hers, until about quarter past nine Malcolm informed us that we were within a dozen miles of our goal.

The name of the place where his aunt lived was Rudley, he said. From his brief description of her dwelling, an eight-roomed cottage almost entirely surrounded by a brick wall, we began to believe that only her good-will was needed to end our troubles. Rhona and I would stay there in hiding until the expiry of a fortnight from the time she escaped in blue pyjamas. After that we would travel to London, where—we hoped—we should find that Malcolm had somehow persuaded the police to overlook my transgressions. On December 6th Rhona would present herself to her late uncle's solicitors, and formally inherit her fortune; and if Dr. Paul turned up then, we should be able to make all the rude gestures or ugly noises of which we were masters.

In much the same way, I imagine, does an opium-smoker plan his paradise, taking no account of unfavourable possibilities but insisting that all be to his exact desire. Yet, at precisely 9.30 by my watch, we had our first intimation that we weren't destined to get things entirely our own way. Or, more accurately, we ought to have realized as much: but the form the warning took was so ordinary, so apparently innocuous, that I think we were all three deceived. Four miles from Rudley we had a burst tyre, and a brief examination taught us two things: that the spare wheel was innocent of air, and that at some time unknown some low person had removed Malcolm's wheel-brace and jack.

After a short consultation we came to the obvious decision. Rather than wait for a passing motorist, which might take all night and include the danger of his recognizing or remembering us, we determined to abandon the car and finish the journey on foot. I profoundly doubt whether, with the utmost concentration of thought, we could possibly have foreseen the difficulties into which that decision would ultimately lead us: yet at the same time I admit to a sneaking belief that we really ought to have known better.

## XIV

WE REACHED MALLOW COTTAGE about quarter past eleven after a walk made difficult by the almost complete darkness. There was no moon, and we had no torch. By the time we arrived our feet were not only sore but filthy from contact with the innumerable ditches into which we had strayed. As a precaution against future enquiries in the neighbourhood by Dr. Paul we talked no more than we could help. Three rowdy strangers might easily attract attention where three silent ones could hope to pass unnoticed.

The various habitations on our route were nearly all without lights. Twice we encountered unseen wayfarers, one of whom bade us good-night in the friendly country manner; once Malcolm stopped by a signpost to verify the way, clambering on my shoulder to read the directions with the aid of a match. When eventually he told us that his aunt lived at the top of the next hill, I for one was very glad. All of us were carrying some sort of baggage, and mine had begun to make my arms ache really painfully. It consisted of only the most ordinary things, too: my personal belongings from the caravan, Imery's still-wet suit, and about half Rhona's kit.

"What's your aunt's name?" I asked, as we slipped stealthily through her gate into the invisible garden.

"Mrs. Grayson," he answered. "She's a widow, and a fierce gardener, so mind where you put your feet. If you squash something she's only got one of, she'll hate you for ever."

By the blackness and silence of the house we judged that she too was in bed. We were right, but the fact didn't seem to affect the warmth of her welcome. Within ten minutes, sitting round the resurrected remains of a log fire, I was feeling I had known her for years, and Rhona said the same thing to me later. Some people—a few—are like that, able to eliminate all hint of awkwardness from a first encounter even in the most unusual circumstances, and Mrs. Grayson was a first-rate example. In appearance she was small and neat, her age being about sixty, and her wide-spaced smiling eyes indicated her good nature.

She let Malcolm explain the situation roughly, and then interrupted him.

"All right," she said briskly. "If you want help I'll do whatever I can—this Paul person sounds just the sort of man I loathe. Now, how do you feel? If you're tired you can have a hot drink, and I'll get the beds ready. Luckily I've just had some friends staying here, so there won't be much to do and I needn't even bother to wake Martha. She's my maid, you know, and the soul of discretion, so you won't have to worry about her. But if you aren't tired then we can all have something to keep us going, and after that perhaps we could talk things over."

It was very evident from her manner that she badly wanted to know more, and even if we had been nodding where we sat I don't believe any of us would have had the heart to disappoint her. As things were, the friendliness of her greeting had done a lot to banish our fatigue, and Rhona, speaking for the three of us, elected to stay up and discuss our plight.

It was after half past one before we went to bed, and as I undressed I felt more at ease than I had done for some days. We were apparently safe for the present, we had found two active allies, and Mrs. Grayson assured us that there wasn't a policeman within three miles of Rudley.

Friday dawned bright and sunny, and we reassembled for breakfast in the highest spirits. Rhona had put off her schoolgirl outfit, being now dressed in the clothes she had bought while at my flat. They would do to be going on with, and Malcolm's aunt said that sixpennyworth of dyes would work wonders.

After we had eaten we went on a tour of inspection. First came the house, a really lovely old place with timbered floors and ceilings, open fire-places, and the kind of furniture which tells of good taste combined with reasonable means. One carved oak chest in particular took my fancy, and when I learnt that it had cost only five pounds ten in a local auction-sale I began to remind myself that there were values of which I was all too ignorant. I recalled some of the things upon which I had squandered money during the last six months, looked at the ancient polished chest again, and resolved that if ever I set about making a home of my own I would enrol Mrs. Grayson's aid and knowledge.

Later we explored the garden, and as this will figure rather largely in subsequent events I think I'd better describe it in some detail. As has been said, the cottage stood on a hill, and was in fact the only building there: a three-storied black-and-white house set forty yards back from the road and flanked on either side by cherry orchards. At this time of the year, we were told, there would be few farm labourers about in the neighbourhood, and provided we didn't deliberately draw attention to ourselves we could expect to remain in undetected isolation.

Now, the thing which made this possible was a ten-foot brick wall surrounding the acre of garden on three sides. The fourth, at the back, was a stream, and beyond this an open piece of ground ran down to yet another orchard. Moreover, even this aspect was sheltered by thick clumps of rhododendrons, so that we could count ourselves secure from casual observation.

In front of Mallow Cottage were lawns, flower borders, a small rose-garden which still displayed a few late blooms, and a spacious rockery. There were espalier pears on the inner side of the wall, but the apples and plums were at the rear together with the greenhouse and vegetables. Normally Mrs. Grayson had a man in every day from the village, but it so happened that at the time of our visit he was laid up with lumbago, and though we didn't wish him any harm we were all glad of his absence.

The point of the foregoing brief description of the grounds is this. If—never mind how—we were traced, we could hardly be taken unawares by day because one person on the roof could command all four approaches. On the other hand, we reckoned, provided we kept watch and found some way of rendering the gate impossible as an entrance, we should be equally safe at night. Nobody could get near without either making enough noise, or showing enough light, to give us warning.

The first stipulation would be simple to arrange for, but the second might prove more difficult, we thought. We couldn't afford to make even one passing motorist wonder, for instance, why an apparently peaceful cottage should need to barricade itself with barbed wire.

Once we determined to take all safeguards—and that happened before lunch on Friday for reasons which I'll explain in a minute—we turned the problem over to Malcolm. He's a useful sort of person with his hands, unlike me, and he showed himself fertile in invention. By tea-time he had rigged up a contrivance of wires and hand-bells provided by his aunt which would effectually notify us if the gate were opened after dusk.

And now I must mention what made us adopt such a cautious attitude. It wasn't anything to do with my resolve never again to underestimate Dr. Paul, though doubtless it should have been. We behaved in that way because of a discovery which worried us all immensely by virtue of its possible significance. About eleven o'clock in the morning Malcolm decided to borrow Mrs. Grayson's maid's bicycle and see that his car was all right. He then planned to make arrangements at a garage—not the local one—for it to be collected and repaired. He told us that he needn't return to town before Sunday night, but that he must be there first thing on Monday morning because he had a brief to prepare.

We watched him set off without alarm: the enemy knew nothing about him, not even his appearance or name. When he returned forty minutes later with an ominously grave expression, though, we weren't quite so perky.

"My dear boy, what in the world are you looking like that for?" demanded Mrs. Grayson. "Did you run over a chicken or something?"

"Don't rot, Aunt—it isn't funny," he answered shortly. "A mystery's happened that I just don't begin to understand—or don't want to, rather. The car's vanished."

We all stared at him, until Rhona's common sense asserted itself.

"You're sure you looked in the right place?" she asked practically.

"Quite sure, thanks—and it hadn't slipped under a stone, either."

"Then it's been stolen!" declared our hostess solemnly. "There was an article in the paper about car thieves the other day."

He sighed, and turned to me.

"Come on, Arnold, for heaven's sake say something sensible!" he urged. "People simply don't steal cars like mine, especially when they aren't in working order. Why, the thing wouldn't fetch more than a tenner in part-exchange, for all it still goes."

I found no difficulty in doing what he requested, much as I disliked the task.

"Obviously Dr. Paul's got it," I said: "that's about the unpalatable truth of the matter. The real question is, how does that affect our plans? I rather think it may muck them."

"Why?" asked Mrs. Grayson. "He still won't know where you are."

"But he'll be able to find out who Malcolm is, and that'll be half way. How long would it take a dozen men to make enquiries within a five-mile radius? 'Excuse me, but does a Mr. Imery live in these parts?' 'Well, not exactly, but he's got an aunt at Rudley.' Why, it would be child's play even for me."

"Oh, hang it, I'm not as notorious as all that!" objected Malcolm: but he readily admitted that he wasn't unheard of in the district.

"Yes, it looks nasty," agreed Rhona, and turned to him.

"How long before they could learn anything from the car?" she enquired.

"About a minute and a quarter," was the wry answer. "Shame on my fat head, but the log-book's in the door-pocket."

She nodded thoughtfully, her blue eyes full of worry. An hour before, I remembered, they had been laughing and carefree: I felt a spasm of hatred for Dr. Paul.

"Very well, then we must prepare for the worst," she said. "What's it likely to be?"

"Well, you're the best person to tell us that."

"Yes, I suppose I am, really—I've certainly known him the longest. Let's think about it."

We pooled ideas at the end of ten minutes, and our conclusions may be summarized as follows. The doctor's probable actions would be first to locate us by question and answer in the neighbourhood of the abandoned car, then to assure himself of our presence at Mallow Cottage by direct observation, and finally to attempt our capture. How long it would take before he was ready for that we could only guess: Malcolm thought three days, but Rhona and I were inclined to shorten his estimate by at least half.

"And how will he capture you?" asked Mrs. Grayson innocently, her grey eyes twinkling. "Surround the place with armed men and deliver an ultimatum in proper international style, or just invade us?"

"Either—or both," she was told: and it was at that point in the discussion that Rhona made a truly sensible suggestion.

"I don't know about you people," she said, "but it's my belief we ought to be moving on while we can."

"And I think the same, although I'd rather stay," I agreed. "It isn't fair to turn this delightful garden into a battlefield."

Malcolm made no comment, but his aunt set her face resolutely against any such proposal.

"I know I'm only an old woman, and not a particularly clever one," she said, "but I honestly can't see why you need run away before anything happens."

"Because they mayn't be able to run away afterwards," her nephew murmured, but she was unimpressed.

"This is rural England, my dear, not Hollywood."

"I know, Aunt, I know: but Rhona's an escaped lunatic, and Dr. Paul's her legal guardian twice over. I admit he doesn't seem too keen on invoking the law, but then nor are we."

"And how can you possibly be sure you won't run straight into him the minute you leave?" she persisted. "You've only got your legs to carry you, remember."

"Well, if it comes to that, how can you be sure he isn't standing on a step-ladder the other side of the wall listening to you now?" he countered, his lean face smiling.

Mrs. Grayson jumped a little at the bluntness of the query, but soon reverted to her contention that for the time being we were safe enough with her.

"All you need do is make arrangements for another car," she declared. "I haven't a telephone, unfortunately, but I can always go along to the vicarage and use theirs."

"Yes, we ought to do something like that," I said. "It's lucky I've got lots of money."

"We shall have to do it," remarked Malcolm decisively. "I've got to get back to town, and I'm not proposing to walk, and I detest trains."

"And there's something else, while I think of it," put in Rhona, frowning at him. "How much safer is it for you than for us? Suppose Dr. Paul kidnapped you, and then told us? We should have to do what he wanted, you know."

"Oh, nonsense!" he laughed. "It simply wouldn't work—you'd only have to notify the police. They've got nothing against me, so far, and as a matter of fact I'm rather good friends with a chap at Scotland Yard. Ring Whitehall 1212 and ask for Inspector David Burns if you receive any sinister messages: 'Imery's in my clutches—surrender by dawn or look out for his ears by parcel post, followed by his eyes, his tongue—'"

"Don't be horrible!" exclaimed his aunt. "We all know your ears stick out, but your poor mother was always so short-sighted."

We finally decided to remain at Mallow Cottage at least over the week-end, unless our rather nebulous fears were confirmed earlier. That settled, we fell to planning our defence against possible aggression, as I have mentioned previously. Malcolm and I would take it in turns to keep guard by night, and during the day there would henceforth always be someone secreted on the roof between the two sets of chimneys. Fortunately this made an excellent observation-post, and there was a way up through the bathroom window, which saved us the necessity of procuring a ladder. In addition, Mrs. Grayson said she had an old telescope which had belonged to her husband, and we found it suited our requirements admirably.

It wasn't till Malcolm had fixed up his alarm by the gate, about four o'clock, that I had what I considered a fairly bright idea.

"If we had the clothes and materials," I told him, "Rhona and I could disguise ourselves really efficiently, and that would mean we could go where we liked. Up till now we simply haven't had the time and the money both together, but this seems a perfect opportunity."

"Except that the village store doesn't sell false beards or wigs," he pointed out.

"I never supposed it did, but the vicar's alleged to have a telephone. Couldn't you think of someone in town who'd buy us the right stuff and shove it on the next train down? Then when we hire that car you talked about we could tell them to collect and deliver for us."

He looked at me to see if I were serious, and then shook his head.

"Have you ever tried disguising yourself efficiently?" he asked in his dry way. "I don't mean in order to take in a lot of people the other side of some footlights, but passers-by, and the man sitting opposite you in a bus. Don't bother to answer—I can see you haven't, so believe me when I say it's no job for an amateur. Whatever you do to your faces won't change your build or height or walk, and Rhona was never cut out for a boy. Unless you're a couple of class actors, which I take leave to doubt, you may just as well stay as you are. Unless of course you're prepared to part company?"

"Well, I'd rather not," I said, and ignored his knowing nod.

"Then give your brain a rest. From what I've heard, there isn't much padding in Dr. Paul's head. You can bet he's told all his toughs to suspect any couple of being you which consists of a tall man and a short girl unless they can prove they aren't."

"Short be damned!" exclaimed Rhona, coming up behind us. "I'm only half an inch out for my weight and age."

"According to the slot-machines in stations?" he queried politely. "Then either they weren't working, or you're too—well, too heavy."

He dodged the piece of soil she threw at him, and went on with his criticism of my idea.

"Disguise is all very fine in story-books," he told us, "but this is no dream. Anyway, just think of what most people look like at a fancy-dress dance."

"Well, I didn't suggest going as a harlequin or Henry VIII," I said.

"I meant their facial make-up, not their costume."

"But what about actors on the films?" asked Rhona.

"They're done by experts, and even then they won't stand staring at in cold blood and sunlight. If you care to order, say, the man who makes up Charles Laughton when he's playing a character part, there might be some hope: only I'm afraid I don't know anyone who could get him for you."

"All right," I sighed. "Forget I was smart."

"Certainly—provided you let me try to be. My aunt was talking about a car just now, but I'm not so sure, because it won't be much use unless it's handy, and there's no place for one here. She walks everywhere, and if it's too far she hires the local ironmongery. All the same we must have a conveyance available, and the faster the better."

"So as you're clever with your hands you'll sit down and make us a nice aeroplane," suggested Rhona sweetly, and dodged in her turn.

"Only if you've got enough elastic about you!" he retorted. "Otherwise I was going to propose that you let me scout round in the morning and buy you a motor-bike. With a pillion, of course, and a good stout frame."

"Look here, you two," I interrupted, a moment later: "if this is a fight, I'm going indoors."

"Well, tell him to stop talking about me as if I was a fat woman at a fair," said Rhona.

"Stop drawing attention to the lady's misfortune," I told Malcolm: which made things no better. In the end we got back to our subject, and I agreed that his suggestion was a good one.

"I haven't ridden a motor-cycle for years," I admitted, when the point was raised, "but I shouldn't bother about that in an emergency. However, it's my turn to crab, so what about licence and insurance? I wouldn't fancy using my own name, and I don't know the ropes when it comes to using a false one for things like that."

"Objection overruled," was the reply. "I'd buy the thing as if for myself, and then kindly lend it to you. I should be using your money, though."

"Or mine by proxy," put in Rhona, quite seriously. "I hope you're keeping a strict account?" she added, to me.

"Very strict," I assured her. "You'll probably have nothing left for yourself. All right, Malcolm, just dispose of one more snag and the thing's on. The bike is presumably to be kept up our sleeve till urgently needed? Then, when that happens, do we sneak out to where it's hidden, or do we go through the gate and hoot meekly for the hooligans to get out of the way? We've agreed that danger will probably come by night, like the business in the Bible, but at night the gate's fitted with your bell-rope system, and I'd hate to have to untie it in the dark without rousing the parish. Yet that's the only place we can reach the road from, with a cycle."

"Yes, I get the point," he smiled. "I hadn't thought about it much, but hiding seems to be the procedure. We must find a place which isn't too near, or the enemy may spot it, nor too far, or you'd never make the distance if you were being chased. I'll see if my aunt can help."

He was back in five minutes with the news that at the bottom of the hill was an old barn which would probably do perfectly, but by that time I had thought of an alteration to his plan.

"How much does a motor-cycle cost?" I asked.

"About £15—the sort I shall get you."

"Good—then while you're on the job buy me a couple. That would give us a second chance if they blocked one line of exit."

He demurred a little, thinking my proposal unduly extravagant, but with Rhona's aid I gained my point. I can safely say that if I hadn't insisted, this chronicle would almost certainly never have been written. It was about the one wise action I performed during the time I was at Mallow Cottage.

There can't of course be any excuse for our criminal carelessness in deciding to stay on after the disappearance of the car, and I feel that I was chiefly to blame. It was up to me to do the best possible for Rhona: far more so than in the case of the other two, since I had no particular position in the world to lose and they had. The fact that she herself consented to our suggestions is neither here nor there, and though she won't admit it I expect she was harbouring dim notions about being all right with two men to look after her.

I repeat, to remain was the behaviour of an imbecile: yet I had no uncomfortable feelings during the next two days, and in that part of the night when I was at liberty to sleep I did so soundly. So might a rabbit with a bad memory, I suppose, engaged in a game of hide-and-seek for life with an especially vicious stoat.

## XV

**B**UT ANTICIPATION IS SUPPOSED TO BE INARTISTIC; so I will revert to life as I saw it then, and say frankly that I considered that Friday and Saturday two of the happiest days I ever remembered spending. Apart from the disappearance of the car, nothing occurred which even hinted at danger. Safety seemed ours, and for the first time I relished it as a positive factor in existence instead of merely accepting it as a foregone conclusion. All the same we kept a strict watch, an irksome but necessary task which sharing made easier.

We divided the day into six periods, Rhona taking two three-hour spells between 7 a.m. and 7 p.m. Malcolm and I split the rest of the time between us. It sounds as if we worked ourselves hard, but in practice the daylight part was hardly more than a matter of form. The person on duty could comfortably take a book for company, and merely glance round every five or ten minutes. It was the night watch which proved a strain, since we couldn't allow ourselves a light. There was even a suggestion, self-sacrificingly made by Malcolm, that we ought not to smoke, but I refused to fall in with it.

"There's no other way I'll be able to keep awake after the first hour or two," I said bluntly, "and anyway we're as good as invisible up there."

He didn't press the point, and naturally we observed every caution else.

I can't honestly say I know a worse method of passing half the night than squatting on a roof exposed to all the winds of heaven. If it had rained I think we should have given up pretty quickly, but that excuse was denied us. How Malcolm got through his two watches is his secret: it would have been cruel to ask. I can only describe my own experiences, and that not very excitingly, because as far as results went my time was wasted.

At seven o'clock in the evening, then, I levered myself unwillingly out of the bathroom window, somehow attained the mainland of the roof in practically pitch darkness, and crawled upwards to my post. Since I'm no mountaineer, even on the smallest imaginable scale, I didn't enjoy that bit at all, but once I was settled I soon recovered from wondering what it would feel like falling through space. When I had arranged myself so that I should remain secure whether I was awake or asleep, I started to envelop myself in protective covering: an overcoat, a blanket, an eiderdown, a woollen tea-cosy for my head, three pairs of socks, and two of gloves. What I had on underneath is nobody's business, but among the items were the black stockings which formed part of Rhona's gym outfit, footless of course, and a peculiar flannel garment which Mrs. Grayson said had been her grandmother's idea of cami-knickers.

Let it be remembered in my defence that the house stood on a hill, that the time of year was late November, and that I was utterly debarred from taking exercise. Very well: when I was apparelled I picked up the telescope and surveyed the district for suspicious lights, at the same time doing my best to listen through my headgear. The only lights I saw, however, were those of a few passing cars—Rudley was really a very deserted place; and the only serious sounds I heard emanated from an owl who seemed to have mislaid his mate. When I got tired of staring round I smoked, or ate a sandwich, or had a drink of hot coffee from a flask.

It may perhaps be wondered what I had to be happy about if I spent at least six hours of the twenty-four in acute discomfort. The answer is that the rest of my waking time more than made up for any inconvenience. A churl could scarcely have been miserable at Mallow Cottage with Mrs. Grayson to look after him, and certainly not if Rhona and Malcolm were available for company. With reference to them, I found myself not only enjoying the comfort of an old friendship, but also the excitement of a new one, and I derived pleasure from the realization—for I had begun to consider the matter—that this might possibly lead one day to something stronger.

I've said earlier, or implied, that I'm no great believer in love at first sight, but that doesn't mean I'm not susceptible to repetition. I liked Rhona immensely, and she behaved as if she liked me: the one thing which gave me some cause for thought was that she seemed equally attracted to Malcolm. But no, that isn't wholly true; it would be nearer the mark to say that when we were both with her she made no difference between us, but that the way she treated me alone was to my mind of another and more intimate quality. The impossibility of knowing how she got on with him when I was absent somehow didn't trouble me.

Nothing much happened on Saturday. Various tradesmen called with Mrs. Grayson's provisions, and since she had a well-stocked larder, and the butcher and baker brought round their wares with them, our presence didn't worry her in respect of food. Also, in the morning, Malcolm duly went out to purchase two second-hand motor-cycles, and after licensing and insuring them put one in the barn as agreed upon and the other in a disused pigsty just over the brow of the hill. The whole business took him four hours, and he declared that he had accomplished it without arousing anyone's curiosity. In addition, he ordered a car to be waiting for him at the village cross-roads at 6 p.m. on Sunday. He was insistent about returning to town that night, but if nothing happened we proposed to stay on in Rudley. Needless to remark, our proposals were still-born.

The alarm was raised on Sunday morning about half past nine. I was shaving in the bathroom at the time, and Rhona called my name softly from the roof. I stuck my head out of the window, and was immediately told that she had just seen a tramp behaving rather oddly in the road.

"He's walked by twice, and turned back, and I'm sure he's trying to make up his mind to come in," she said.

"A real tramp?" I asked, and she shrugged.

"He seems all right to me, but I'm no connoisseur. Hurry up and get your whiskers off—then you can look for yourself."

By the time I was ready to do so he had entered the gate, now clear of bells, and was ambling up the path as if he had trouble with his feet. I took a hasty glance at him from behind the curtains, and intensely disliked what I saw. The fellow appeared genuine enough, to judge from his filthy bearded face and ragged clothes, but he had the sort of expression that inspires distrust. His eyes shifted restlessly from side to side as he walked, and from the way he held his head one might have supposed he was sniffing for something. His age was about forty, I judged, and he was powerfully built: slung over his shoulder was a bundle on a stick, and his hat was shapelessly antique.

It was out of the question for me to show myself, in case he should be a spy and familiar with my description, so I did the only thing I could think of: informed Mrs. Grayson, and went quietly upstairs to wake Malcolm.

"Hush!" I said, prodding him. He grunted sleepily, opened his eyes, and was alert in an instant. When he heard the news he at once scrambled out of bed and began dressing.

"Thank heaven they don't know my mug!" he whispered as he pulled on a sweater. "Keep still, and don't come down whatever happens. Where's the girl—on deck? Then creep into the bathroom and signal her to stay out of sight. It's probably a false alarm, but we daren't risk anything."

I did as he suggested, and Rhona nodded to show she understood my gestures. Then I waited anxiously for the outcome of the interview which was going on downstairs. I fancied I could hear faint voices, but wasn't at all sure, and I resisted the temptation to return stealthily to the front of the house: movements overhead might cause suspicion. Instead I spent five worrying minutes telling myself what fools we were to have remained at Mallow Cottage. All our piffling precautions were suddenly disclosed in thentrue light: worth about as much to us now as an umbrella to a man falling out of an aeroplane. We could have been safe in Yarmouth or Blackpool or the wooded beauties of the Quantocks, I thought regretfully: but no, we had chosen to stay in Rudley!

Malcolm came slowly upstairs, his face a study in uncertainty.

"I don't know—I simply don't know," he said. "The fellow looked like a tramp, and talked like one, and his story seemed the real thing, yet he was such a foxy sort that I'm half inclined to doubt him all the same."

"What did he say he wanted?"

"Oh, the usual—food and a few coppers, and a pair of old boots because his own were done for. That part was the truth, anyway."

"Did he offer to work for what he got?"

"No, as a matter of fact he didn't. But then, I don't suppose they ever do if they think they can dodge it. Let's go into the bathroom."

Rhona was at her post once more, and didn't turn round immediately. Then at my suggestion she made her way indoors: if the tramp were one of the enemy, nothing would happen till he had reported, and if he were only what he seemed, we could chance a few minutes without a watch. She listened to Malcolm's account, and then filled in the visitor's movements after he had been despatched with a shilling and a pocketful of food.

"He limped down the path," she said, "and when he got outside turned to the left, opposite the way he'd come. The wall and hedge hid him till he was about fifty yards off, but when I did see him again I got the idea he wasn't hobbling quite so much. That may have been only imagination, though, and perhaps going downhill made a difference. Was he as nasty close to as he looked at a distance?"

"Probably nastier—and he didn't smell like roses. I wish to goodness I could make up my mind about him."

We were unable to help, but a moment later Mrs. Grayson came upstairs followed by her maid Martha. The latter was a middle-aged woman with a pale plain face, and it appeared that she thought she could throw light on the question which troubled us.

"Did he say where he came from, sir, while I was getting his food together?" she asked Malcolm.

"Yes, from Marsham. That's the next town, about five miles on," he added, for the benefit of Rhona and myself.

"And did he pick up another bundle or anything outside the gate, miss?" continued Martha unsmilingly. She knew about our chimney-haunting activities, of course, but not why they were being carried out. Mrs. Grayson had led her to believe we were trying to win a big bet over some glorified paper-chase.

"Nothing at all," Rhona told her. "When I saw him again he was just the same as when he came up the path."

This information was received with a grim nod, succeeded by some seconds of silence. Then Mrs. Grayson's maid proceeded to remove all doubts from our minds, and incidentally to give us a lesson in elementary detection.

There had been a heavy dew in the night, she said, as Malcolm would confirm. Yet if the tramp carried no luggage apart from what we had seen, then he couldn't have slept out in the open because his clothes were bone dry. He had—perhaps unwittingly—obstructed her in the hall, and she had pushed him away to teach him his place, as she put it. On the other hand, he hadn't sheltered in a barn or shed on the Marsham side because his boots were not muddy, only dusty. She knew the district thoroughly, and there was nowhere he could have gone without crossing at least one field, when his feet would have been certain to bear traces. It had rained hard on Wednesday and Thursday, and all the paths in the neighbourhood were sticky. Finally, the nearest workhouse was at Marsham itself, but he couldn't have stayed there or he would never have been in Rudley by half past nine on a Sunday morning.

We regarded her with respect, even if we weren't pleased by the obvious meaning of her remarks.

"Well, the emergency is arising," declared Rhona thoughtfully, when we were alone again. "I think I'd better get back on the roof in case we're being surrounded. Meanwhile you two must hurry up and decide our next move—I'll agree in advance to make it easy."

"No, I shan't go to bed any more," said Malcolm, in answer to my question. "Ten to one old Martha's right. Of course, it's always *possible* the chap got a lift in a lorry or something, but I doubt it. We must get ready for the worst."

He accompanied me below to share my waiting breakfast. We ate gloomily, both busy with our thoughts, and at once returned to the bathroom. The instant he was inside, though, he muttered something under his breath and tore downstairs again as if he were in a panic.

"The hall!" he told me briefly a minute later, his expression one of deep concern. "All our hats and coats are hanging up—he's bound to have seen them. I was thinking he wouldn't have much news, but that alters things. It strikes me that the sooner you two slope off the better. Oh lord, what's up now?"—for Rhona was descending again, and hastily.

"Pull your socks up—we're for it!" she whispered, unintentionally kicking me in the ribs as I tried to help her through the window. "There's four men coming up the hill, and a car following, and two men the other way, and some at the back. Think quick, or I'll be back in the asylum by lunch-time."

## XVI

WE HELD A COUNCIL OF WAR downstairs in the kitchen, first drawing the curtains and posting Martha in the front room to watch the gate. Mrs. Grayson immediately began to say how sorry she was that she had persuaded us to stay, but I cut her short.

"If it's anybody's fault it's mine," I told her. "What we've got to decide now is how to get away."

"You can't—yet," asserted Malcolm quietly. "Not till we know exactly how many people we're up against, and what line they're going to take. Anyway, it's Sunday, and that may help: there's more chance of casual traffic on the roads, and so on. I shouldn't really be surprised if they held off till dark. You know, somebody ought to be on the roof—shall I go?"

"No, you're too valuable," responded Rhona at once. "I shouldn't have come down, only I felt such an ass stuck up there watching us being caught. I'll go back—at least they'll have a job to get me if they decide to attack."

When she was gone Malcolm spoke again.

"What does one traditionally oppose force with?" he asked.

"Trickery," I answered. "The trouble is that I've rather run out of ideas at the moment. I can only think of the maddest things, like building a boat and trying to get away down the stream at the back."

He didn't bother to shake his head, though his aunt was kind enough to smile.

"We shall have to create a diversion," he observed: "somehow gather all the enemy into place A, while you two sneak off at place B. I don't fancy we shall find it easy, but all the same I believe I've got the beginnings of an idea."

"Yes?" I prompted eagerly, but he sat frowning.

"It wouldn't work unless we could count on being overheard," he murmured, mostly to himself. "And how could we possibly arrange that? Still, there's always the chance somebody'll try a bit of snooping over the wall."

"It's a still day," I said. "A cloud of tobacco smoke would indicate our presence in the garden."

He nodded more hopefully at that.

"It'll mean sacrificing one of the motor-cycles, though, and also the car I've ordered, and we shall need your help, Aunt, and anyway we can't start till this evening."

He went on to give us an outline of his plan, and when I understood I approved of it immediately. It offered us a far better chance than anything I could propose.

"The only point that isn't clear is what happens to you," I told him, and he smiled.

"You'll have to fix that," he said. "The minute you get far enough away to stop, arrange for me to be picked up somehow: we'll settle details when we see the way things shape. Now let's find out how Rhona's getting on."

"Two men at the back and two on each side," she informed us: "and Dr. Paul's just over the hill in a car. Yes, really—I saw him a moment ago. Hullo! There's a girl opening the gate—it looks like Gloria. Yes, it is, and she's holding a letter."

"Keep out of range," advised Malcolm, and departed downstairs. A couple of minutes later he was back with an envelope bearing my name.

"Is Gloria the wench who pretended to let you go the other day?" he asked. "Not what you'd call ugly, is she? This thing was stuck through the door, but I got a peep at her from the dining-room."

"She isn't nearly so nice as she looks," I assured him. "Let's read the ultimatum."

Dr. Paul's letter was mostly to the point. He had dated it Sunday morning 10.00 a.m., and there was no address.

*Dear Mr. Dane* it said, *I am aware that you and Miss French are concealed at Mallow Cottage. My excellent scout saw jour outer garments in the hall, which surely argues carelessness on someone's part? Naturally I expect you both to surrender, and promise that if you do so quietly I will consider treating you with clemency. In case you aren't in a position to know, I may say that you are surrounded by ten men, and haven't the faintest hope of escape. I will add that should you elect to be obstinate I shall have no option but to come and fetch you by force. You will hardly need to be told that I desire no quarrel with either Mrs. Grayson or Mr. Imery, and can dispense with their company, charming as I should doubtless find it. Please inform them that after your departure they will be well advised to keep their own counsel. Upon their continued silence will depend your personal safety, so you will probably manage to persuade them that discretion is vital. Two further points: it will suit my convenience if you will please to remain where you are till dusk—I will call for you at six o'clock. You will also oblige me by returning this note at once. Attach it to a stone and throw it over the wall, where one of my men will be at hand to retrieve it. Failure to comply with this request will cause me to send for a particularly powerful weed-killer, one which unfortunately doesn't differentiate between the weeds and the flowers of even so obviously excellent a gardener as Mrs. Grayson.*

"His style strikes me as a trifle florid," remarked Malcolm thoughtfully, and stood kicking his heels against the bath. "I told you he wouldn't fancy any rough stuff in daylight," he added. "He's not even giving you the chance to be awkward."

There was no signature to the letter, and Rhona said the writing was not the doctor's own. Since there was no immediate hurry she had once more descended from the roof, and after a short discussion we decided to return the document forthwith. None of us wanted Mrs. Grayson to suffer on our account, and I felt sure that Dr. Paul was quite capable of carrying out his threat.

After that we were free to elaborate Malcolm's plan, which we began to do by telling Rhona about it. She paid careful attention, and said she thought it might work if handled properly, though we should need a large slice of luck.

We got it four hours later in the shape of Brett, the man who had organized my capture in Thames Ditton. From the chimneys I saw him slinking through the cherry orchard on the downhill side of Mallow Cottage, a safe enough action on his part because he was sheltered from the road by a tall hedge. I could almost have clapped my hands, for he was carrying a hurdle, which meant that he intended to look over the wall. For ten minutes after he disappeared from sight I waited anxiously, my eyes alert to detect the slightest movement above the brickwork. Twice a trembling branch deceived me, and then my patience was rewarded. A hand came over the top holding a small mirror: before Brett began spying he wanted to be sure he wouldn't be observed.

It was the work of a moment to indicate his position on the pencil sketch of the garden which I had ready, and toss it to Rhona in the bathroom. I don't suppose it was more than a minute later when she and Malcolm sauntered out of the front door and turned left towards the rockery. In the middle of this was a wooden seat, and by and by they disposed themselves upon it, their backs to the watcher. In a straight line their heads were about eight yards from the wall, and provided they didn't mess things Brett was bound to hear every word. That's the great point about a sharp whisper: although it bears all the hall-marks of stealth, in actual truth it carries a good deal farther than a low-pitched mumble.

The fact that they could utilize the seat was accidental, but everything else had been rehearsed a dozen times, and I knew what they were saying as well as if I had been with them. That was impossible, of course: I dared not leave the roof in case I were heard. The time, by the way, was five minutes past four, and if by half past no one had turned up to hear our plot we should have tried to attract attention: first by my suggested cloud of smoke, and if that failed by firing the pistol and then cursing one another for being ham-handed. As it was, we were spared the necessity for any such feeble artifice.

Malcolm began the conversation upon which all our hopes relied, and Rhona told me later that his manner was impressive.

"You're not frightened?" he asked, with a friendly pat on her arm.

"Not a bit."

"And you're sure you've got everything clear?"

"Well"—hesitating, "not absolutely. It's all got to go off like clockwork, and I don't want to make a howler."

"No fear—it might be your last! Would you like me to go through it again?"

"Yes please. I—I suppose it's all right talking out here?"

"Why not? They won't come up close—they've no reason to. All right, listen carefully, because I shan't be able to explain twice. The car's booked for six o'clock at the cross-roads down the hill, and my aunt says Dicksons are always punctual. It's a pity about the time, but it can't be helped—we couldn't possibly guess Dr. Paul would turn up.

"Well, what we've got to do is to make him think it's Auntie who walks down to the village and gets in, but you and I know different. Only you'll have to walk like her as near as you can— remember you're a woman of sixty and not a young girl, and don't go prancing along. Take it easy, and get in a bit more practice when you've dressed up. It's darned lucky you two are about the same height and build, and it'll be dark by then, which gives us a chance.

"Now, it would take her about ten minutes, and she's always early, so you'll start off at quarter to six, and Martha with you. At any rate she'll be genuine enough, and somehow you've just got to get through. There's no reason why you shouldn't, really, because we shall be doing our damndest to lure them away on a false scent. Auntie'll rig herself up in your togs, and she and I will make a dash for it at the back of the house—or pretend to."

"What time will that be?" interrupted Rhona. "How long before I go, I mean?"

"Three minutes—-we can't make it more in case they spot us and nip back after you."

"I see. Your aunt's an awful sport, Malcolm, I must say. And if you get away? It might happen, you know."

"And it might not!" he retorted with a meaning laugh. "If we do fluke through we shall just have to walk till we get somewhere—it doesn't really matter. On the other hand, if we don't then I shall have the pistol handy, and I wouldn't wonder if I used it."

"Only don't go killing anybody—that would spoil everything! And poor old Arnold follows me."

"Yes—about the worst job of all, because he's got to go as himself. Still, don't worry—I think he'll manage his part if you can manage yours, for all he's still a bit lame. He'll give you ten minutes' lead, and then make a burst for it. The barn's about three hundred yards down the hill, and the motorbike's ready to start at a kick. Thank heaven we had the sense to hide one, just in case! You'll be past there long before he gets going, of course, and probably in the car if Dicksons' man is early. If you're both lucky you'll meet in Southampton around eleven o'clock, and once you're safe for pity's sake stay safe. It's a bit doubtful if you'll find anywhere open at that time, but if I possibly can I'll put a trunk-call through and book you a couple of rooms at the *Railway Hotel*. There's bound to be one, so call there first.

"Now"—looking at his watch, "it's after half past, and you've got to change and make up, so we'd better start moving. Feel more hopeful now?"

She nodded and giggled.

"It's all terribly exciting," she said. "If only it comes off! I wish Arnold hadn't hurt his ankle, though."

During that discussion I watched Brett listening to it. To my delight he became so interested that he ventured to put his head above the top of the wall, and I was confident that he had heard all he was meant to. My belief was borne out when Rhona and Malcolm came in: almost before the door shut he had abandoned his perch and was tearing away across the orchard.

The bait had proved attractive enough to the small fish, and had seemingly been swallowed whole: but was it good enough to catch the big fish too? How would the cold-eyed Dr. Paul receive his lieutenant's account of our conspiracy? It was a question we possessed no means of answering until we made our break for freedom: we could only pray that Brett would convince him. There was a fair chance of that because the story could be tested at two obvious points, and both would ring true. An enquiry at Dicksons' Garage—its whereabouts easily discoverable in the local telephone directory—would reassure the enemy that there was indeed to be a car at the cross-roads at 6.00, and a search of the barn would reveal the motor-cycle.

And our real plan? Simplicity itself, and a good sample of Malcolm Imery's worth. The person who went through the gate with Martha at 5.45 would be the real Mrs. Grayson pretending to be Rhona pretending to be the real Mrs. Grayson. (I know that's a mouthful, but I can't find any other way of saying it.) Similarly, the apparent Rhona who made a dash for it at the back at 5.48 would be equally real: and would, we hoped, be allowed to depart unmolested, especially as her companion was reputed to carry a pistol. As for myself, I should indeed attempt to get hold of a motor-cycle, but not the one in the barn. I should turn the other way, and do my utmost to reach the pigsty in record time. If I succeeded I should pick up Rhona at a point about a mile distant, and somehow contrive to give Malcolm a lift too as far as the next town. We should leave him there to shift for himself, and meet him again not in Southampton but in London. Incidentally, my lameness was only imaginary, but there had to be some reason why I wasn't in the garden with the others.

One other point deserves mention. We thought it likely that, unless steps were taken to ensure the contrary, Dr. Paul might feel inclined to vent his anger at being tricked upon Mrs. Grayson and Martha; either directly, by harming their persons, or indirectly by damaging Mallow Cottage. It was the remark about the weed-killer which suggested that thought, of course, and I was deputed to devise some safeguard. The letter I composed was held to be satisfactory: Malcolm's aunt would take it with her, and hand it to her captors.

*Dear Dr. Paul* I wrote, *In case it should occur to you to ill-treat Mrs. Grayson or her maid, or alternatively to assault this property by fire, water, explosives, or arsenic in commercial form, let me advise you not to do any such thing. Why not? Because in the event of any harm befalling her, or anyone or anything connected with her, we shall immediately make a full statement to Scotland Yard. If you care to ring up Detective-Inspector David Burns anonymously, and ask if he knows a Mr. Imery, you'll be told that he does. Friends at headquarters are valuable, Doctor, and you might find some difficulty in accounting for the fact that you haven't enlisted police support towards your recent efforts. In addition, we possess an excellent photograph of your epistle this morning. I'm told that by enlarging sufficiently there would be enough evidence for a handwriting expert to pass an opinion about the character of the author. Not yourself, of course, but certainly someone in your employ, so perhaps you'd better start murdering him or her without delay. Finally, don't overlook the possibility that if it came to a public show-down our reputations and past histories might bear closer investigation than your own, or those of the two medical monstrosities who certified Miss French as being insane. She isn't alone now, you know: not before they're needed she has supporters at work on her behalf. Enclosed please find twopence in cash wherewith to buy yourself a comic paper to read on the way home. Yours faithfully,*
*Three Ill-Wishers.*

# XVII

AT PRECISELY QUARTER TO SIX, wireless reckoning, Mrs. Grayson and Martha issued from the front door of Mallow Cottage and walked soberly down the garden path. At least, Martha was sober enough, but the way her mistress contrived to instil an unnatural springiness into her step, and at the same time give the impression that she deliberately held back, was stimulating to see. She proved herself a clever actress in the hour of need, and from behind the dining-room curtains I found courage in watching her feet. I was enabled to do this, I may say, because her maid carried an electric torch: even the straightest track is hard to keep to at night without illumination.

The others, playing the parts assigned to them, were secreted among the rhododendron bushes at the back, and so missed the performance. In three minutes they were to set out themselves, while I waited for a favourable moment to make my own escape. It was an unenviable position, for I had no means of knowing Dr. Paul's attitude. If he saw through our trick then he would certainly retain the watchers on either side of the cottage, but unless I got on the roof again I shouldn't find out till too late. I was tempted to do that, but refrained because I could hope to see nothing unless they were very careless and showed a light.

It would have been an easier task to tackle with the moral support of a companion, but I had no one to turn to. For a minute or so I dithered, but that was useless. My chance was as good as my friends', and if I were captured it couldn't be helped. The person whose safety really mattered, after all, was Rhona: she was the one the enemy sought to catch.

My palms were clammy as I mounted a small pair of steps and vainly peered from the top of the right-hand wall. Beyond lay silence and darkness: I was crouching poised upon the edge of the unknown. Perhaps there were hands waiting to seize me, I thought; perhaps I should have no other company but my own fears. For some five seconds I remained thus, hesitating: then I told myself to get on with it, and dropped.

I landed fairly well, having remembered to relax my muscles and keep my arms outstretched, and an instant later was on my feet prepared to run. No sound came to me, no shadows closed in. I had only to make my way through the leafless unseen trees and I should be clear.

My goal was about a furlong distant, the way to it leading across the cherry orchard. I accomplished first part of the journey in safety, protecting my face from invisible branches by stooping down and only twice bumping into obstacles. When presently I reached a ditch I knew I was near the road, and widened my eyes for a gap in the hedge which Malcolm had mentioned. After a short search I found it, which pleased me: using the utmost care I forced myself through, and was standing on firm ground. Thence, obeying instructions, I turned to the right, walked a couple of dozen paces, crossed and saw dimly before me the blackness of the pigsty which housed my motor-cycle.

I approached on tip-toe, in case of danger: it was always possible that the hiding-place had been discovered. Yet I hardly thought so: surely even Dr. Paul wouldn't foresee our purchasing two machines, I told myself. And then, with my hand outstretched to avoid a collision, I suddenly paused, for very close, a little ahead to the left, I felt certain I had heard a throat cleared. The noise was nowhere near so loud as a cough, but it served to put me more thoroughly on my guard and also to make me believe that so far my presence was unsuspected. I must have trodden more quietly than I knew.

The position was a tense one, for a false step now would spell disaster. 'If only I had a torch!' I thought, as still as a dead man and listening intently. 'It would be worth showing myself to find out how many there are.' But I hadn't, and it was a waste of time wishing: I must employ other means for determining the question.

I felt I could reasonably hope to deal with one man, and just possibly with two, but more than that would mean capture. If there hadn't been Rhona and Malcolm to consider, I should have chosen the line of least resistance and tried to depart as softly as I had come, but that was inconceivable. Provided they had escaped they would be awaiting me, and I knew that in similar circumstances neither would have let me down. So I stood there, hardly daring to breathe for fear of betraying myself and them: my feet felt frozen to the ground, as in a nightmare.

Half a minute probably elapsed before my wits began to work. There was only one way to find out what I wanted to know, and I acted accordingly. With nervous fingers I explored my pocket for the bagful of sandwiches which Martha had cut me; a fraction of an inch at a time I withdrew it, not making the slightest rustle. For a second it lay poised in my hand, and then I tossed the thing over my shoulder: it fell with a clearly perceptible swish into some grass, and I waited.

There was no sound whatever from the pigsty, which I had decided to treat as a favourable sign. Of course it was possible that whoever lurked inside hadn't heard the package fall, but I doubted that. My reading of the situation, partly dictated by hope as it might be, was that I had to contend with one man only. If there had been two, I argued, they could scarcely have resisted warning one another audibly at what they must suppose to be my approach.

'Unless they're so close together they can use their hands' I thought, but dismissed the idea. If I was wrong, so be it: I had done what I could to estimate my chances.

My left foot moved from the ground as I started to creep forward, and then came the clearing of the unseen throat again. An instant afterwards the truth penetrated, for there succeeded the unmistakable scampering of tiny feet. I had merely heard a rat abroad on some nocturnal business, and my imagination had done the rest. In a moment my brow was cold and damp, and I began to shiver violently. It has since been explained to me that I was reacting to a period of intense strain, but at the time I was immensely puzzled by the waywardness of my body.

'You half-baked fool!' I muttered disgustedly, lit a match when I had recovered control, and entered the pigsty. There was nothing tangible inside but the motor-cycle, which I bad-temperedly wheeled out. For a moment I propped it up while I retrieved the sandwiches, because the rat had had enough fun at my expense: then I reached the road, kicked the starter, and was off as fast as I could go. The machine made such a deafening noise that I was certain I should be chased, but again my fears were groundless. At 6.20, having experienced no further troubles real or unreal, I rode up to the place where I had arranged to meet the others; and there they both were at the edge of the road.

"All right?" came Malcolm's voice softly.

"Except for my nerves," I answered. "And you?"

"As good as new!" said Rhona, with something between a laugh and a sob, and put her hand for a second on my shoulder as I straddled the bike.

"I knew you'd do it," she added, and I felt thankful it was dark: I suddenly thought of the rat, and blushed.

We were naturally anxious to get going, since Mallow Cottage lay only a mile away, but it soon became apparent that we couldn't make our conveyance carry three. None of us was sufficiently expert to take a passenger on the handle-bars as well as one on the pillion, and that was the only way of doing it.

"Very well, I'll walk," declared Malcolm. "Go on, don't argue: you're the people with prices on your heads, not me. Clear off quick, and don't stop till you reach Maidstone. Then if you've got time, and enough money left, you can send a car back for me. Tell the chap to make for Long Reach: I shall be in the pub, I dare say—*The Maid of Kent,* not *The Traveller's Rest."*

We bade him farewell regretfully: it seemed a shame to leave him so near to danger, but it was our only course.

"I don't mind," he assured us. "It'll give me a chance to telephone the vicarage and get them to send over for news of my aunt. I hope the old dear's all right."

We hoped so too, and made arrangements to ring him at his chambers in the morning. Then we departed, stopped for a short time in Maidstone, and eventually reached London by 9.00 after a cold uncomfortable run.

On the way we discussed what should come next, and agreed that our main difficulty was a complete absence of luggage. Coupled with the fact that it was Sunday, this meant that we couldn't book rooms at a hotel without drawing considerable attention to ourselves: yet neither of us liked the thought of spending the night in some railway station, and we dared not return to the caravan or the flat.

"And anyway we're still wearing the same old clothes," remarked Rhona. "Somebody said something about dyeing them once, but it never happened. Do you suppose people will remember what they read in a paper last Thursday? I'm sure I shouldn't."

"Not unless they've had their memories jogged," I answered. "But I can think of one or two Sunday rags which simply eat up stories about escaped lunatics and unknown drugs."

"Then we'll have to steal some luggage," she said, as if it were the most commonplace suggestion in the world. "After all, it's in a good cause, and I'd rather do three months' hard labour than be caught by Dr. Paul. Or don't you agree?"

"I believe I'd rather do three years in a chain-gang," I told her. "All right, invent ways and means for stealing two suitcases, preferably containing clothes that fit. I'll have a go too, and we'll compare results later."

In the end we decided to try my way first, because although she would have to do most of the hard work it seemed to contain an element of safety. As a general method of pilfering other people's kit, though, I can't truthfully recommend it. One not only needs to be lucky, but may very well lose money over the business.

What happened was this. After parking the cycle in a garage near Charing Gross we entered the station separately, Rhona having in her possession a pound-note and a ten-shilling one. As if we had no possible connection with each other we sauntered towards the left-luggage counter, by which I presently took up my position. I pretended to be waiting for someone, and I suppose in actual fact I was: for a suitable person to rob. The qualifications for the part were few but essential. My victim must be a woman with luggage to deposit and no male companion to thwart our plans.

It's enough to say that she turned up within a quarter of an hour—a portly middle-aged female puffing along behind a porter. He carried two large cases, and ideal ones from our point of view: as well as being shabby they were unmarked by labels or initials. In a matter of three minutes more the stuff was disposed of, the receipt tucked into her handbag—also an essential—and the porter dismissed with a tip. The unsuspecting woman then waddled away, but couldn't have got a dozen yards before Rhona was after her at a wink from me. I had seen some paper money inside the handbag, and because this consisted of pounds I winked with my left eye: had it been ten-shillings I should have used the other.

"Excuse me, madam," said Rhona, tapping the stranger's broad shoulder, "but you dropped this"—and she held out a pound-note.

"I beg your pardon? I don't think so," was the answer, given with a surprised stare.

"Oh, but you did—I saw you! It fell out of your bag just now over there"—with a vague gesture towards me.

"Oh, but really!" protested our intended benefactress. "I'm sure it couldn't have—I'd have been bound to notice."

Rhona frankly grinned.

"Well, I suppose you must have your own way," she said. "I'm equally sure you did drop the thing, but I expect it'll find a home, and I needn't have told you, need I?"

The smiling question had effect: the woman she had accosted began to look dubious, for most people resent the suggestion that someone is getting the better of them.

"I dropped it over there, you say?" she queried, turning rather red.

"Yes, when you were putting something away. Still, it really doesn't matter—I may have been wrong."

"Oh, but it *does* matter if it's mine!" was the sharp retort.

"Well then, why don't you count what you've got? If you're a pound short it'll be yours, and if you aren't it won't. Only please be quick, because I've got a train to catch. Look, come into the waiting-room—it's cold standing about."

They went, sat down at a table in a deserted corner, and the all-important handbag was unfastened: whereupon I made my entry. I gazed round with an anxious expression, appeared to catch sight of Rhona, and hurried across.

"I've been looking for you everywhere, Ruth!" I said breathlessly, raising my hat with a fleeting look at her companion. "We've exactly seven minutes or you'll have to spend the night here. What's the fuss?"

"This lady dropped a pound-note, only she doesn't think she did."

"Well, what are you waiting for?" I demanded brusquely, glaring at the woman. "She ought to know, oughtn't she?"

"Yes—but she doesn't seem to."

I snorted and turned to our victim, now getting extremely flustered and staring from one to other of us stupidly.

"Look here, madam," I said, "did you or did you not drop that pound-note? We've a train to catch, even if my sister is a fool."

"Well, I can't just be sure—I was just going to count and see," she stammered.

"Then kindly do so," I requested, eyeing her handbag with cold disfavour. "And the next time you venture out alone, I should advise taking some elementary precaution against carelessness," I added grimly. "Really, I never saw anything like it! Do you realize, my good woman, that murders have been committed for less than you're carrying round as if it was so much toilet-paper?"

"Albert!" exclaimed Rhona with prim severity. "Please remember you're not at home now."

"Oh, sorry!" I muttered. "Only it makes me sick the way some people treat good money. Well, give her the wretched thing and let's go."

Rhona obeyed, putting the note rather regretfully on the table. The stranger followed the action with her dull eyes, and that gave me my chance. In my gloved hand I held another note, screwed up, and with a quick movement I let it fall behind her chair. Then I glanced down and gasped.

"Good night alive!" I ejaculated. "She's a witch or something—look! Just look on the floor!"

But it was the poor wretch herself who did so, goggling in amazement at the crumpled green scrap: Rhona had other business to attend to. In a second her fingers darted into the open handbag, and out again with the luggage-receipt. The trick had worked.

After that we removed ourselves as speedily as possible: total cost, £2—value received, the means of claiming two suitcases. If anyone says we had no right to expect success, I shall agree, while firmly maintaining that the outline of the plan was prearranged. Most of the conversation had to be extemporized, of course, and I naturally picked our dupe with care. Nine women out of ten will put an odd slip of paper into their handbags, though, and Rhona's apparent honesty disarmed suspicion.

We allowed ten minutes to go by; then gave a porter the job of completing our theft. Twenty minutes after that we were safe in a hotel. Our name was Stanley, and if anyone wanted to know, we were cousins. Also, our rooms adjoined, and in defiance of possible regulations to the contrary Rhona came into mine, so that we could find out what we had got for our pains.

Frankly, we were disappointed as far as clothes went. One case contained male attire seemingly designed for a stout giant, and the only garment in the other which Rhona felt like wearing was an embroidered linen nightdress. Strangely, it appeared that either our victim's husband never went to bed or else he slept in his shirt, for there were certainly no pyjamas. I managed to obtain materials for shaving, however, and some clean handkerchiefs. In addition, we discovered the owner's name and address from the fly-leaf of a prayer-book: John Griggs, Acacia Avenue, Sutton Coldfield.

The rest of that day can be passed over. The following morning we put our stolen luggage in a tube-station cloak-room, and posted the receipt to Griggs. If I had dared I would have asked for half my money back, but deemed it unwise. The next hour was spent in purchasing cases of our own, and suitable garments for our immediate use. After that we treated ourselves to a cocktail apiece, and by half past eleven were squashed into a call-box telephoning Malcolm. Five minutes later we were outside again, but frowning now instead of smiling. Neither his chambers nor his flat knew anything about him since the previous Tuesday, the day he went to Leicester.

## XVIII

"IF I UNDERSTOOD what a kettle of fish was," I remarked with false gaiety, "I'd say here's a pretty one. Look, Rhona, we've got to do something: let's sit down and decide what."

She nodded gloomily, her blue eyes staring at the pavement. Then she glanced up, and once more I felt grateful for her sturdy common sense.

"You mustn't rule out other possibilities," she told me—"accident or illness, for instance. If anything like that's happened we're helpless, of course, but if on the other hand Dr. Paul's got him, then we shall hear about it soon enough. You see, Malcolm's only valuable as a hostage, and the time's getting short."

"Yes, that's fair enough," I agreed. "But will he be able to convince Dr. Paul that he really doesn't know where we are? If not he'll probably get the treatment I was promised, and I don't suppose he'll like it any more than I should have done."

"Damn, I hadn't thought of that!" she muttered. "Paul's a positive devil—somebody ought to go and shoot the man. Only—only I don't believe I could do it in cold blood—not even him."

"I could, if I had to," I said, though by no means certain if I were telling the truth. "Anyway, let's have a coffee."

We finally determined to telephone Malcolm's flat and chambers every half an hour from midday to five o'clock, and also to get in touch with both the Maidstone garage and the vicarage at Rudley. We might at least learn something that way: more than if we just sat still and worried.

At ten minutes past one we felt slightly more hopeful. There was still no news of Malcolm, but the information from other quarters proved encouraging as far as it went. The Maidstone driver declared that he had set down his passenger on Westminster Bridge at 2.15 on Monday morning, and Mrs. Grayson sent us a message by the vicar's parlourmaid that everything was well with her.

We felt more hopeful, I say, until the possible truth of things occurred to me, which was at 1.20. I turned to Rhona, and spoke my mind without hesitation.

"I'll bet Dr. Paul's got him, just the same," I told her. "I've just remembered the log-book in his car, and log-books carry addresses. They could have been there hours before him, waiting, and I don't expect he had the slightest chance."

"Yes, that's about what happened," she said in a miserable voice. "Then let's not do nothing till 5.00—let's ring up *Holmwood* now. Good lord, aren't we slow! That's what we're meant to do, of course, once we know Malcolm's disappeared! Dr. Paul's probably sitting by the telephone promising the most awful things if the bell doesn't go in the next five minutes. Come on, let's get it over."

We were in a Soho restaurant at the time, and had just begin to eat. In spite of that I got ready to leave, and then sat back again: for yet another possibility had struck me.

"Look here," I said, "Malcolm's no fool. Suppose he approached his flat with an eye open for trouble? Then he might have seen he was walking into a trap, and sheered off. Else why should he get out on Westminster Bridge, the draughtiest place in London?"

"Well, where's his flat?" demanded Rhona. "All I know is the phone number."

"Oh, it's Westminster all right, round by the passport offices in Queen Somebody's Something. All the same it's a good six or seven minutes on foot from the bridge, so why get rid of his car there unless he intended to explore? I don't think we ought to be too hasty. If we ring up Dr. Paul, and Malcolm hasn't been caught, we'll be giving away our whereabouts—he could get the call traced if he made enough fuss. I know that London's a big place, but if you remember we came back here because we reckoned they'd expect us to go anywhere else first. It's a rather different proposition if there's a dozen men doing their level best to hunt us down."

"Yes, that's true enough," she agreed. "And he wouldn't stop at a dozen, I don't suppose. We ought to be safe even so, of course, but that won't do Malcolm much good if he's in trouble. Do you really think he may be all right?"

"Well, put yourself in his place," I said. "You get somewhere near home, and since your eyes are wide open you see things that put you off going any nearer: a parked car, or a couple of shadows in a doorway. All right, where do you go then? Or the next day? Not to your chambers, because the enemy could easily find someone to tell them you're a barrister, and immediately look you up in the right book. Also, how do you start trying to make contact with us? When you daren't telephone a message in case some idiot blabs, and Paul realizes we're in London? It strikes me as a stinker, to put it politely."

"Well, give me a cigarette and try not to say what you really think," she suggested with a smile. "Then I'll see if I can be clever for once. It's about time—I don't somehow feel I'm pulling my weight in this affair. Considering the things that have happened to you since you got to know me, it's a wonder you don't quietly walk out, Arnold," she added. "But please stay if you can possibly bear it."

"You try to get rid of me!" I said. "I wouldn't dream of deserting anyone who was going to be worth three-quarters of a million."

She wrinkled her nose at me.

"I see. To you I'm just an investment?"

"Well, among other things," I agreed lightly, and felt it was time to change the subject. "Meanwhile you were going to work out what Malcolm did," I reminded her. "Here's the cigarette: now pull like blazes."

"Pull?" she echoed uncertainly. "Pull what?"

"Your weight," I explained, with my most diplomatic smile. "Where did Malcolm go when he couldn't go home, and what did he do about us?"

Rhona sat silent for several moments.

"Well, the first part's too hard," she decided, "and anyway it isn't important if we can manage the second, so let's concentrate on that. To begin with he'd try to put himself in your place, and imagine what you'd do when you found you couldn't find him. That makes sense?"

"Undoubtedly," I said, and gave in; but she persisted quietly, frowning most of the time and making a few pencil notes on the back of the menu. Presently she looked up and helped herself to another cigarette.

"You'll promise you won't laugh if I'm wrong?" she asked.

"Of course not. Anything you suggest will be one up on me—I haven't an idea in my head."

And that, in passing, was no more than the truth. Try as I might I could think of no alternative to ringing up *Holmwood* and demanding point-blank if my friend were there.

"No?" said Rhona. "I can't really believe that—you were extremely bright last night."

"And what was the result?" I countered, a trifle bitterly. "So far as I can see, I simply spent a couple of quid for the doubtful benefit of a shave with a very blunt blade."

"But I had a nightie to sleep in," she reminded me, "and it wasn't your fault the cases were full of junk. Still, this time it seems to be my go, so here you are—a question to start with. How many common friends have you and Malcolm got?"

"None," I said. "And I'm not trying to be funny—I was brought up to respect the word 'mutual' too. It just happens that we've never had the chance to mix in one another's social circles."

"Then where in the world did you meet?"

"Oh, at Cambridge: but we were in different colleges, and we've both lost touch with the other men in the XI."

She regarded me with pretended awe.

"Corks, are you a blue?" she demanded. "This must be where the light comes out of its little bushel. The XI—now what would that indicate?"

"There's only one game worth talking about that fits," I asserted. "Some people pass the winter playing barbarities like soccer or hockey, I believe, but nobody could call them games: one's a profession and the other's usually a massacre with blunt instruments. But don't bother about that—it's not summer yet. Malcolm and I know nobody well enough to think of using him as a private post-office."

"Ah, that's a pity. Still, it does simplify things. Now another question: is he friendly with any reporters?"

"Yes, several, I believe."

"Right: then here's your answer. He'd somehow get a message inserted in the *Personal* column of a daily paper, and if he couldn't manage that he'd at least be in time for an evening one."

"I say, that really *is* clever!" I exclaimed in genuine admiration. "I should never have thought of anything so—so sensible."

"Obvious is what you mean," she corrected. "But it's always on the cards he didn't think of it either: shall we buy some papers and see?"

Is it necessary to say that she had guessed right? There was the message in both *Times* and *Telegraph,* and pretty plain once we knew what we were looking for. All the same, I shall never be certain that Malcolm ought to have expected me to work it out: but perhaps he had summed up Rhona's wits at somewhere near their true worth. This was our cue.

> MAKE-UP FAN: *Adore see you* 1200 *HQ.* 7.00. *tonight bring strong man's burden can hardly wait love:* BIG-EARS.

I may mention in his defence that he's temperamentally the sort of person who enjoys solving *Observer* acrostics. The inscription and signature aren't too difficult, one referring to our conversation in Mrs. Grayson's garden on the previous Friday afternoon and the other to her remark about his mother's short sight. I solved those myself, and also the reference to Rhona, but 1200 *H.Q.* baffled me completely. She spotted it at once, though, and teased me for a long while before asking who governed my beloved game of cricket, and what M.C.C. represented in Roman numerals.

"We thought Dr. Paul had got you," said Rhona as we walked away from *Lord's.*

"And was busy inventing new tortures," I added.

"And we very nearly rang up to find out," she went on, "but Arnold suddenly realized you might have changed your plans."

"But it was she who suggested looking in a newspaper," I assured him: "and solved your beastly conundrum, incidentally. Anyway, what did happen?"

It was much as we had foreseen. Though he felt sure he hadn't been followed from Long Reach, he took the precaution of finishing his journey on foot, and so saved himself from being trapped. There were three men waiting for him in the opening of a nearby mews, he said.

"So I decided to go elsewhere," he told us, smiling. "I walked back to the Abbey, found a taxi, and persuaded a friend to let me borrow an arm-chair. It was a puzzle to know how I could get in touch with you two until I thought of advertising, which was quite late. I only just got the thing phoned through in time—hence the obscurity."

"And your aunt?" asked Rhona. "We've heard she's all right, but no details."

Malcolm had a fuller account, and gave it to us over a meal.

"They let her go as far as the cross-roads and actually into the car: only it wasn't Dicksons', but one of theirs. The doctor himself was sitting in the back, looked at her once, she says, and immediately began to apologize. He must be a cool sort of cuss—he didn't even seem to mind being tricked, according to her. She handed him your letter, Arnold, which he read with one or two chuckles, and remarks to the effect that apparently your brains were more developed than your face had led him to suppose. Then he asked if he might drive my aunt home, and started complimenting her on her roses."

He paused, grinning to himself at what came next.

"And, believe it or not, when they reached the cottage the old brute spent half an hour with her in the garden examining the things by torchlight," he continued, "talking about how to prune and when to bud and what bone-meal does that stable-manure doesn't, or *vice-versa.* Just as if there'd never been a Rhona French, she says, and the Bank of England was a kind of spare money-box he'd lost interest in. But he had a parting shot to dispose of, and here it is more or less accurately.

"'Tell your nephew not to meddle any further with my affairs, Mrs. Grayson. Otherwise I won't answer for the consequences. With regard to the other two, they're no safer now than if they were already in my charge, because I pledge you my word that I shall be entertaining them—or they me—in forty-eight hours from now. If I prove to be mistaken I will send you a root of *Herman Paul,* the only striped moss-rose in existence. I devised the variety myself, and it's really extremely rare.'

"So there you are, chaps. My aunt begs you to keep clear till seven o'clock tomorrow evening, because she likes the sound of a striped moss-rose."

"We'll do our best," promised Rhona. "He's an amazing man, isn't he? And you really must be careful, Malcolm—you'll never be a judge if you get into his clutches."

"Oh, I doubt if that would make much difference," he told her with amusement. "I'd rather stick to the active side of the business—I haven't the patience to sit still all day taking notes laboriously. And by the way, Arnold, I've some news for you—something a little brighter. I saw my friend Burns this afternoon, and sounded him on your position: you said I might, you know."

"Of course: what's the verdict?"

"Rather a surprising one: apparently Dr. Paul cleared your name on Friday."

"What!"

"Cleared your name. He went to Scotland Yard and confessed he'd got hold of erroneous information, and that the man who assaulted him and the girl was someone entirely different. Burns tells me the police weren't altogether satisfied, but accepted his apologies and didn't open their mouths too wide."

"But this is incredible. Does it mean I can go and ask a copper the time without being arrested?"

"As often as you like—provided he's good-tempered."

"But why? What's the game?"

"I've no idea, or only the vaguest. We might think about it presently."

"And how do I get on?" demanded Rhona. "I suppose nobody whitewashed the poor lunatic?"

He hesitated a moment, his grey eyes staring at her solemnly, and she was alert in a flash.

"Oh Malcolm, what is it?" she cried. "You're hiding something—tell me, *please!*"

If I break in for a moment to mention my own feelings, it must be forgiven me. Either her tone, or the way she was looking at him and the light grip of her fingers on his arm, suddenly caused me to experience a horribly empty sensation at the pit of my stomach. 'My god, I believe she's in love with him!' I thought, and was in such a daze that I scarcely heard his reply. Yet it was momentous enough news, in all conscience.

"All right," he agreed quietly, "I couldn't decide if I ought to or not, but you're too sharp. The official position is this, Rhona: Dr. Paul has also notified the police that you were recaptured last Thursday evening near Dorking in an exhausted condition. What's more, I met a reporter today who swore he'd been down to *Holmwood* and actually seen you in bed 'recovering', and his description fits you absolutely pat."

## XIX

FOR A MOMENT WE WERE STUPEFIED: then both together began to ask questions. What did it mean? we demanded. Why had there been nothing in the papers? How were we to treat the situation?

Malcolm hushed us at last and ordered a round of drinks.

"You can imagine I've been thinking till I felt dizzy," he said. "Here are my conclusions, for what they're worth. I found out by patient enquiry that Dr. Paul did his utmost to see there *wasn't* anything in the press, and succeeded except in one case, which doesn't happen to be the paper my aunt takes. That means he didn't want you to know you needn't be afraid of the police, and the reason seems fairly obvious: you might go and endanger his game by throwing in your hands."

"Eh? What was that?" I asked.

"I'm sorry—I haven't made it very clear. In my opinion, he's gone past the stage where he's prepared to exhibit Rhona *in person* on her twenty-first birthday. 'Here you are, gentlemen, one certified lunatic by the name of French: in return please hand over her fortune.' It also strikes me as more than possible that he never intended to do that, because you can't get hold of a really convincing double at a minute's notice.

"As I see things, your escape temporarily spoilt his plans for producing a fake Rhona, because he couldn't be sure you wouldn't go straight to the police. Accordingly, until he knew you weren't likely to do that he admitted he'd lost a patient, but as soon as he felt safe enough he went on with his original plot, taking what steps he could to ensure you didn't hear about it. The way things stand at present is this, Rhona. You're free, but as far as Scotland Yard's concerned you've stopped being Rhona French. If you insist you are her you may perhaps be landing the doctor in trouble, but at the same time you'll be doing yourself out of the money for an absolute certainty."

"But why?" she queried, frowning. "If I can *prove* I'm me, then I can't also be the lunatic he's supposed to be showing reporters."

"Admittedly: but you don't know all the facts yet. I told you I met a man who said he'd seen you, but I didn't tell you who the man was. His name's Jenkins, and he's the kind of sweep who'd swear he saw three elephants asleep on the Monument for a ten-pound note. In other words he's been bought, body, soul and fountain-pen, and if it turns out inconvenient for you to have been stared at in bed, then you won't have been. The story isn't published yet, I may say."

"Gosh, you do save the nasty bits till last!" she exclaimed.

"I'm sorry: but I thought you might be sick if I told you all at once."

"You mean that if Dr. Paul really does recapture her, as per his promise to your aunt," I said, "she and the understudy change places?"

"More or less: though possibly not for the birthday party."

"Well, leave that out for a moment. What I want to know is, how does he get on if the police find out, and ask him what the devil he meant by saying Rhona was recaptured at Dorking on Friday or whenever it was?"

Malcolm smiled again.

"Mind, I'm only giving you my own impressions, but if that happened I should expect him to deny ever having been to Scotland Yard in his life. He'd suggest he'd been impersonated by somebody employed on your behalf, and probably bring a dozen witnesses to prove he was miles away at the time. It's no good, Arnold: he's got the whip-hand for the present, and you must face the fact."

"All right," agreed Rhona: "but let's get it so clear that even a lunatic can understand. Officially I'm not me, and as such don't get any money: but if I tell a copper I am me, Dr. Paul immediately wangles things so that I officially start being myself again, with the same result. Then what *can* we do?"

"Well, I've been thinking about that too, and I simply don't see any way out. Which isn't to say there's not one, of course: only that I've missed it. While you're at liberty you're helpless, as you've just pointed out: but if he catches you again you won't be a halfpenny better off and maybe a dickens of a lot worse. I mean, you are *alive* now."

"But how does that square with what he told me about her survival being so important?" I asked.

"Oh, he wouldn't kill her till he'd got the money, just in case his understudy didn't look like being good enough. In that case he'd probably dress Rhona up as a child of six and shove straws in her hair and give her a good strong dose of the most appropriate drug, and then even her best friends wouldn't back her claim. Yes, that's far more feasible than what I suggested to begin with, as a matter of fact. I rather think it gets my vote."

"And what happens to the fake?"

"Oh, that's simple: she s merely a reserve in case Rhona can't play—catches pneumonia and pops off, for instance."

"Now do stop being morbid!" exclaimed the victim of his speculations. "I don't doubt you're right, but there's really no need to talk about me as if I were something in a puppet-show. I certainly seem to be in a worse hole than ever, although I'm here and not there, but I'm convinced there's a way out if only we can think of it."

"And so am I—positive," I put in.

"On principle?" asked Malcolm shrewdly. "Or have you had an idea?"

"Yes, I believe so."

"Good man! Out with it."

Rhona said nothing, but the encouraging smile she gave me sufficed. For the time being my suspicions that Malcolm was more to her liking than myself no longer mattered: the main thing was to put her in a winning position.

"Don't expect me to be too coherent," I advised, "but this is a rough outline. If we keep Rhona hidden until her twenty-first birthday, Dr. Paul will then be forced to produce his bogus lunatic before he can claim the money. At the same time the real one will automatically have become legally sane, because she'll have been free for a fortnight. Correct?"

He nodded, looking at me gravely.

"Good: then all we have to do, surely, is to join in the party and prove conclusively that Paul's Rhona *is* bogus. It won't matter admitting that ours was a lunatic once—that wouldn't disinherit her. Nor will it matter if we get let in for assault and battery and theft and exceeding the speed limit. There'll be enough money at stake to make anything the police can do worth while: but we mustn't attempt a move of any kind till after midnight next Sunday. Until then, Rhona's in baulk."

Malcolm went on looking at me for a moment, and then laughed.

"I agree with the dear doctor," he said: "there's more in you than meets the eye, Arnold. You've gone straight to the only possible solution, while I've been walking all round dodging it. Sorry."

"Now don't start belittling yourself," I told him. "You got us out of the caravan, and you got us out of Mallow Cottage."

"Yes: but first of all I got you in, both times, so that was only fair."

He turned to Rhona energetically.

"The question is, *can* you prove you're you?" he asked. "Against the enemy's deliberate assertion that you're not?"

"Well, I should have thought so," she answered, smiling confidently: but when we came to discuss the matter we realized it mightn't be so easy. To begin with, she had no surviving blood-relations, and because of her secluded life with her uncle at Kingston could think of no one likely to remember her at all well since she was sixteen. Furthermore, all her personal belongings—clothes, books, childhood toys—were in Dr. Paul's hands.

"But there's always my birth certificate," she said hopefully.

"Which proves precisely nothing," Malcolm informed her: "except that such a person as Rhona French exists, or did once. No, you don't look like being able to produce much tangible evidence: your line will be the test-of-memory one. For example, you went to school, and something happened to you there which you know about but the fake Rhona doesn't. You sat on a netball and burst it, say, or hacked the geography mistress on the shin, or giggled in church and got sent out three Sundays running."

"Yet even there Dr. Paul will have a loop-hole," I observed, after Rhona had denied performing any such actions. "He'll ask how in the world you expect his ward to remember things when she's mad. Also, you can bet he'll contradict every word about life at Kingston, especially as he must have prepared for opposition. The servants, for instance: I wouldn't insure their lives, nor the accuracy of their memories."

The girl reluctantly agreed with me.

"There were only ever three, although it was such a big house," she said: "a cook, a housemaid, and a manservant who also looked after the garden. What's more, the cook's dead and the other two got married to each other—Dr. Paul told me about it while I was at *Holmwood*. I couldn't imagine why he bothered, at the time, but I see now all right. They're probably in New Zealand with a nice fat cheque and his best wishes, and I've got about a week to find them!"

"But there's bound to be *some* evidence," I objected.

"There will be," agreed Malcolm significantly. "The trouble is that evidence and truth aren't the same thing."

"Then they ought to be," I maintained. "Anyway, what about fingerprints? They don't alter when you grow up, except I suppose that they get bigger."

He laughed, though kindly.

"You try finding a fingerprint *you* made when you were an infant!" he suggested. "The only hope would be to burgle *Holmwood,* and if you're thinking of that you can count me out."

"Then let's try handwriting," I persisted, to Rhona. "I know he's got your school books and things, but didn't you ever send people any letters or post-cards?"

"I dare say I did, but I honestly don't remember, and in any case I was made to do script till my grandmother died. Look here, Malcolm, be frank: what sort of a chance would we have if we set about proving my identity by this memory business?"

He shrugged rather pessimistically.

"In view of the fact that Paul's candidate's officially demented," he told us, "and the difficulty of bringing forward reliable witnesses to cover the last four years, I wouldn't call it more than evens at the best. Still, don't be disheartened: it *is* a chance, and apparently the only one. What we must do is to present our case in the most favourable light possible, and as you say there isn't a great deal of time."

He paused, glanced at his watch, and scowled.

"It's close on 10.00," he said. "You know, I really think we could do with a good night's sleep first—anyway, that's how I feel. I'm staying at a pub in Holborn, by the way, and my name's Hood, not Imery. Shall we meet tomorrow and thrash the matter out?"

"Yes, let's," agreed Rhona, and then hesitated a moment. "There's just one other thing I want to say," she went on, rather shyly, "and please don't argue, either of you. We three are sharing the danger, not to mention the brain-work, so if there's a fortune at the end of it all we'll go shares in that too."

"Ass!" said Malcolm, surveying imaginary diamond rings.

"No, I mean it."

"Then I shall begin to think you really are a loony," I remarked. "Besides, think of what I told that poor woman last night about being careless with money!"

Malcolm hadn't heard that story, so I related it while Rhona went off to powder her nose. He found it amusing, but doubted if a magistrate would have agreed.

Well, that's how matters stood on the evening of Monday November 28th. Rhona had been at liberty for almost eight days, and if she could hold out for a further six she would become legally sane. Yet this fact no longer promised to supply us with the end of our troubles. Unless we were very careful, Dr. Paul might walk off with the money while we looked on helplessly.

'Not if I can stop him, though!' I thought, as I sat down to remove my shoes. 'And not if Malcolm can stop him, either.'

We were again in a hotel, but a different one: also, we had registered separately, and of course in assumed names. Although it seemed unlikely that our presence in London was known or even guessed at by the enemy, we were taking no risks.

Now, it's obviously impossible for me to mention the establishment in question, but there's no harm in saying it was in Bloomsbury, tucked quietly away among the squares and not above a quarter of a mile from the British Museum. It wasn't a particularly high-class hotel, but on the other hand Malcolm told us that it had the reputation of being respectable. Not that I'm finicky, especially when I'm in hiding; but respectability, of a rather dignified old-fashioned kind, promised a pleasant contrast to the life we had been leading recently.

Unfortunately I shall never know if the promise would have been fulfilled, because I was destined for other experiences.

I sat down on my bed to take off my shoes, the time being just short of 11.15. Then, searching my pockets, I discovered that I had neither cigarettes nor tobacco, and accordingly shod myself again. That done, I made my way along dim carpeted corridors and down a wide deserted staircase on the ground floor, but was unlucky. All the clerk on duty in the office would provide were cigarettes with cork tips, which I abominate.

"Very well, I'll go out and get some," I said. "Which would be the best way?"

"Turn to the right outside, sir, and take the first right again. You'll find a machine on the next corner—it's only three minutes away."

He may still be sitting there awaiting my return: I've never been back to see.

The night was cold but fine: overhead the stars glittered frostily, and in the distance I could hear the dull rumble of traffic. Yet the immediate neighbourhood lay shrouded in repose: there wasn't a person in sight, and only the clack of my new shoes on the pavement disturbed the sleepy square.

And then, without the least warning, things began to happen. A car slid quietly round the corner towards which I strode: a sleek black Daimler driven, surprisingly, by a girl. It stopped a yard or two in front of me, and in a moment the near-side door was open and an elegant silken leg protruded.

"Oh, please!" said its owner in an urgent husky voice. "Have you seen a policeman anywhere? Or perhaps you know the nearest doctor or hospital? My chauffeur's been taken sick—he's lying in the back and he looks pretty queer."

Instinctively I glanced behind her, but could see nothing because of the darkness, so I turned towards the front again. It's hard to remember now what impression I received of her then: the light was none too good even with the door open, and all I could make out clearly was the provocative leg. There was more than enough of that in evidence to be interesting, but after all legs of the better kind are much alike. Her face was shadowed by one of those ridiculous hats with veils which reach the nose, the rest of her to the knees being covered with an expensive fur coat and her hands daintily gloved.

"No, I haven't noticed," I answered, "but I dare say they'll know at my hotel. Look, it's only just down the street—I'll hop in and ask them for you."

"Oh, thanks!" came her curiously throaty voice. "That's real kind of you."

'Ah, an American!' I thought stupidly as the leg retreated and I usurped its place: but only for a second. As soon as the door was shut the Daimler moved forward with scarcely a sound, and it took me next to no time to realize that it wasn't going to stop again in a hurry.

"Here!" I expostulated: and then jumped. Something had pricked me in the left arm, just below the shoulder.

"How truly providential!" purred Dr. Paul smoothly from behind. "We were about to call upon you, and here you are to meet us."

"You devil!" I cried, or tried to: but already I was feeling faint and fuzzy. Whatever he had dosed me with, it acted quickly.

"Now don't struggle!" he told me softly, seeming to speak from a great distance. "Just relax—just relax."

I did so, but not because he ordered. I was fighting the waves of nausea sweeping over me, weakening my limbs and burying my head in clouds of burning cotton-wool.

"That was excellent, Gloria!" I dimly heard him say. "I always knew you were clever, but not that you were brilliant . . . the admirable agility of mind . . . a totally different voice . . ."

Then I became aware that I was sinking—that if I continued to lie back I should slither into a gaping pit. It would be a sensation something like sleep, only deeper. I should go down and down, I was perceiving, and what should I find at the bottom?

The thought that I might come upon a permanent oblivion stirred me. If I were indeed to die, I would at least go out with some show of energy. With a desperate effort I regained momentary control of my arms, lurched towards Gloria, and strove to push out my hands. I reached the steering-wheel, as if through syrup, and tried to force the car into the curb or across the road or anywhere out of its true course.

And then I lolled backwards laughing feebly, for my utmost grasp upon the polished ebonite was lighter than a child's caress: so feathery that the girl didn't even bother to brush away my fingers. I was probably still sniggering when I lost consciousness.

## XX

I CAME TO MYSELF SLOWLY, painfully, not realizing for some minutes that I still lived. Then, as my eyes began to focus more correctly, I observed that I was out of the pit and lying in bed in a darkened room. On a small table to my left a night-light flickered wanly; further off was the glow of a coal fire, and beyond the foot of the bed curtains flapped gently at a window.

I felt a certain amount of vague curiosity about my surroundings, but was more concerned over the throbbing in my temples. There seemed to be an active piece of machinery inside my head: now perhaps a clock which ticked solemnly and consistently, and now for an instant a furious roaring dynamo. I tried to raise my hand to my brow, but failed, discovering that I had power only over the upper joints of my fingers.

'That's silly—they won't work!' I thought. 'I wonder what's happened? I wonder where I am? If only my head would keep quiet for a little while and let me think!'

And then Gloria came in dressed as a nurse, and I remembered.

"Hullo, did you wake up?" she asked me brightly. "I was beginning to reckon you weren't going to."

"What time is it?" I enquired: or that was my intended question, but what issued from my mouth sounded like nothing so much as the noise a bee makes inside a nasturtium.

"Now don't start worrying!" she said. "You won't be fit to talk for ages yet, so you may just as well lie quiet. All right, I'm not going to hurt you—don't be afraid."

She had approached the bed, and now with cool fingers took my pulse. Apparently satisfied, she distended one of my eyes and examined it gravely, then nodded.

"You'll get over it," she told me. "All you want is food and sleep."

"What time is it?" I tried again, but with no better result: on this occasion she took no notice whatever, but went briskly out. A few minutes after she returned with a bowl of broth, with which she fed me slowly in spite of my angry glances: nourishment of any kind was the last thing I felt I could bear. After that she made me swallow a black capsule, and within a short time I fell asleep.

Time passed, though I had little idea of how much or how quickly. At intervals I awoke, then slept again, but each waking found me stronger. Apart from Gloria and a taciturn male nurse I received no visitors, and since my voice was the last of my faculties to come under control I gave no trouble to either.

Eventually, for perhaps the hundredth time, I attempted my question and achieved intelligible words. At once I experienced a feeling of profound relief: I had resolved with myself privately that when I could make myself understood I should be well on the way to recovery.

"Good lord, is that all you've been sweating to ask me?" said Gloria amusedly. "You've no idea how funny you sounded—just like bath-water running away."

She opened the door and consulted a clock somewhere outside.

"It's just a minute to half past seven, if you must know," she told me. "In the evening, of course."

"Yes, but what evening?" I demanded, my voice becoming clearer.

"Ah, that's a different matter. I don't think you're supposed to know, but you've been very good on the whole, so if you like I'll find out."

During her absence I lay in almost a fever of apprehension. Although I felt physically weak my wits were working properly now, and I was master of all the circumstances connected with Rhona's inheritance. We were to have met Malcolm to discuss them, I recalled: on Tuesday for lunch at *Simpson's*. Yet it must be long after that—perhaps even as late as Wednesday evening. And what of Rhona herself? I hardly dare think, because since Dr. Paul had known where to find me, it seemed to follow that he must also have known where to put his hand on her.

Gloria came back with an apparently friendly smile.

"Yes, I am allowed to tell you," she said. "It's twenty-five minutes to eight on the evening of Friday December 2nd."

*"Friday!"* I gasped, and she frankly chuckled.

"Friday as ever was—my word, that's bucked you up! How d'you feel now?"

I explained, briefly and ungallantly.

"And if I was strong enough I'd get out of bed and throttle you!" I finished.

"Now, naughty! I'm much too nice to throttle"—and she stroked her white throat softly.

"Yes," I agreed: "it was made for a rope, not hands. Where's Dr. Paul?"

"Coming along to see you by and by—don't be impatient. Is there anything else you'd like me to tell you?"

I hesitated a moment. Would it be wise to ask where Rhona was, even after what seemed a direct invitation? But I badly wanted to know.

"Oh, she's safe enough," replied the girl coolly. "I dare say they'll let you see her soon. By the way, I hope you aren't too sore about what happened here the other morning? I was only carrying out orders, you know."

"Oh, don't apologize—it was my own fault. One day I'll do as much for you."

She laughed again, good-humouredly, and sat down in a wicker arm-chair at the far side of the fire-place.

"And you needn't worry about the money," she told me with an impudent grin. "Though I believe you would have sent it if I'd really let you go. And I'm afraid I can't give you back your £40, because I've spent most of it."

"What on—that ghastly hat you were wearing in the Daimler."

"Why, didn't you like it? Yes, that was one of the things I bought, and I must say the veil came in jolly useful. Even then I think you ought to have recognized my legs, though—you've seen enough of them lately. I got quite a nice fox fur, too—a girl has to look smart to get anywhere these days."

"You won't need to look smart where you'll end up," I said—"there aren't any fashions in the gutter. Tell me how they got Rhona."

She shook her head.

"Ask Dr. Paul if you want to know. In any case, I don't much like the way you're talking to me."

"Well, did you expect to? I'm not feeling very polite."

"No, I suppose not—I probably wouldn't myself if I were in your place. And now you tell me something, for a change. Are you in love with Rhona?"

I stared at her, trying not to go red.

"I'm more in love with her than I am with you," I replied. "What do you ask for?"

She said nothing for a moment, but when she spoke seemed momentarily serious.

"Oh, it doesn't matter—I don't know. At least, I do: I was really hoping you aren't."

"Because you've got designs on me yourself? Don't bother. If I was dead and in my grave, and you climbed in beside me, I'd jump out before you had a chance to corrupt the remains."

Yet she still regarded me soberly.

"There you go again!" she remarked. "Good heavens, I've cleaned my shoes on better men than you—*and* they liked it! I was hoping you aren't in love with her for your own sake—not that I care an awful lot. Well, I shall have to be running along, but you can always ring the bell if you need anything."

"Bell? What bell?"

"On the wall behind—hadn't you noticed? You can't be as bright as I thought."

Her smile was mischievous again, and I had to admit to myself that she made a pretty enough-picture standing there in her trim uniform, her golden hair peeping from under her white headdress and her red lips slightly parted. Then she turned towards the fire, knelt down, and poked it into a blaze.

"You can't say we don't look after you," she observed, and in the same breath swore violently as she got up.

"That's the third —— suspender that's gone today," she informed me, and putting her foot on the bed began to inspect the damage with as little regard for my presence as if I had been a block of wood.

"You ought to have spent my money better," I said. "Surely you could have got a long enough pair of stockings for £40?"

"Well, give me some more and I'll try!" she retorted. "Now go to sleep till Dr. Paul arrives. Sure you're all right?"

"I'd be better with a cigarette: is it allowed?"

"Don't know—I don't see why not."

"But you ought to know—you're a nurse."

"What, me a nurse? Don't crack jokes or you'll make me bust something else. I'm only an ornament—it's useful for the gentlemen visitors to have somebody to wink at when they think no one's looking. Not meaning you, of course: you're—you're not really a visitor."

"No, I'm just one of the prisoners," I agreed. "All the same, I would like a cigarette, please."

'So Rhona's caught at last!' I thought miserably, alone again. 'After all our efforts—it's too foul to be true.'

Yet I felt little doubt that the worst had happened, until it struck me that perhaps the doctor was going to try out his fake heiress. If I were deceived, he might argue, so would anyone else be. If I accepted an impostor as the girl I had been seeing daily for a week, then he need fear nothing from outsiders. Malcolm Imery's words came back to me, about the difficulty of building up a disguise which would withstand serious scrutiny. I determined that if I had the chance I would thoroughly test the identity of whoever should be shown to me as Rhona.

At the time I believed I had been really clever; yet it would have required a great deal more penetration than I shall ever possess to prepare me for what lay in store. Lying there in bed smoking, and not much enjoying the taste of the tobacco, I was like a man about to play with a firearm which he thinks unloaded. He suspects nothing until the explosion staggers him: he is merely an ignorant fool, as I was then.

Half an hour later Dr. Paul came in to see me. His greeting was mildly triumphant, and he readily answered all my questions.

"How did I discover where you were staying? My dear fellow, that wasn't very hard. When your friend Imery failed to spring the trap I set for him on Sunday night—there are embryonic signs of intelligence in that young man, you know—I simply waited. After all, he's a person with qualifications and a career, and consequently traceable. I intended to invite him here—let's put it that way—and see how much information he possessed, but fortunately that wasn't necessary. You and Miss French aren't the only people who can decipher somewhat tortuous messages, and I happen to have heard of your cricketing interests and achievements."

"So you followed us?"

"Precisely: from the moment you broke up your party on Monday evening. Not myself personally, of course, but someone acting for me. When you so kindly saved me the trouble of inveigling you out of your hotel I really felt that fate was smiling"—and he did so himself, benignantly stroking his cleft chin with long fingers.

"And how would you have got us out?" I asked.

"Oh, surely that doesn't matter now? But I can assure you I had worked out three separate methods, any one of which would have sufficed. And now you'd probably like to hear about Miss French?"

"Very much," I said. "She's here?"

"Of course—where else should she be? I'm afraid your friend's aunt will have to do without her moss-rose after all. A pity: but then it really is scarce, and I should never have felt certain she appreciated it. However, I mustn't exasperate you. That same night, Monday, I left a note at the hotel explaining your absence, and suggesting that Miss French might care to redeem you. Which, I am happy to say, she did, after a long telephone conversation the next morning."

"Redeem me? I don't quite understand."

"Well, nor do I, Mr. Dane, to be perfectly frank. Facts are inescapable, though, and I can only conclude that she must have taken a liking to you. She returned here voluntarily on condition that I released you upon the morning of her twenty-first birthday, alive and unharmed. I shall keep my word because I always do, and that means you've nothing whatever to be nervous about. Nor, incidentally, have I, for I shall naturally take steps to ensure your silence."

"Really?" I remarked coldly. "Then you'll have to be a damnably clever man, Dr. Paul. Short of cutting my tongue out and my hands off, which would hardly fit with your promise, I don't think you can do it."

He shook his head in disagreement and leant forward—he was sitting in the wicker chair by the fire.

"I can, because I *am* a damnably clever man," he declared calmly. "That's to say, I don't let the simple truth slip under my nose as so many people do. Let me give you an illustration of my meaning. Imagine that I have two objects—say two cricket balls—connected by a yard of elastic. I place one here"—indicating the mantel-piece, "and the other there"—pointing to the window. "The distance is about nine feet, which implies that the elastic is tightly stretched. Now, suppose I wish to bring about a particular event—namely, the conjunction of those two cricket balls. How am I to accomplish it?"

He broke off to smile at me encouragingly, but I frowned: I didn't follow his discourse at all.

"You would rather I told you myself? Very well. The ordinary man answers 'By releasing one of them', and the clever man answers 'By releasing *either* of them', and there you have the whole difference between wit and wisdom. The first says 'One of the balls' because he has a narrow vision: the second says 'Either of the balls' because he can see the problem in its entirety. He has learnt one of life's golden rules, that most things work both ways.

"But you're still frowning, Mr. Dane, and I forgot you may not be at your best. In the plainest of plain language, then, my reply to your suggestion is this: *what silenced her will silence you.* She surrendered herself in order to save your life. Similarly, you'll promise what I require in order to save hers.

"And kindly refrain for once from being facetious," he added, as I was on the point of speaking. "I'm touchy upon one subject only—the value of my pledged word. The question cropped up on a former occasion, when I offered you your freedom in return for information of Rhona's whereabouts. You then behaved untruthfully, by saying you would have betrayed her if you could, only you were very sorry but you weren't in a position to: yet I bore you no grudge for that. But if you had dared to doubt the worth of my promise, Mr. Dane, I should probably have become angry, and when that happens, anything may.

"Still, don't let's be too intense"—with one of his whimsical smiles. "You'll be set at liberty at eleven o'clock on the morning of Tuesday next, without fail. Even though you told me to my face that you'd be back in an hour with a regiment of artillery and the whole police force, you should still go: but you would return at Rhona's peril, not your own. Silence for a period of three months is the price of her safety, my friend, and if you observe the conditions honourably you can look forward to being reunited in due course."

He took a cigar-case from his waistcoat, and prepared to smoke. At the same time he nodded towards the packet of cigarettes which Gloria had left on my bedside table.

"Help yourself," he said—"I'm sure the young woman won't mind. She's taken quite a fancy to you, too, so I suppose you're what people call an attractive man. From your clothes, and some of the contents of your flat, I imagine you aren't quite a pauper, and there will always be Rhona's two thousand guineas. In addition you may possibly receive a small wedding-present from myself, should circumstances lead that way. I suspect the future is rosier than you realized?"

"Slightly," I admitted.

"Then you accept my terms?"

I had only a moment in which to decide my answer, and played for boldness.

"I accept them as binding from eleven o'clock onwards on Tuesday morning," I said, "providing that Miss French and myself are still in your—in your abominable care, Doctor."

He laughed as delightedly as if I had made an excellent *bon mot*.

"Aha! Hope survives, eh? Even as last man in, with a hundred runs to go and five past six by the pavilion clock—or should it be three-quarters of a million runs? Well, well, I was young once, and I like a good fighter. The agreement stands!"

## XXI

I ASKED IF I MIGHT BE ALLOWED to see Rhona that evening, but the request was refused.

"You can visit her in the morning—you'll feel stronger then," I was told, and had to be content. As a result I spent a restless night, unable to sleep for thinking of how she had sacrificed herself to save me, and full of contrition that I had never grasped the truth. Yet the action accorded well with her nature as I had come to know it, and I determined that somehow I would make things up to her.

The more I brooded the more I realized the wretchedness of the position in which she must have found herself, and admired the gallantry of her conduct. Then I began to wonder if she had got in touch with Imery first. It was a point the doctor hadn't mentioned, and I made a mental note to ask him at the earliest opportunity.

Once, in the dead of night, I got out of bed and tried to walk round the room, in the hope that I was strong enough to contemplate escape. The attempt was a failure: I could go no more than a dozen steps without feeling faint and having to hang on to the nearest support. For the moment it seemed that my attitude towards Dr. Paul had been a vain one: that I should still be where I was when Rhona's birthday came.

I heard 5.00 strike distantly, the sound probably carried from some church clock by a favourable gust of wind. Then I must have dozed off, for the next thing I became aware of was Gloria looking down at me.

"Come on!" she was saying. "I've brought you some special medicine which'll make a big strong man of you again, and then if you're very good you shall see your lady-love."

She handed me a small glass containing a violet-coloured liquid, and I drank it obediently: it tasted faintly musty, but not nearly so unpleasant as I expected. Then I was given a basin of steaming bread-and-milk, and coffee, and by ten o'clock felt considerably fitter. An hour later, still clad in pyjamas and dressing-gown, I was being strapped into a wheel-chair. The clothes were my own, incidentally, Dr. Paul having obtained my suitcase from the Bloomsbury hotel. When I asked the reason for my bonds, Gloria merely shrugged.

"They're what the doctor ordered," she told me, and refused to say more. I looked at her sharply, and thought she seemed on edge about something, but altogether failed to suspect why.

The male nurse wheeled me down a long flight of stairs, negotiating them so skillfully that I scarcely felt a bump. Then at the bottom I caught sight of Dr. Paul, standing in a beautifully furnished lounge before an electric fire. He was reading a newspaper, but at my arrival smiled and put it away.

"Ah, here you are—good morning," he said genially. "All right, Amos, you can go. That's the man whose coat you borrowed," he added in a whisper, as the attendant departed. "An interesting fellow—he'd probably have been a bishop by now but for a regrettable desire to over-populate the country at the expense of his female parishioners. Still, every profession has its black sheep, they say.

"And now I'll take you to see Miss French, as promised, but first I think we might pay another call. You shall inspect the substitute I provided in case the real one didn't return in time."

I made no comment, but I thought a lot. So Malcolm had been right! And the doctor didn't mind my knowing. I felt obscurely troubled, but wasn't acute enough to discover upon what grounds.

The false Rhona was in bed and apparently asleep: a girl with hair of the same auburn shade as the original's and remarkably similar features. Only her head was visible, but I should never have been deceived in a thousand years, and said as much.

"Why, of course not: but please remember you're seeing her in quite the most unfavourable conditions. For one thing she isn't conscious, which makes a considerable difference, and for another she hasn't been made up in any way. Her face at the moment is perfectly natural, if inanimate. Again, we hadn't to deal with anyone who's recently had so excellent an opportunity as yourself for studying the real Rhona—here for the last six months, you recollect, and reputedly insane at that. In the circumstances I think this one would have passed muster, but fortunately we needn't employ her. After the 5th of this month she can go back to the chorus where I found her: a little richer, perhaps, and a little fuller in the hip through so much repose, but none the wiser. She's been under the influence of an opiate for some weeks."

"Very interesting," I remarked, and my brevity made him frown. When he had wheeled me outside he walked round to the front of the chair and stood looking at me gravely.

"You know, you don't seem particularly surprised," he observed, with a questioning inflection.

"Well, no: you see, I'm not. My friend Imery worked all this out days ago—bogus claimant and crook reporter and so on. You'll keep that poor wretch here till after Tuesday, just in case Rhona accidentally dies, and then as you explained you'll send her packing."

Yet even as I spoke I knew that wasn't the whole of it. Malcolm had mentioned something else as being part of Dr. Paul's probable plans, but for the life of me I couldn't remember what.

"Really?" said the doctor keenly. "I told you there were gleams of intelligence in that young man, and I'm always glad to have a diagnosis confirmed. Would it have been he who devised your mode of escape from Mallow Cottage, may I ask?"

I nodded: I was still trying to get my brain going.

"Then I've done you both an injustice!" he declared. "Him by withholding well-earnt credit for the achievement, and you by supposing that your looks belie your abilities," he added slyly.

"Oh well, I may surprise you yet—I've got three days!" I answered lightly, having given up my problem. "And where *is* Imery, by the way? Have you taken steps to silence him too?"

"Of course. I hardly cared to mention it last night, for fear you might think I was wearing a delicate subject threadbare, but the same applies to him now as will apply to you from Tuesday onwards. He's pledged to silence by knowledge of the consequences if he speaks."

"But how *can* he be?" I protested. "I mean, you're going to release me because you've promised Rhona, and do the same for her eventually because you've promised me. Both agreements are quite free from subordinate conditions about what Imery does or doesn't do in the meanwhile."

"Undoubtedly," he smiled. "But you still aren't exhibiting quite that breadth of outlook I could have hoped for. There are other people in the world besides yourself and Miss French, let me remind you. In particular, there's a certain Mrs. Grayson, to whom I have attached your friend by *his* strip of imaginary elastic. I should prefer not to detail the terms of our compact, but I don't mind saying that you'll be wise not to count upon him any longer."

It was a profound blow to my prospects, but I contrived to keep my face cheerful.

"Not even if I escape?" I asked, and he pretended to consider the question with appropriate gravity.

"Nothing was arranged about such a contingency," he informed me, "but I don't object to relaxing a point in favour of an incorrigible optimist"—and he chuckled hugely. "If you leave here before Tuesday, Mr. Dane, you may tell your friend that he resumes full liberty of action: but the odds are incredibly against you. I wonder"—looking at me again with a speculative stare from his amber eyes: "have you a plan in mind?"

I laughed.

"That's a secret anyone can share," I told him truthfully. "At this minute I don't possess the faintest vaguest notion how to get out of this place. It's just that I was brought up to believe in the ultimate triumph of right over might."

"Then you were badly brought up. In an ideal state the dictum might hold good, but not upon this sterile promontory, not amid the pestilent congregation of vapours we breathe. The man with a sword beats the man with a stick every time, my friend: but a pistol is better, and a machine-gun better still. And that leaves out of account the really dangerous fellows—the one with a million pounds or the one with brains. The latter I have, and it will help me to the former, and then let the world watch out! Money is like quicksilver: a big piece absorbs a smaller, and the more you have the quicker it grows. A million pounds makes a fair beginning, and I shall appreciate it, yet in five years' time I don't doubt I should be able to write you a cheque for that amount and not need to inform my bank."

He paused, his bushy eyebrows lifting a little at his own eloquence.

"I'm sorry if I bore you," he said, in quieter tones. "I merely wished to emphasize how much more useful the money will be to me than it could ever be to you two, for I shall do things with it that you never imagined possible."

"But I thought you were going to investigate the core of weakness in the western mentality," I reminded him, and he smiled suddenly.

"And I shall do: even a multi-millionaire may have a hobby, surely? Others amuse themselves with racing or yachting or games of chance in a casino. I shall direct my own attentions to such topics as the real hardships experienced by a Jew or Jewess in a concentration-camp, and if some of the stories one hears are authentic, then I may well have to revise the suggestions I made to you the other day.

"But we're delaying, and it's cold in this passage. I shall now take you to see Miss French."

I saw her, and understood why I was bound, and why Gloria had queried the state of my affections, and remembered the part that was missing from Malcolm's prophecy; and I'm ashamed to say I could do nothing more practical than faint.

Rhona occupied a cell similar to that from which I had been freed nine days before, except that the grille was low enough for me to look through it without leaving my chair. She sat on a divan, horribly clad in some shapeless sacking smock, and her arms were roped to her sides. But it was her face which sickened me: everything else I could have stomached. Of her identity I had no doubt, but never in my worst dreams had I met such fearful empty eyes, or a mouth which muttered and yet produced no sound. I stared at her aghast: and she in return stared through me, her vision not myself but a thing of twisted thought. Then she glanced away inanely, her lips working with wordless diligence, and a moment later she began to rock softly backwards and forwards, giggling.

Then, I suppose, I was wheeled away and taken upstairs, for when I came to my senses I lay once more in bed. Gloria sat near, and her expression seemed genuinely solicitous.

"It's all right!" she kept saying. "It's all right—it's all right. Can you understand me?"

"Yes," I answered, weakly.

"Then do *please* stop worrying—I promise you it's all right. She isn't really like that—it's only the dope he's given her. Truthfully."

I nodded, and closed my eyes: but the instant I did that I was confronted with Rhona's twitching lips and idiotic stare, so I opened them again quickly.

"How do you feel?" asked Gloria. "You've been out stone-cold for two hours. I told him it was a damn-fool thing to do, only he would insist. Look, drink this"—holding out some more of the violet medicine. "It'll buck you up."

I allowed her to pour it down my throat, and presently roused myself enough to sit up, she helping me with an arm behind my back.

"That's better!" she said, more kindly than I would have believed possible. "Now, listen—I've something for you. Dr. Paul's gone away and he won't be back till tomorrow night, but he left a letter. Can you read it yourself, or shall I tell you what it says?"

I put out my hand in silence, and she gave me an envelope still sealed. Then after I had fumbled vainly for a few moments she took it away again, returning the contents spread out for me to see.

*Dear Mr. Dane* wrote the doctor, *Forgive me for inflicting such a cruel shock upon you. I hasten to tender you my professional guarantee that the reality is far less disturbing than the appearance. In actual fact Miss French is still as sane as yourself. She merely reacts at present to an almost unknown South-American drug which I have perfected in medicinal form during the last few weeks, and with which I have treated her. Its effects are calculated to deceive even well-informed observers, so you need feel no self-reproach. I have unfortunately to absent myself from here until tomorrow evening, or I would make amends for this morning by restoring her temporarily to her natural condition of health especially for your benefit. However, I promise that should you continue as my guest until then you shall see her thus at noon on Monday, and converse with her for an hour. She will recall nothing of her present abnormality, so you must of course abstain from mentioning it. H.P.*

*P.S. I shall require the return of this letter before I permit you to see Miss French.*

I read the thing through twice, then passed it to Gloria.

"Does he mean it?" I asked. "Is he telling the truth?"

She scanned the note, and declared that I had no cause to worry myself: yet the double assurance failed to make my mind easy. For hours I lay there in a kind of waking coma: my eyes open, because only so could I keep my imagination within bounds. The picture of Rhona as a lunatic lurked ready to unfold itself if I shut them even for an instant: Rhona vacant-faced and strange, absurd in sackcloth, muttering and giggling.

Occasionally it occurred to me to wonder that I hadn't lost my own reason in looking at her, yet what worried me still more was another consideration. Even supposing Dr. Paul's letter to be strictly accurate, could I ever forget what I had seen that morning? Would it not always come between us two, clouding the brightest prospect with an odious memory? But there was no answer for the moment to that question: only time would show.

# XXII

IT WAS SOON AFTER EIGHT O'CLOCK in the evening—still Saturday—that the event took place which altered the whole situation. At Gloria's repeated request I had bestirred myself into some sort of activity, and was doing my best to eat an omelette. I was alone at the time, and seriously considering how to dispose of the thing: it had grown cold during my slow consumption of its edges, and now tasted like wet flannel. Then the door opened, and Nick slipped softly in.

"Hullo!" I greeted him. "Come to visit the sick?"

His only reply for a moment was a morose stare, and in a very short while my nose divined the truth: he had been at the bottle. I returned his gaze, to my dismay soon noticing signs which bore out my first impression. He swayed a little on his feet, and the scar which stretched from ear to nostril was prominent, showing as a dull red weal against his pasty skin. His hands were buried in the pockets of his green tweed coat, and I couldn't help suspecting him of being armed. This made me feel rather shaky: I wasn't attracted by the idea of entertaining a drunken gunman, however great his skill.

Then he spoke, enunciating his words with thick deliberation.

"You're the b——!" he told me solemnly, his brown eyes spectacled and bright. "Yep, you're the b——I've been looking for! I got a few things to settle with you."

"Yes?" I said. "What would they be?"

" 'What would they be?' " he mimicked, with slow scorn. "I guess you reckon you've forgotten, hey? I guess you take me for a sucker, hey? I guess *you* never threw no stink in my face and coshed me on the nut? I guess *you* wouldn't be so——rough!"

"As a matter of fact, you're quite right," I agreed. "It didn't happen to be me in either case."

"Aw, punk! You or your pals, who cares? And who mashed up my lamps? Hey?"

I said nothing: there I was guilty, but didn't feel like telling him so. His manner seemed too hostile, his pockets bulged too ominously.

"I don't like you, see?" he went on, thrusting his face forward. "An' I never did like you, an' when I don't like a guy he don't laugh about it."

He shook his head to emphasize the statement, and with an unbelievably swift movement exposed his right hand. It held a black automatic, one with a silencer attached.

"Get a load of this!" he suggested, waving it carelessly above the bed-rail. "I pulled it on you once, only I missed 'cos the boss said to miss. Now I reckon I'd like to pull it again, and I ain't so sure I will aim to miss."

I didn't fancy my position at all, and wildly wondered what to do. How much would Nick care for Dr. Paul's promises, in his present state? What would it matter to him that I had been guaranteed my liberty in three days' time? I suddenly saw myself leaving *Holmwood* not as a free man, nor even as a prisoner on parole, but as a bullet-stricken object conveyed away secretly in a sack.

"Don't be a confounded idiot!" I exclaimed sharply. "If that gun goes off you'll be up against the boss for the rest of your life. I'm his meat, not yours."

The answer was a sneer, and a heart-chilling twirl of the automatic.

"Huh! He don't give a bent cent what happens to you—why should he? So Nicky mustn't fire his little gun—big brother might be frightened! You think again, pal!"

Immediately there came that muffled hissing noise, with which I should soon be familiar, and something passed very close to my left ear. I can't say I saw it, because I instinctively shut my eyes for a second, but I heard the impact on the wall behind. Stupidly I turned to observe the damage, and then even in my terror found an instant to be thankful. Whether by accident or design—probably the latter, for all his nonchalance—he had hit the bell plumb in the centre and smashed it to shreds.

"Not bad," I said, trembling with anticipation. Which would reach me sooner, Gloria or another bullet?

*"Nick!"* she cried furiously from the doorway. "What the hell are you doing upstairs?"

He wheeled round at once, and snarled.

"Say, you keep your trap shut!" he ordered. "You get outa here—quick!"

"You're drunk!" she told him, with biting truth. "Give me that gun, you souse!"

The girl had pluck, no doubt of it. She walked straight up to him as if he had been holding only a banana, and put out her hand. In a moment his pale face contorted with passion: he snarled again, vicious as a wild-cat.

"*Get—out!*" he screamed, brandishing his arm, and his tone was poisonously fierce. But she stood her ground, glaring at him, and I remembered how it had struck me in the flat that these two were bad friends. Yet what could she do against an armed drunkard? What could either of us do?

For perhaps three seconds they remained like that, myself forgotten, and then he moved. He feinted with the pistol as if to strike, she ducked, and with a brutal kick in the stomach he sent her sprawling.

A moment later I joined in too, more by instinct than thought. I had only one possible weapon, my pillow: with all my force I flung it at his pistol arm, at the same time leaping out of bed. Then we were all three in a tangle on the floor, Gloria gurgling and sobbing for breath while Nick and I fought madly.

In the ordinary way I could have tackled him with something to spare, because I'm a fairly large person and he was a pretty small one, though wiry; but conditions now were all against me. For one thing I was far from being fit, and for another I didn't understand quickly enough that fair play would be a dangerous waste of time. You don't expect a sporting spirit in anyone who can deliberately kick a girl in the wind, I suppose, yet I was foolishly surprised when I found his thumbs almost gouging my eyes out.

Somehow I rolled over and shook him off, but already I felt limp. There seemed to be no air in my lungs and no strength in my grip upon his thick arms. I had one cause for thankfulness, though: since both his hands were free, he must have dropped the pistol.

The pair of us grunted bestially, and his breath came to me whisky-laden as we struggled. Now he was on top, now I had squirmed free and was battering vainly at his jaw. It seemed to have little effect, so I forgot Queensberry rules and tweaked his glasses off. How they had ever stayed on was a mystery, but the action worried him, especially when I followed it up by banging his skull against the wall. I got in three or four solid-sounding blows and then he was at me again, slashing and kicking and punching.

Whatever his shortcomings he didn't lack vigour, nor singleness of purpose. He meant to beat the life out of me, and there was no pretence about it. In spite of my sternest resistance I was soon in grave difficulties: not helped by the fact that Gloria's legs became mixed up in things. During a brief instant I glimpsed once more their slender length, and her taste for flimsy underclothing. In another she had disappeared, and my head began to sing as Nick grabbed me by the hair, jerked my face towards him, and brought one knee up smartly beneath my chin.

That, I'm not sorry to say, made me lose my temper, and for ten seconds I was all over him. Then I started to feel faint again, and the force went out of my blows. I doubted if I could hold out for another half-dozen gasps: but I didn't need to. For the second time that evening I heard—though dimly now through burning ears—the sizzle of the automatic, and then it was all over. The little ruffian fell back inert with a bullet through his brain, while Gloria stood motionless watching the blood well out from the small neat hole above his nose.

There succeeded a period of intense silence. Then the girl understandably went to bits for a while, moaning and shivering. After I had staggered up I did my best to quiet her, removing the pistol from her hand and making her sit down while I covered the body with a blanket. That done, I flopped on the bed myself to recover from my own exertions.

We were neither of us in very good trim. I bled from various knocks received in the fight, and my pyjamas were torn; so was her dress, gaping badly at one bared shoulder and the rest of it crumpled. Both her stockings sagged round her calves, and the affair she had worn on her head turned up in the grate. In addition she was as white as flour, and said she felt sick. For a moment I was inclined to sympathize, but decided not to. I wanted urgently to know what came next.

"Then be sick, and get it over!" I advised. "We can't hang about like this for long."

"All right," she whispered. "Sorry to be a fool, but I never killed anyone before."

"Well, you couldn't have made a better start," I told her, and meant it. Perhaps my attitude will be censured, but somehow I didn't consider her for a second as a murderess: she had simply done the obvious thing, and one which incidentally saved my life. If she hadn't settled Nick's account I don't doubt he would very soon have settled mine, and probably hers too.

"Now, what are we going to do?" I asked presently. "What will Dr. Paul say?"

"God knows—I'll never dare tell him!" she muttered, and frowned at her rumpled stockings. Another interval of silence followed, and then she smiled with some return of her old spirit.

"But it was nice of you to stick up for me," she said. "I don't know anyone else who'd have lifted a finger."

"What, none of the better door-mats? You obviously don't mix with the right people. Still, chattering won't help. The thing is, what do we do?"

"We?" she queried pointedly. *"You* haven't got anything to worry about. You just climb back into bed and pretend you were asleep—I'm the one in a mess."

"Oh, nonsense!" I scoffed. "What's to prevent you telephoning the doctor and telling him I did it?"

She stared for a moment at that, before shaking her head.

"Well, it's certainly an idea—only I shan't."

"Why not?"

She didn't answer for a bit, her fingers busy trying to do up her dress. Then she faced me defiantly, rather red and plainly embarrassed.

"Partly because I didn't come from that kind of gutter," she told me. "I mean, there's a difference between gutters and sewers. And partly because I'd never get away with it: he'd have the truth out of me in a couple of shakes. No, I guess I'll have to skip."

For some odd reason that solution had never occurred to me, but now I seized upon it eagerly.

"And leave me here?" I asked, as if I didn't believe she could.

"Well—I don't know. If I'm going I suppose you may as well come too, but I'm darned if I see how. There's other people in the house besides me."

"Then why hasn't the shindy brought them up?"

"Because they're probably at supper—it's twenty past eight. And Amos is out anyway, so we'll be all right till the morning. He won't come back before breakfast."

It was then that I had my idea, and in a turmoil of excitement I sat forward to think it out.

"Hush, don't talk!" I gabbled. "I believe I've found the way. Corks, talk about luck! This beats everything."

You see, I had just remembered Jervis Brown, and Jervis Brown was an undertaker, and Nick was a dead body.

## XXIII

**B**Y AND BY I LOOKED UP, to see her offering me a cigarette.

"Thanks," I said. "You know, I feel a devil of a lot better than I did an hour ago."

"Do you? I don't."

"But you will. Wait till you're clear of Dr. Paul and an honest woman again—you won't recognize yourself."

She giggled at that, and I saw that she was recovering.

"I bet I wouldn't!" she agreed. "What's the plan?"

"I'll tell you, provided we understand one another first. I mean, no more double-crossing, Gloria."

She was honest enough not to quibble about my right to make the demand.

"I give you my promise, if you think it's worth having," she said.

"All right—but I don't suppose there'll be any £2000 for you, mind. Unless I can rescue Rhona before Tuesday, which looks blooming doubtful."

"Don't waffle—I'm not broke, and anyway you're helping yourself now, not me. You did that a few minutes ago, the best you could. Show me how to get us both out of this hole and I'll do it. Otherwise I shall clear off and leave you, and that's flat. And please don't suggest taking Rhona too, because it simply isn't possible with her in the state she is. Dr. Paul's the only person who can put her right."

"I'd guessed that—curse him. Very well, here's my idea, and this time you listen carefully. First, do you know where the doctor is? Can you get in touch with him by telephone? If you can't then there's the door, because my plan'll be as dead as Nick."

"Yes, I do know. He's in Portsmouth, and he left a number in case anything went wrong."

"Good—that's a beginning. Now, did you mean what you said the other day about winking at visitors?"

"Winking at visitors? Oh, I remember: you mean, am I really a nurse? Yes, as a matter of fact I am—was."

"Well, you couldn't have had Amos's complaint, anyway," I murmured. "As it happens I don't care if you're a contortionist and a girl-guide into the bargain. What I want to find out is, do visitors come to inspect this place, and if so can you invent an important one who'd insist on poking his nose everywhere and making a fuss if everything wasn't just so? One who's alleged to have wired he's coming tomorrow afternoon before Dr. Paul returns?"

She regarded me with puzzled eyes, but nodded.

"Yes: one of the big bugs pops down here at odd times. He's as nosy as sin, and sometimes I have to be very busy keeping him—well, occupied."

"Better and better! Luck knows its job at last, so this is what you do to start with. You ring up the doctor and explain I've just killed Nick, telling him exactly what happened except that I pulled the trigger instead of you. Then tell him this nosy-parker arrives tomorrow for lunch, and suggest getting the corpse out of the house first. Would he fall for that?"

"I don't see why not—he certainly wouldn't want it lying around. But are you sure it's all right to say you did it? Won't he take it out of Rhona, maybe?"

"No, don't worry about that—work it my way. And one more point, to complete the first part: say I know you're phoning, and mention that I've been badgering you to ask if the agreement still stands. Nothing more than that—'Dane wants to know if the agreement still stands'. Got it all clear?"

She repeated the message, made herself as presentable as possible, and departed. I spent the time till her return twenty minutes later in trying to decide if I could trust her, and came to the conclusion that I had no choice. If she let me down again I was done for as far as hopes of escape went: but there seemed a fair chance that this time she was genuinely on my side.

Her report proved entirely favourable, and more than ever I became convinced that the luck had turned.

" 'Tell Mr. Dane that the bargain still holds good'—those were his words. And I'm to get Nick cleared away as early as I can tomorrow. I pretended Nugent was coming at midday, and the doctor's trying to be here by 3.00. All right so far?"

"Perfectly: but what did he have to say about Nick's death?"

"Oh, he didn't seem to like it, but he was very quiet. I rather think there must have been someone else in the room, because he spoke in a soft of whisper. I explained what had happened, just as you told me to, and I rubbed it in about the little rat being drunk and trying to shoot your ears off."

"Well, that's not far from the truth: now for the next act."

"Only, first, what *is* your bargain with Dr. Paul? Or mustn't I know?"

"I'd prefer to keep it to myself," I admitted. "It's a question of moral values, really—when a promise is binding and when it isn't."

I wasn't at all keen on telling her I was to go free on Tuesday anyway, in case she decided to leave me where I was, but to my surprise she seemed satisfied.

"He's a crack-pot about promises!" she remarked. "Pledging one's word, he calls it, and I always think of pawnbrokers. Now go on with how we get out of here—I'm darned if I can see where Nugent comes in."

"He doesn't—he was merely the excuse for removing Nick. As for that bit, it's simple: get hold of a telephone directory and look up a man called Jervis Brown. He's an undertaker, he lives in Thames Ditton, and he firmly believes I saved his life once. Consequently he's offered to do a job of work for me free whenever I want him to, and this is when. Say you're speaking on behalf of John Clive—not Dane, Clive—and arrange for him to come here with a van—I mean a hearse—at six o'clock tomorrow morning."

"Six o'clock!" she echoed. "But he'll never do that—nobody would."

"I think he will," I contradicted. "Anyway, ask him, and if he jibs remind him about what happened last Thursday week. We must be well away before Amos arrives. Also, tell him to bring a good-sized coffin—one that *I* can get into."

At last she fathomed my intentions, and laughed excitedly.

"And if I jump in beside you, then you'll jump out!" she said. "But I bet you wouldn't, all the same."

"That was a grave, not a coffin," I pointed out. "I'm not proposing to be buried, you know. All that's going to happen is that I'll be carried out openly and driven away, while Nick stays here for Dr. Paul to cope with."

She nodded, still smiling.

"Why, we could shove him in your bed and pretend he's you!" she suggested. "I'm getting my nerve back, you see," she added rather unnecessarily, as she saw me looking at her. "Only I still don't fancy staying here to be questioned. And—and I forgot to ask, but you won't give me away?"

"Of course not—you needn't be afraid. Now, is there anything I've left out?"

We both thought intently, and made two amendments. The coffin was to be provided with air-holes, in order that I shouldn't expire in transit, and if possible Jervis Brown would bring a man with him. We preferred not to obtain inside help for the task of carrying the thing to the road.

By the time she had made fitting arrangements it was 10.00. No one had come near my room, and Gloria had remembered to collect our suppers from the kitchen to avoid rousing comment. It then struck me that I didn't yet know how many other people there actually were in the house. I queried the point, and was relieved by her answer.

"Five, but none on this side of it," she said. "You see, you're in the private part—Dr. Paul's. I told Jervis Brown to leave the hearse out in the road and go across the lawn to the french windows in the drawing-room. There won't really be any need for them to come upstairs at all, will there? You can go down instead."

"Yes, I should think so," I agreed. "But where's the gang? Mappin and Sam and Wilson and Brett, and all the wretches who surrounded Mallow Cottage?"

"Well, half of them are Nick's men, not the doctor's. Brett's gone to Portsmouth with him, and Mappin's in hospital because the ammonia got in his eyes at your flat. I admit Sam's still here, but he sleeps on the other side, and anyway I can settle him. I'll put some dope in his cocoa—he always has a cup before he goes to bed. The rest of them don't matter."

"Good lord, cocoa for Sam? He didn't look the type, somehow."

"But it's true—and a stale sponge cake. He *says* he likes it. And what are we going to do with that?"

She indicated the heap on the floor, still covered by a blanket. For some reason its presence hadn't in the least bothered me, though I might have felt differently if the body had been exposed.

"I don't know," I said. "I don't much care about rigging it up in bed."

"No, nor do I, really. Let's just push it underneath, and pull the quilt down. Then it won't show if anybody does happen to come in."

So under the bed the gunman went, a stiff and heavy lump of dead flesh. We both sighed when the task was done.

And what of Rhona all this time? it may be asked. Was it a case of out of sight out of mind with her too? The answer would be a difficult one to state clearly: in brief, it is that for the present I was trying my hardest not to think of her. I knew without need for much reflection that all hope of ultimate happiness for us two, other things being equal, depended on my ability to cleanse my mind of its persistent vision: its haunting tableau of the girl I loved sitting silently muttering in a cell. I believed that when I saw her sane and well again I should forget: in fact, I was determined to, if the feat were possible. Of course, she *might* still prefer Malcolm, but I no longer felt frightened of that. Her action in giving herself up to save me had put things in a different light.

Neither Gloria nor I were inclined for sleep, so we sat up playing innumerable games of cribbage. We hadn't really much to talk about to one another, except our present predicament; and even if I had wished to—which I didn't—I don't fancy I could have made love to her with a carcase a yard away. Her chief concern now seemed to be about the stores of clothing she must leave behind: her jewellery she made into a parcel, and a fair-sized one at that. I promised I would do what I could subsequently to salvage the rest of her belongings, and advised her to wear what she valued most. While she was absent changing I shaved and dressed, and also made a discovery which will come in again later. Then, as I say, we played cards, to pass the time.

## XXIV

WHILE I WAS WAITING in the drawing-room I began to think that perhaps there wasn't much point in the hearse business after all. As dawn broke mistily I could gauge the distance across the lawn, and felt certain I might have covered it and been away in a matter of seconds. Yet later events proved that caution paid.

When Jervis Brown appeared, accompanied by a man who was obviously his brother, I took him aside and hurriedly explained the position. They had brought the empty coffin with them, an affair of polished ochre elm and glittering brass handles, and sinister enough it looked on Dr. Paul's Aubusson carpet: yet Brown's simple face was the more reassuring by comparison.

"There's no time to go into details," I told him quietly. "You said you'd repay me for anything I did the other day: well, here's your opportunity."

"And glad of it!" he informed me earnestly, bowler hat in hand. "You give the orders and I'll see they're done."

"Thanks. The idea is that I hide inside that coffin, and then you carry me out to your hearse. This young lady's coming too, and the moment we're loaded up you must drive back to London as fast as you dare. Did you put some air-holes in the thing?"

"Yes sir: all along the side—see? I sort of guessed there was something funny up. Just one question, please: do you want us to screw you down just the same as if you was a late?"

"A what?"

"A late—deceased—body. It'd stop anyone looking in—if there was anyone."

"Yes, but it would also stop me getting out. Still, perhaps you'd better, only for heaven's sake unscrew me as soon as you can, just in case I choke."

"Never you fear, sir—I'll see you're all right. I say, this wouldn't be for the films or anything?"

His weak blue eyes were full of hope, and I was sorry to disappoint him.

"It wouldn't, Jervis. This is dead serious—let's get on with it."

Until I actually lay down I never knew how small a coffin is inside. I read somewhere once of a Parisian hairdresser who habitually sleeps in a glass one, but I'll wager it's an outsize model. Things weren't improved when they put the lid in place, thus contracting my world to a narrow strip of varnish-scented gloom; but my mind was fairly easy until Gloria raised the covering and put her scarlet lips an inch from my ear.

"I've just remembered—I clean forgot to dope Sam!" she whispered. "Is the pistol in your pocket? Which one?"

I told her and she took it out, screening her action as far as possible with her new fox fur.

"Just in case I need it," she whispered again. "Good luck!"

'Drat the girl!' I thought waspishly, as they screwed me down. 'That was villainously careless—unless she did it on purpose? But hardly, or something would have happened before now, and anyway I suppose I ought to have reminded her.'

A moment later the escape really began. They hoisted me up, and I went careering about in space: a ghastly experience which I don't recommend to anyone with weak nerves. The sense of confinement was more terrifying than anything I had yet gone through: I would rather have faced a dozen intoxicated gunmen. I wanted to hammer on the sides of my dark prison, to beg that they should put it down and release me, and for one appalling instant I plunged to the very depths of hopelessness. I wasn't on my way to freedom, I was about to be interred alive. Soon I should feel earth being shovelled on top of me, and what little air I had to breathe would diminish, and I should suffocate slowly and horribly.

I told myself not to be a fool, and was cheered by the discovery that I could hear quite plainly through the wood: footsteps, the sound of someone fastening the catch of the french windows, Jervis Brown's slight cough. The steps became inaudible, and I knew we were crossing the lawn: and then came the first intimation that there was sand in the works.

"What the devil's all this?" demanded a harsh voice, and I recognized the speaker at once. It was Sam, the man in the leather coat who had followed me into the butcher's shop.

"The result of an accident!" was Gloria's immediate answer. "That lout Dane shot Nick last night, and Doc says to get him away because Nugent's coming."

"Dane shot Nick!" he echoed. "Say it again, sister."

"Why, didn't you wash this morning? Dane shot Nick—murdered him. Got it?"

"Garn—that's a fine tale!"

"All right, telephone Dr. Paul if you don't believe me. You'll find his number on the pad—if you can read. The body has to be got rid of, and he said the fewer people who know the better: some of them talk too much."

Apparently her words produced some effect, for he grunted a trifle uncomfortably.

"Well, I guess I ain't broken-hearted—I reckon somebody ought to dib up a medal. But what are you all dolled to glory for? You look more like a wedding than a funeral, and you smell like a honeymoon. And who's looking after Dane now?"

She chuckled, and I marvelled at her coolness.

"Oh, him! He got a dose of what he gave me—a needleful of No. 6 where it'll do most good."

Sam too laughed: evidently she was reducing any suspicions he might have had.

"But that doesn't explain your get-up," he said less roughly. "What's the fur-piece for?"

"Good lord, you don't half want to know something! Maybe you'd like to see what I've got on next to me? I've been given my orders, and I'll carry them out. If you did the same yourself now and again you might get on better."

That was possibly an allusion to Thames Ditton, I thought, and smiled: but not for long. As Gloria went on talking I became suddenly and desperately uneasy: I began to wish that she would stop dawdling and get on, because haste would soon be essential. For no special reason my nose had started to itch furiously, and I knew that very shortly I should sneeze.

My feelings for the next few minutes can only be described as agonizing. The onset of the irritation was so abrupt that I had no time to think what I would do: I just had to do it, and I can truthfully say that I strove not to betray my presence with all my might. I rubbed my nose desperately against the lid of the coffin, but in vain. It simply wasn't practicable to reach the right spot, and my hands of course were useless: the highest I could raise them was to the middle of my waistcoat. In torment I tried putting my tongue out and curling it upwards, but it wouldn't stretch far enough, and blowing with my lower lip distended merely seemed to make things worse.

Consequently I lay there and suffered, my fingers clenched, my toes doubled up inside my shoes, my eyes streaming with tears. And all the time Gloria continued to talk as if she had several days at her disposal, explaining to Sam how she was to call at Sir Edward Nugent's house and do her best to delay him till after three o'clock. Her story was a clever effort in the circumstances, and some of the impromptu details almost convinced even me. From my point of view the performance had one gigantic drawback, however: it took too long.

Why Jervis Brown and his brother hadn't disposed of their burden passed my comprehension, but there I was still suspended on their shoulders. For perhaps another two minutes the girl chattered while I writhed, believing every moment that I couldn't last until the next. Then she mercifully desisted, and my bearers moved. In my misery I both heard and felt the coffin touch solidity: it was pushed into position, and I lay at last within the hearse.

'Thank heaven for that!' I thought, and sighed as noiselessly as possible. From the amount of air which came out of me I realized that I must have been holding my breath, and to replace it I inhaled deeply, of necessity. The action proved disastrous: before I could stop myself I had shut my eyes and exploded.

To myself the din seemed terrific, echoing in my head like the discharge of a howitzer in a cave. Gloria told me afterwards that to her it sounded fairly normal, but Sam didn't agree, she said. He turned deathly pale, stared in stupefaction at what was ostensibly a miracle, and then unluckily for us regained his wits. By that time the girl too was on board, and urging Jervis Brown to hurry. She had lugged the automatic from her handbag, and swears she would have used it, but she got no chance. Sam shot from his pocket and sent her weapon spinning: after which he removed his hand and took deliberate aim at the coffin.

I heard the reports to the exclusion of all other sound, for he used no silencer. There were four or five, and so deafeningly loud that they quite drowned the tinkle of the hearse's broken glass. As well, I felt something strike the wood at my side, moving me a few inches. Then we were off, and a second later I became aware that I was wounded in the right arm.

As soon as it was considered safe they halted in a lane and unscrewed the lid. I was still conscious, but feeling very weak from loss of blood. The bullet had ploughed its way up my arm from elbow to shoulder, doing no serious damage but making a fair mess. Gloria showed herself a genuine nurse by bandaging me as skillfully as the conditions and lack of suitable materials allowed. We then completed our journey with all possible speed, and at Jervis Brown's they gave me a lot of brandy and made me as comfortable as they could. I was in a good deal of pain but no danger, and submitted to the girl's ministrations with some pretence at stoicism. She pulled out the bullet with a thin pair of pliers sterilized in lysol and boiling water, and bound up the wound more efficiently. Then at my request she telephoned Malcolm, and by nine o'clock he had collected me in a taxi.

Gloria assured me that she could look after herself for the time being, but we made arrangements to meet the following day, Monday, in the afternoon. As for Jervis Brown, I promised him a full explanation and recompense for his invaluable help at some later date. The first he was clearly eager to receive, but the second he declined to hear of in any form. I left him looking a little bewildered but cheerfully aware that he had faithfully discharged all conceivable debts to me.

At Malcolm's flat—now considered fairly safe—we talked and talked. He was surprised to learn he was free to oppose the doctor again, and told me that for the last few days he had been living in utter despair.

"I simply couldn't let anything happen to my aunt," he said: "yet you two were in a worse jam than ever. I really don't know what I should have done if I hadn't heard anything by tomorrow night. I hope you don't think I let you down?"

I told him not to be ridiculous: then put before him my suggestions for a plan of campaign. He listened very attentively, but without interruption.

"I *must* get Rhona away!" I finished. "I'll go mad myself if she stays in that condition a moment longer than I can help."

He nodded understandingly.

"You're in love with her," he said calmly. "I can't pretend I blame you."

"Does that mean you are too?" I blurted out, and he stared at me almost open-mouthed.

"My dear good dolt!" he exclaimed. "They must have shot you in the head, not the arm. For one thing I never poach, not even heiresses. For another, she wouldn't look at me once if you were in the same hemisphere. For a third, I'm becoming very nicely acquainted with a damsel of my own when I can spare the time, thank you for not asking."

I was immensely relieved, but still had a question to ask.

"You're sure she doesn't like you better than me?" I pressed him.

"Well, she never asked *me* if I was engaged, or ever had been, or was ever likely to be."

I didn't follow, and said so.

"She didn't ask me either," I protested, and he laughed.

"I'll say it again, with a different emphasis. She didn't ask me if *I* was engaged, and so forth, but she did ask me if *you* were. Only you mustn't tell her, because she told me I was never to tell you she'd asked me: if you can sort it out. And now I'd better get busy, and you'd better go to bed."

## XXV

THE SETTING UP OF ANY RECORD PERFORMANCE is a tricky business nowadays: one has to be so careful to be sure of breaking new ground. Hence I will put forward my own claims modestly, saying no more than that I rather expect I'm the only fast bowler in the world called Dane who quitted a lunatic asylum in a coffin, returned in a taxi twenty-eight hours later, and survived to tell the story.

I prepared my arrival by a telephone call, and Dr. Paul was in the drive to meet me: his smile as broad, his manner as pleasant, as if I had been perhaps his favourite son home from Australia after a ten-year absence. We exchanged polite nothings until we were in his study, and I realized as I walked beside him the vastness of his self-control. He could have been a great man, I thought a little tritely, if only he had been a good one.

"And now you must tell me why you've come back," he said, when we were seated with sherry and biscuits between us. "You were somewhat vague when you rang up earlier. Incidentally, I must congratulate you yet again. I suspected that Gloria liked you, of course, but I admit I didn't grasp to what extent. The coffin idea was ingenious, too, and I hope Sam didn't hurt you seriously?"—looking at my sling. "He was inspired with the best of intentions."

"I'm sure of it," I answered gravely. "In a few words, Doctor, I'm here to bargain with you."

He nodded, regarding me attentively with his yellow eyes.

"I thought as much," he declared: "though I don't quite see what pressure you propose to exert. Still, I dare say you're ready to tell me that?"

"More than ready—anxious to: but first you must let me ask you three questions, and I shall appreciate concise replies. To begin with, is Miss French still in the same state as when I saw her on Saturday morning?"

"Exactly the same, Mr. Dane."

"Thank you. Secondly, how long would it take you to restore her to normal.?"

"Between four and five hours—it cannot be done with safety sooner."

"And finally, how long would be required to de-certify her?"

He half closed his eyes at that, sitting as motionless as a sphinx, with his fingers interlocked across his breast.

"That's a peculiar suggestion," he remarked at last. "I don't think I wholly grasp the implications."

"Then let me put it more clearly. If you were offered every inducement to do so, could you arrange for Miss French to be, by six o'clock this evening, as legally sane as at the moment she's legally insane?"

For a second more he drowsed: then looked up blandly.

"Given sufficient inducement, I believe I could exert sufficient influence," he told me.

"I'm sorry, Doctor, but that isn't quite good enough. Could you guarantee it absolutely?"

"Why, yes—I *could.*"

"Thank you: and now I'll explain my proposals."

"Just one minute," he interrupted, entirely wide awake again. "Do you really mean proposals, or is that a polite synonym for demands? I should like to know just how I stand."

"No, I do mean proposals," I said: "in one sense, very strictly. Unfortunately I'm not in a strong enough position to compel you, much as I should wish to be. All the same, I don't advise you to ring your bell and have me taken away before I've finished, because you might just possibly regret it."

"The thought had never so much as entered my head," he asserted smoothly. "Please continue—I find the situation extraordinarily interesting."

So did I: and full of pitfalls, too. If I made a false move I might as well never have escaped: everything depended upon my ability to present my ultimatum tactfully.

"A fortnight ago I'd never met Miss French," I said, "and because of ignorance, or my bad upbringing, I'd never heard of you either. I was a young man with a fair amount of money, nothing particular to do, and no particular personal ties. A week ago things were different. I found myself caught up in what I might almost call a whirl of excitement, and I had a definite object in view: namely, to help Miss French secure her fortune in spite of your plans to the contrary. Today, Dr. Paul, things are different again. I have another ambition, in comparison with which money becomes of trifling importance. In short, I now put Miss French as a human being first, and her position as an heiress nowhere. For that she may not thank me, of course, but it can't be helped. Her sanity and freedom have become vital: her wealth or poverty doesn't count.

"As you suggested the other day, and I just now, I'm not a pauper. By the standards of her late uncle I can't call myself rich, but I believe two can live quite comfortably upon the interest from £45,000, leaving out the possibility that I might be able to earn something on my own account. I'm putting my financial standing before you Doctor, because you're Miss French's guardian. You see, my proposal is that I marry her by seven o'clock this evening."

"Well, well!" he exclaimed, in apparent surprise. "That would certainly be a most novel solution of the affair. But why not suggest it before, Mr. Dane? When I myself gave you the lead, for instance? Why wait till you're at liberty before surrendering?"

Luckily I had my answer ready.

"For a very simply reason. I had no chance to broach the subject earlier because until I saw Miss French on Saturday morning I didn't realize the full gravity of her present position, nor that her freedom and happiness were the only things which ultimately mattered to me. By the time I regained consciousness after so stupidly fainting you were absent. Accordingly I resigned myself to awaiting your return and then putting the idea of an early marriage before you. In the meanwhile, however, certain events occurred which enabled me to escape, and I assure you I've put the interval of freedom to good use."

"Yes?" he encouraged me warily. "In what way?"

"This," I replied, pulling a large envelope from my pocket. "A lot of yesterday my friend Imery was raising heaven and earth to get me a special licence—here it is. Miss French and I are entitled to be married anywhere at any time by any clergyman, and as I said a little while ago I propose that the ceremony takes place this evening. Since she'll still be a minor it will effectually invalidate her claims to her uncle's fortune, which is exactly what you want. I honestly can't see a single reason why you should withhold your consent: can you?"

"Certainly not—I think it's an admirable way out," he agreed readily, to my enormous relief. "But aren't you forgetting one thing? A marriage is like a quarrel, you know: it requires two parties to set it going."

I laughed.

"I hope ours won't be a quarrel!" I said. "I see your point, though, and that was why I asked how quickly you could restore her to her normal condition. I want you to do that, so that I can ask for her approval myself."

"And if it shouldn't be forthcoming?" he enquired gently. "Or perhaps you've reasons for feeling sure it will be, of which I know nothing?"

"I haven't," I told him frankly. "All I've got is hope: effrontery, if you like."

He smiled amiably.

"Some people might call it that," he observed. "I mean, is anybody worth the difference between £45,000 and £800,000? But as there's no question of her inheriting, I think she shouldn't object upon that score. Nevertheless, we must face the odd chance. If she refuses to marry you, what then?"

I shrugged.

"Hocus," I said, trying to sound hardened. "Surely you could drug her so that she wouldn't realize she was being married? I tell you, Doctor, I'm desperate—I can't see any other way out. With all due respect for your word, I can't bear to think of her being a prisoner for three more months, and nor can I imagine how to ensure her inheritance.

"For instance, I could have gone to Scotland Yard this morning instead of coming here, but what good would that have done? None whatever: it would merely have published her insanity to the whole world. The hateful truth is that you've been too clever for us: we simply can't stop you nobbling the fortune, and consequently I appeal to you to do it by marriage and not by madness."

He gave me a very searching glance from under his thick black brows.

"I wonder if you're being honest, really?" he murmured. "I would willingly believe so, but I don't feel at all confident. In the past I fear I've underrated you at times, Mr. Dane, and I should be loath to do so again. Tell me, what safeguard have you now? If I *were* to ring that bell, why should I perhaps be sorry for my action later?"

"Well, naturally I took what steps I could to look after my own skin," I answered. "The position is this: I hold just three weapons against you, two of which aren't very reliable. Imery and I think they might embarrass you if used collectively, however: therefore, should you not fall in with my suggestions or attempt to detain me, he'll test their worth.

"As a start, he'll hand over your letter to Scotland Yard—the one you left for me on Saturday, which I fortunately found when I was dressing to leave. I don't know if it's in your writing, but the police and the solicitors in charge of the estate might find the wording of interest, not to mention the lunacy commissioners and the B.M.A. After that, he'll do his utmost to get an incriminating statement from Gloria, who could doubtless help us a lot if she chose to."

I paused, looking Dr. Paul straight in the face.

"And finally," I informed him, "Imery will apply for an exhumation order in respect of Rhona's uncle's body, and only you can say whether that would be a good move or a bad one."

By no slightest facial movement did the man convey his feelings: he continued to gaze at me evenly and imperturbably.

"I see," he remarked. "Thank you for explaining. Are there any other stipulations bearing upon my acceptance or rejection of your terms? I beg your pardon—your proposals."

"Only small ones. For example, Malcolm would very much like to have his car back."

"Of course. It's in one of the garages, and I shall make no charge for the repairs. And in addition?"

"Gloria would be glad of her clothes, and I promised to do what I could for her. As well, there's the question of her personal safety, of course: she'll undertake to keep your secrets if you'll do as much for hers."

"Yes, that seems reasonable. I accept all your conditions, Mr. Dane, provided you in turn accept mine. There are two only, and I think you'll find them fair. Once you and Rhona are married, then—I presume you *do* know her Christian name?—it must be clearly understood that neither of you makes any attempt whatever, directly or indirectly, to reinstate her as heiress to her late uncle's fortune."

"Agreed—how could we?" I asked. "By contesting the will? But if there'd been a chance in a million of that I shouldn't be here now. There isn't, unfortunately: Malcolm says the confounded thing's water-tight and solicitor-proof and as sound as the Old Bailey. I suspect you of helping to draw it up, Doctor—am I right?"

"Perfectly," he assented, his eyes twinkling. "I felt I had better be thorough. My second condition is that you permit me to be present when you propose to Rhona."

I pretended to hesitate.

"Well—I can't say I shall welcome company, but if you insist I suppose I've no choice. I expect I'll make a howling fool of myself, though."

Again his eyes gleamed.

"All I'm concerned about is that you don't make one of me," he declared. "I confess I don't think it possible, but I prefer to take no risks."

"Oh, I understand! You're looking for desperate last-minute conspiracies. I'm afraid you won't discover any, but come along by all means—perhaps you'd be good enough to back me up if necessary? I mean, if Rhona doesn't fancy me for a husband, you could always make up a little piece about my worthiness and eligibility and untarnished reputation."

"Omitting all mention of the body under the bed, of course!" he chaffed me. "Though I should be quite ready to hear that you didn't kill Nick at all."

"I'm afraid I don't remember," I said evasively. "I wasn't in a very coherent state of mind, you know."

By the time we had gone over the conditions on both sides again, and made sure we fully understood one another, it was midday. Dr. Paul then prepared to carry out his side of the contract, relating to Rhona's restoration to normal health and legal sanity. How he proposed to achieve those two things I had no idea, but he assured me that if I returned at 6.00 p.m. I should find nothing to disappoint me. Accordingly I departed in Malcolm's car, first filling the back with the contents of Gloria's wardrobe and trunks. Amos helped me in the task, and not once did he speak unless I first addressed him. I saw nothing of Sam or Brett, and wasn't sorry.

Malcolm received my news with satisfaction, and willingly agreed to accompany me to *Holmwood* later.

"You don't think he's got anything hidden up his sleeve?" he asked.

"No, I believe everything will be all right provided Rhona agrees. It's a bit of a nuisance he wants to hear what I say to her, though."

"Still, you could hardly expect him not to: but I hope to goodness he *doesn't* smell rats. And now all we've got to do is to wait."

"Except for finding a parson," I reminded him. "Know any?"

"My brother," he answered simply. "He's just the chap we want."

After lunch I spent half an hour having my arm done by a doctor whom he recommended to me. Then I realized that I had very little money left, and that it's customary to give one's bride a present, so I went round to see my cousin and her husband. After obtaining £500 in return for a minimum of information I met Gloria as arranged. We had a short talk, and then explored Bond Street together wildly looking for something that Rhona might like. At first I could see absolutely nothing, and at the end of an hour had bought only half a dozen wedding-rings of different sizes and a box of chocolates. As a result of considerable thought I added some flowers, some stockings in case she hadn't any, a dress which Gloria said would fit her, and in desperation a carved jade Buddha with a most benignant smile. Then it was time to hurry back for Malcolm.

Rhona was in Dr. Paul's drawing-room, the same from which I had escaped by coffin a few hours before. One glance was enough to tell me that I need fear no bogies of my own creation: she was her old self, smiling and delightful. In fact we were all smiling: she, the doctor, Malcolm, his burly parson brother, and myself. A stranger might have supposed we were all to share a fortune.

"Well my dear, here are your friends," said Dr. Paul: then turned to me.

"I find I needn't intrude after all, Mr. Dane," he loudly whispered. "The fact is that my ward—I think I may call her that still for a few more minutes?—divined the situation by some uncanny process of which we males know nothing.

"Come, Mr. Imery," he added, in his ordinary voice. "And you too, sir"—to his brother. "Let me show you my birds' eggs—or my modern first editions, if you prefer."

He chortled happily, took Malcolm's arm, and in a moment Rhona and I were left alone, she still before the fire-place smiling at me and I speechlessly staring. My trouble wasn't that I had nothing to say, but that I had too much, and in consequence could get none of it out. I felt, and must have looked, positively stuffed; but at last I managed to make my tongue behave.

"You *do* know?" I asked, and she nodded.

"You're going to propose," she told me, almost gravely.

"And you? What are you going to do?"

"Oh—well: oughtn't you to wait and see? I won't bite you, anyway."

And then, as I began to gaze not at her but past her, and my lips fell open a little, she changed her tone abruptly.

"Arnold, what is it?" she cried. "My dear, what's the matter?"

I had to think and act quickly, for I had seen something which made me realize how near I had been to disaster.

"Nothing," I said, as if in pain. "It's only my arm—I got a bullet in it, you know."

"A bullet? But when? How? Let me see!"

"Not now—I'm all right again. I'm not hurt, really, only I didn't want to wear the sling in case it worried you. It's only a graze, but it made me feel a bit silly for a moment: because I'm all worked up, I dare say."

In truth I was mostly master of myself once more by now, though, sitting in Dr. Paul's arm-chair as calmly as could be expected considering that Rhona was a mere two yards away. Yet inwardly I still trembled, for I alone knew how close to failure I had gone, how nearly he had bluffed me.

The drawing-room mantel-piece was of oak, supported by a deeply carved panel; and in the centre of this, well enough hidden in a gargoyle's mouth to serve for nine cases out of ten, was a microphone. How I had ever spotted the thing still mystifies me: perhaps some instinct warned me to beware of guile. However, the fact remained that in another moment I should have said too much, and so given away the whole game. I felt as certain as if I watched him that the doctor had made some excuse to Malcolm, and was now intently listening to every word that passed my lips.

"Well, about this proposed proposal," I resumed with a smile. "You understand what it means, of course?"

"Of course—and I don't give a damn. There—could a modest girl go further? Do get on, Arnold!"

But I still held back, for I had an audience of two.

"No fortune—nothing but two thousand guineas and me," I declared. "Yet it's the only way of freeing you, my dear."

"And that's why you're doing it?" she demanded, colouring. "If you propose like that I'll never let you say another word to me!"

I sighed, for I was plainly making a hash of things.

"Well, I'll put it this way," I tried again. "I'm asking you to marry me for two reasons—because I love you and because I don't know how else to get you away from here without at least three months' delay. If you accept only on account of the second reason, I shall understand. If you could possibly like the first one as well, then—then I'm afraid I shan't understand, but just be very happy and very—very—Oh Lord, help me out, Rhona—I'm getting worse!"

But her answer was in her blue eyes.

"Well, I must say defeat's extremely pleasant," I told her presently. "Maybe that's because I'm the winner and not the loser, though."

"Bunkum!" she retorted. "It's only the money I've lost, and I'd a million times rather have what I've found. And anyway, it was an honourable defeat."

"Yes, I think we could call it that. Tell me how you guessed."

But she shook her head, smiling mysteriously.

"I couldn't," she said. "I don't think I even know. I just—guessed. You're *sure* we can really get married tonight?"

"Certain, so long as the doctor's done his part and got you made sensible again."

"Oh yes, he filled in all the forms before you came."

"Well, I'll believe you: but I shouldn't have thought so, the daft way you're behaving."

"Now be careful!" she warned me. "I haven't yet—I can always change my mind now I'm in it."

A few minutes later Dr. Paul returned, and by his manner unwittingly satisfied me that I had disposed of his last suspicions.

## XXVI

**M**ALCOLM LEANT ACROSS, tapped me on the arm, and whispered in my ear.

"Oh lord!" I muttered foolishly, and looked at Dr. Paul.

"I'm awfully sorry, Doctor," I said, "but I clean forgot the parcels—left the wretched things in the back of the car."

"The parcels?" he repeated.

"Yes, odds and ends I bought this afternoon: a present or two for Rhona, and a new dress."

"Oh, how nice!" she exclaimed. " 'Something old and something new, Something borrowed and something blue'—isn't that how it goes? I think you ought to make quite a good husband, really."

Dr. Paul agreed slyly that it was possible, rang the bell, and sent Brett out for the packages. When they were undone Rhona's pleasure was evident in her eyes.

"Will the dress fit?" I asked.

"I'll make it, somehow," she assured me. "It looks absolutely perfect."

She turned to her legal guardian, lately her persecutor and foe.

"Could I go somewhere to put it on, please?" she enquired.

"Of course, my dear, of course." He was all geniality. "I'm sorry Gloria isn't here to help you, but doubtless Mrs. Miggs the housekeeper will do her best."

He rang again, and Rhona departed in the wake of a hard-faced woman of forty with bony hands. At the door she glanced back smiling, and the doctor nodded approval.

"She likes you," he observed innocently. "Mutual affection is a good beginning."

For some five minutes we chatted idly: then he picked up the jade buddha.

"It's a fine specimen," he told me after intent examination, and with the air of one knowing about such things to the last detail. "If you paid less than £50 for it you obtained a bargain."

"Really?" I murmured. "This seems to be my lucky day."

I spoke a trifle bitterly, and he gave me an understanding smile.

"And mine too, I would say, if it didn't seem heartless."

"Oh, don't let that stop you. By the way, Doctor, I suppose Rhona's been properly de-certified?"

"Of course," he answered, and patted his coat. "But one signature is needed to complete every formality—my own. The moment you two are married my pen shall be at your service—I pledge you my word on that."

"Thank you," I said, and relapsed into silence. It appeared that he didn't mean to be caught napping.

"You'll want the usual number of witnesses, I presume?" he went on, addressing Malcolm's brother. "Exactly—it will be a pleasure. Have you ever married anyone by special licence before?"

"Never," replied the young clergyman amiably. "My work lies in the East End, you know. They don't go in much for this sort of thing down there."

Three minutes later the doctor looked towards me again.

"Nervous, Mr. Dane?" he asked.

"Yes, a little," I admitted. "They say one always is, the first time."

"So I believe. And you're somewhat depressed too, perhaps? But it was a good chase while it lasted, and you put up a really splendid fight. A losing one, of course, but then you could scarcely hope to succeed almost single-handed."

I nodded glum agreement.

"Now, I don't quite like that 'almost'!" put in Malcolm, more lightly, and the doctor laughed, his amber eyes amused.

"I take it back!" he said generously. "You fought well, all of you, but more is necessary than luck and the energy of youth. What a long time Rhona's taking! I shall soon begin to think she's changing her mind instead of her frock."

"If so, there'll be a row," I remarked. "At least you shan't be the only person to get what you want. Still got the ring, Malcolm?"

"I've still got all six of them," he replied solemnly.

"Six?" echoed his brother. "Why so many spares?"

But he was never answered, for at that instant came the sound for which I had been waiting: the sharp sudden screech of a car horn. A second later it was repeated, and in that moment we three acted. The parson slid quietly to the door, in his hand now a most unclerical-looking pistol, Malcolm displayed himself as similarly armed, while I rose to my feet and faced Dr. Paul.

"Not definitely a losing fight, sir," I said, and saw his black brows meet grimly. Suddenly he appeared to be crouching rather than sitting, and the atmosphere was electric.

"Your present safety depends upon raising your hands above your head and keeping them there," I continued. "Also, there will be no marriage, for the simple reason that Rhona's no longer here."

He obeyed my hint slowly, his face again impassive. Not by the blink of an eyelid did he betray his feelings for quite ten seconds: then he smiled, subtly scornful.

"Strong-arm stuff at the eleventh hour?" he asked mildly. "Really, I thought better of you."

But I too smiled, for I knew more than he did.

"The eleventh hour is just the right time for it," I said. "Especially when it's going to be effective, and I promise you this lot is. Shall I explain the position, just in case you aren't clear?"

"Please do."

"Then it amounts to saying that when we came here this evening there were four of us, and not three. We dropped Gloria a couple of hundred yards from the gates, but of course she knew how to get in without attracting attention."

That seemed to shake him slightly. His yellow eyes narrowed, and his smile grew less apparent.

"I see—a turncoat," he remarked.

"Well, I prefer to call her a convert," I rejoined. "The car hooter you doubtless heard just now was a signal that she had accounted for Mrs. Miggs and got Rhona safely away. That being so, there's nothing between us and success but the matter of the certificate in your pocket."

"No?" he murmured, but as if he were not altogether sure of his ground.

"No," I said. "Of course, things might have been different if I hadn't spotted that microphone in the mantel-piece, but luckily I did. Hence I was able to deceive you when I proposed to Rhona by deceiving her too: not in saying I wanted her to marry me, but in suggesting it happened tonight. Still, that didn't matter. I managed to tell her afterwards under my breath that at all costs she must trust Gloria."

"And you're sitting there waiting to be rescued!" Malcolm broke in, rather mockingly. "You think Brett and the other ruffians are bound to have heard, but you're wrong. They're all fast asleep by now, thanks again to Gloria. The second toot on the horn told us that."

"So!" grunted the doctor softly, and sat frowning. His hands were still uplifted, and his manner was distinctly troubled, more so than I had ever seen it. Yet for a moment only: then his rigid self-control enabled him to look up and smile almost whimsically.

"And to round things off you'd like me to sign in the appropriate place and send you away with my blessing?" he suggested. "Very well: *how are you going to persuade me?*"

"So you're game to the end," said Malcolm. "I thought you would be, somehow. Still, we never supposed we'd have everything our own way just for the asking."

He leant forward, felt inside the doctor's coat, and pulled out a long white envelope. This he tossed to his brother, still on guard at the door.

"Just vet it, Tom," he requested. "Incidentally, he's qualified to," he explained. "He spent the day learning how, with the help of sundry friends."

"It needs only his signature," was the verdict, "and the sooner the better as far as I'm concerned. Then we can go somewhere and eat—I'm hungry."

"Which means I'd better cut things short," I said. "Now, Dr. Paul, I expect you'll recognize a hypodermic needle when you see one?"

He nodded, in no way alarmed to judge by his face.

"You're not murderers, any of you," he declared firmly. "I'd stake my life on that, and shall do if the occasion arises. In fact, in my opinion you're incapable of anything which could make me alter my determination not to sign that form. There, gentlemen, that's my answer to all these heroics. Rhona comes of age tomorrow, and she has been here in the presence of witnesses since last Tuesday, which annuls any question of her automatic reversion to legal sanity by reason of having been at liberty for a fortnight. I admit, reluctantly, that you bamboozled me very cleverly over this proposed marriage, but three plain facts remain. Without that certificate you're powerless to claim the fortune, in its present condition it's useless, and I will *not* amend it."

"There was never any thought of murdering you," I pointed out. "Nevertheless, Dr. Paul, I fancy you're going to sign and be thankful for the opportunity. Death isn't the only weapon that counts: you yourself showed me a better. This needle contains my version of your amorous dentist—you remember you once threatened me with his activities? Very well: I threaten you now with the effects of that South-American drug you employed on Rhona, and you know as well as I do just how hideous those effects can be.

"In other words, you old scoundrel, if you don't fill up that form double-quick then in half a minute, or half an hour, or however long it takes the stuff to work, you'll be indistinguishable from a maniac."

"And in case Arnold forgets to mention it," interrupted Malcolm, "let me remind you that by your own account—so Gloria says—you're the only person who knows how to counteract the drug: and you mightn't be able to make anyone understand."

"I might also add that the contents of this needle are entirely genuine," I observed. "Gloria pinched it for me on Saturday night. It smells of faintly a cross between garlic and orris root, doesn't it? I thought so."

And now, in defeat, we saw the full quality of the man. What I should have done in his place I can't say, but I'm certain I should never have schooled myself to behave with such stupendous coolness in the face of what must have been the ruin of all his plans. He glanced at the needle which Malcolm held, stared at me closely until he was satisfied that I meant business, then shrugged. He was beaten, and he knew it, for his experience of insanity was too deep for him to relish contracting even an artificial brand.

"Give me a pen, please," he requested. "Not one person in a thousand would have noticed that microphone, and that's the only thing which saved you apart from Gloria's defection. However, I consider it extremely improbable that you'll always be so fortunate, Mr. Dane"—and for a second his eyes held nothing but naked hostility.

"Perhaps—perhaps not," I said. "I should hate to prophesy. And finally, Doctor, now that you've signed you're going to receive instead a shot of what I believe is technically known as No. 6. We'd rather have you out of action, just in case."

Before he could expostulate Malcolm had given it to him from a second needle, and a minute afterwards Dr. Herman Paul lay inert and senseless in the middle of his drawing-room carpet: in almost the exact position, as far as I could tell, which had not so long ago been occupied by Jervis Brown's coffin. It was all over, and without fireworks, and if the conclusion of so much hurrying and scurrying, capture and escape, move and counter-move, seems tame, I can only say that none of us regretted it. We had had enough of excitement: we felt we deserved a spell of peace.

We left him there, his head pillowed by a cushion, his breathing even but stertorous. I wondered as I went out if in similar circumstances he would have treated me as kindly, and had my doubts.

And so, in the end, the luck of the game was ours, and we look well on it. The following day, Tuesday, Rhona came of age and claimed her fortune. She also did me the honour of becoming my wife, and so far has never said she regretted the action. Malcolm had his share of the money, all we could make him accept, and his aunt and Gloria and Jervis Brown were not forgotten.

Yes, life goes very smoothly now, and very very happily: yet sometimes I wonder if it will endure. Six months have passed since I last saw Dr. Paul, and beyond the fact that he sailed for Egypt at the beginning of December we have heard nothing of him. He did not appear to contest the will, needless to say, and he sent us neither present nor good wishes. It may be that he has gone out of our lives, and it may be otherwise. I still remember the significant wording of the last remark he made to me, and the expression in his eyes. One day, perhaps, he will turn up again: then it will be time for us to watch out.

Meanwhile, Doctor, kindly take note that we both go armed.

THE END

# RAMBLE HOUSE's
## HARRY STEPHEN KEELER WEBWORK MYSTERIES
(RH) indicates the title is available ONLY in the **RAMBLE HOUSE** edition

The Ace of Spades Murder
The Affair of the Bottled Deuce (RH)
The Amazing Web
The Barking Clock
Behind That Mask
The Book with the Orange Leaves
The Bottle with the Green Wax Seal
The Box from Japan
The Case of the Canny Killer
The Case of the Crazy Corpse (RH)
The Case of the Flying Hands (RH)
The Case of the Ivory Arrow
The Case of the Jeweled Ragpicker
The Case of the Lavender Gripsack
The Case of the Mysterious Moll
The Case of the 16 Beans
The Case of the Transparent Nude (RH)
The Case of the Transposed Legs
The Case of the Two-Headed Idiot (RH)
The Case of the Two Strange Ladies
The Circus Stealers (RH)
Cleopatra's Tears
A Copy of Beowulf (RH)
The Crimson Cube (RH)
The Face of the Man From Saturn
Find the Clock
The Five Silver Buddhas
The 4th King
The Gallows Waits, My Lord! (RH)
The Green Jade Hand
Finger! Finger!
Hangman's Nights (RH)
I, Chameleon (RH)
I Killed Lincoln at 10:13! (RH)
The Iron Ring
The Man Who Changed His Skin (RH)
The Man with the Crimson Box
The Man with the Magic Eardrums
The Man with the Wooden Spectacles
The Marceau Case
The Matilda Hunter Murder
The Monocled Monster
The Murder of London Lew
The Murdered Mathematician
The Mysterious Card (RH)
The Mysterious Ivory Ball of Wong Shing Li (RH)
The Mystery of the Fiddling Cracksman
The Peacock Fan
The Photo of Lady X (RH)
The Portrait of Jirjohn Cobb
Report on Vanessa Hewstone (RH)
Riddle of the Travelling Skull
Riddle of the Wooden Parrakeet (RH)
The Scarlet Mummy (RH)
The Search for X-Y-Z
The Sharkskin Book
Sing Sing Nights
The Six From Nowhere (RH)
The Skull of the Waltzing Clown
The Spectacles of Mr. Cagliostro
Stand By—London Calling!
The Steeltown Strangler
The Stolen Gravestone (RH)
Strange Journey (RH)
The Strange Will
The Straw Hat Murders (RH)
The Street of 1000 Eyes (RH)
Thieves' Nights
Three Novellos (RH)
The Tiger Snake
The Trap (RH)
Vagabond Nights (Defrauded Yeggman)
Vagabond Nights 2 (10 Hours)
The Vanishing Gold Truck
The Voice of the Seven Sparrows
The Washington Square Enigma
When Thief Meets Thief
The White Circle (RH)
The Wonderful Scheme of Mr. Christopher Thorne
X. Jones—of Scotland Yard
Y. Cheung, Business Detective

## Keeler Related Works

**A To Izzard: A Harry Stephen Keeler Companion** by Fender Tucker — Articles and stories about Harry, by Harry, and in his style. Included is a compleat bibliography.

**Wild About Harry: Reviews of Keeler Novels** — Edited by Richard Polt & Fender Tucker — 22 reviews of works by Harry Stephen Keeler from *Keeler News*. A perfect introduction to the author.

**The Keeler Keyhole Collection:** Annotated newsletter rants from Harry Stephen Keeler, edited by Francis M. Nevins. Over 400 pages of incredibly personal Keeleriana.

**Fakealoo** — Pastiches of the style of Harry Stephen Keeler by selected demented members of the HSK Society. Updated every year with the new winner.

# RAMBLE HOUSE's OTHER LOONS

**The End of It All and Other Stories** — Ed Gorman's latest short story collection
**Four Dancing Tuatara Press Books** — *Beast or Man?* By Sean M'Guire; *The Whistling Ancestors* by Richard E. Goddard; *The Shadow on the House* and *Sorcerer's Chessmen* by Mark Hansom. With introductions by John Pelan
**The Dumpling** — Political murder from 1907 by Coulson Kernahan
**Victims & Villains** — Intriguing Sherlockiana from Derham Groves
**Evidence in Blue** — 1938 mystery by E. Charles Vivian
**The Case of the Little Green Men** — Mack Reynolds wrote this love song to sci-fi fans back in 1951 and it's now back in print.
**Hell Fire** — A new hard-boiled novel by Jack Moskovitz about an arsonist, an arson cop and a Nazi hooker. It isn't pretty.
**Researching American-Made Toy Soldiers** — A 276-page collection of a lifetime of articles by toy soldier expert Richard O'Brien
**Strands of the Web: Short Stories of Harry Stephen Keeler** — Edited and Introduced by Fred Cleaver
**The Sam McCain Novels** — Ed Gorman's terrific series includes *The Day the Music Died*, *Wake Up Little Susie* and *Will You Still Love Me Tomorrow?*
**A Shot Rang Out** — Three decades of reviews from Jon Breen
**Mysterious Martin, the Master of Murder** — Two versions of a strange 1912 novel by Tod Robbins about a man who writes books that can kill.
**Dago Red** — 22 tales of dark suspense by Bill Pronzini
**The Night Remembers** — A 1991 Jack Walsh mystery from Ed Gorman
**Rough Cut & New, Improved Murder** — Ed Gorman's first two novels
**Hollywood Dreams** — A novel of the Depression by Richard O'Brien
**Seven Gelett Burgess Novels** — *The Master of Mysteries*, *The White Cat*, *Two O'Clock Courage*, *Ladies in Boxes*, *Find the Woman*, *The Heart Line*, *The Picaroons*
**The Organ Reader** — A huge compilation of just about everything published in the 1971-1972 radical bay-area newspaper, *THE ORGAN*.
**A Clear Path to Cross** — Sharon Knowles short mystery stories by Ed Lynskey
**Old Times' Sake** — Short stories by James Reasoner from Mike Shayne Magazine
**Freaks and Fantasies** — Eerie tales by Tod Robbins, collaborator of Tod Browning on the film FREAKS.
**Six Jim Harmon Double Novels** — *Vixen Hollow/Celluloid Scandal*, *The Man Who Made Maniacs/Silent Siren*, *Ape Rape/Wanton Witch*, *Sex Burns Like Fire/Twist Session*, *Sudden Lust/Passion Strip*, *Sin Unlimited/Harlot Master*, *Twilight Girls/Sex Institution*. Written in the early 60s.
**Marblehead: A Novel of H.P. Lovecraft** — A long-lost masterpiece from Richard A. Lupoff. Published for the first time!
**The Compleat Ova Hamlet** — Parodies of SF authors by Richard A. Lupoff – A brand new edition with more stories and more illustrations by Trina Robbins.
**The Secret Adventures of Sherlock Holmes** — Three Sherlockian pastiches by the Brooklyn author/publisher, Gary Lovisi.
**The Universal Holmes** — Richard A. Lupoff's 2007 collection of five Holmesian pastiches and a recipe for giant rat stew.
**Four Joel Townsley Rogers Novels** — By the author of *The Red Right Hand*: *Once In a Red Moon*, *Lady With the Dice*, *The Stopped Clock*, *Never Leave My Bed*
**Two Joel Townsley Rogers Story Collections** — *Night of Horror* and *Killing Time*
**Twenty Norman Berrow Novels** — *The Bishop's Sword*, *Ghost House*, *Don't Go Out After Dark*, *Claws of the Cougar*, *The Smokers of Hashish*, *The Secret Dancer*, *Don't Jump Mr. Boland!*, *The Footprints of Satan*, *Fingers for Ransom*, *The Three Tiers of Fantasy*, *The Spaniard's Thumb*, *The Eleventh Plague*, *Words Have Wings*, *One Thrilling Night*, *The Lady's in Danger*, *It Howls at Night*, *The Terror in the Fog*, *Oil Under the Window*, *Murder in the Melody*, *The Singing Room*
**The N. R. De Mexico Novels** — Robert Bragg presents *Marijuana Girl*, *Madman on a Drum*, *Private Chauffeur* in one volume.
**Four Chelsea Quinn Yarbro Novels featuring Charlie Moon** — *Ogilvie, Tallant and Moon*, *Music When the Sweet Voice Dies*, *Poisonous Fruit* and *Dead Mice*
**Five Walter S. Masterman Mysteries** — *The Green Toad*, *The Flying Beast*, *The Yellow Mistletoe*, *The Wrong Verdict* and *The Perjured Alibi*. Fantastic impossible plots.
**Two Hake Talbot Novels** — *Rim of the Pit*, *The Hangman's Handyman*. Classic locked room mysteries.
**Two Alexander Laing Novels** — *The Motives of Nicholas Holtz* and *Dr. Scarlett*, stories of medical mayhem and intrigue from the 30s.

**Four David Hume Novels** — *Corpses Never Argue, Cemetery First Stop, Make Way for the Mourners, Eternity Here I Come*, and more to come.

**Three Wade Wright Novels** — *Echo of Fear, Death At Nostalgia Street* and *It Leads to Murder*, with more to come!

**Eight Rupert Penny Novels** — *Policeman's Holiday, Policeman's Evidence, Lucky Policeman, Policeman in Armour, Sealed Room Murder, Sweet Poison, The Talkative Policeman, She had to Have Gas* and *Cut and Run* (by Martin Tanner.)

**Five Jack Mann Novels** — Strange murder in the English countryside. *Gees' First Case, Nightmare Farm, Grey Shapes, The Ninth Life, The Glass Too Many.*

**Seven Max Afford Novels** — *Owl of Darkness, Death's Mannikins, Blood on His Hands, The Dead Are Blind, The Sheep and the Wolves, Sinners in Paradise* and Two Locked Room Mysteries and a Ripping Yarn by one of Australia's finest novelists.

**Five Joseph Shallit Novels** — *The Case of the Billion Dollar Body, Lady Don't Die on My Doorstep, Kiss the Killer, Yell Bloody Murder, Take Your Last Look*. One of America's best 50's authors.

**Two Crimson Clown Novels** — By Johnston McCulley, author of the Zorro novels, *The Crimson Clown* and *The Crimson Clown Again*.

**The Best of 10-Story Book** — edited by Chris Mikul, over 35 stories from the literary magazine Harry Stephen Keeler edited.

**A Young Man's Heart** — A forgotten early classic by Cornell Woolrich

**The Anthony Boucher Chronicles** — edited by Francis M. Nevins
Book reviews by Anthony Boucher written for the *San Francisco Chronicle,* 1942 – 1947. Essential and fascinating reading.

**Muddled Mind: Complete Works of Ed Wood, Jr.** — David Hayes and Hayden Davis deconstruct the life and works of a mad genius.

**Gadsby** — A lipogram (a novel without the letter E). Ernest Vincent Wright's last work, published in 1939 right before his death.

**My First Time:** The One Experience You Never Forget — Michael Birchwood — 64 true first-person narratives of how they lost it.

**A Roland Daniel Double: The Signal and The Return of Wu Fang** — Classic thrillers from the 30s

**Murder in Shawnee** — Two novels of the Alleghenies by John Douglas: *Shawnee Alley Fire* and *Haunts*.

**Deep Space and other Stories** — A collection of SF gems by Richard A. Lupoff

**Blood Moon** — The first of the Robert Payne series by Ed Gorman

**The Time Armada** — Fox B. Holden's 1953 SF gem.

**Black River Falls** — Suspense from the master, Ed Gorman

**Sideslip** — 1968 SF masterpiece by Ted White and Dave Van Arnam

**The Triune Man** — Mindscrambling science fiction from Richard A. Lupoff

**Detective Duff Unravels It** — Episodic mysteries by Harvey O'Higgins

**Automaton** — Brilliant treatise on robotics: 1928-style! By H. Stafford Hatfield

**The Incredible Adventures of Rowland Hern** — Rousing 1928 impossible crimes by Nicholas Olde.

**Slammer Days** — Two full-length prison memoirs: *Men into Beasts* (1952) by George Sylvester Viereck and *Home Away From Home* (1962) by Jack Woodford

**Murder in Black and White** — 1931 classic tennis whodunit by Evelyn Elder

**Killer's Caress** — Cary Moran's 1936 hardboiled thriller

**The Golden Dagger** — 1951 Scotland Yard yarn by E. R. Punshon

**A Smell of Smoke** — 1951 English countryside thriller by Miles Burton

**Ruled By Radio** — 1925 futuristic novel by Robert L. Hadfield & Frank E. Farncombe

**Murder in Silk** — A 1937 Yellow Peril novel of the silk trade by Ralph Trevor

**The Case of the Withered Hand** — 1936 potboiler by John G. Brandon

**Finger-prints Never Lie** — A 1939 classic detective novel by John G. Brandon

**Inclination to Murder** — 1966 thriller by New Zealand's Harriet Hunter

**Invaders from the Dark** — Classic werewolf tale from Greye La Spina

**Fatal Accident** — Murder by automobile, a 1936 mystery by Cecil M. Wills

**The Devil Drives** — A prison and lost treasure novel by Virgil Markham

**Dr. Odin** — Douglas Newton's 1933 potboiler comes back to life.

**The Chinese Jar Mystery** — Murder in the manor by John Stephen Strange, 1934

**The Julius Caesar Murder Case** — A classic 1935 re-telling of the assassination by Wallace Irwin that's much more fun than the Shakespeare version

**West Texas War and Other Western Stories** — by Gary Lovisi

**The Contested Earth and Other SF Stories** — A never-before published space opera and seven short stories by Jim Harmon.

**Tales of the Macabre and Ordinary** — Modern twisted horror by Chris Mikul, author of the *Bizarrism* series.

**The Gold Star Line** — Seaboard adventure from L.T. Reade and Robert Eustace.

**The Werewolf vs the Vampire Woman** — Hard to believe ultraviolence by either Arthur M. Scarm or Arthur M. Scram.
**Black Hogan Strikes Again** — Australia's Peter Renwick pens a tale of the outback.
**Don Diablo: Book of a Lost Film** — Two-volume treatment of a western by Paul Landres, with diagrams. Intro by Francis M. Nevins.
**The Charlie Chaplin Murder Mystery** — Movie hijinks by Wes D. Gehring
**The Koky Comics** — A collection of all of the 1978-1981 Sunday and daily comic strips by Richard O'Brien and Mort Gerberg, in two volumes.
**Suzy** — Another collection of comic strips from Richard O'Brien and Bob Vojtko
**Dime Novels: Ramble House's 10-Cent Books** — *Knife in the Dark* by Robert Leslie Bellem, *Hot Lead* and *Song of Death* by Ed Earl Repp, *A Hashish House in New York* by H.H. Kane, and five more.
**Blood in a Snap** — The *Finnegan's Wake* of the 21$^{st}$ century, by Jim Weiler
**Stakeout on Millennium Drive** — Award-winning Indianapolis Noir — Ian Woollen.
**Dope Tales #1** — Two dope-riddled classics; *Dope Runners* by Gerald Grantham and *Death Takes the Joystick* by Phillip Condé.
**Dope Tales #2** — Two more narco-classics; *The Invisible Hand* by Rex Dark and *The Smokers of Hashish* by Norman Berrow.
**Dope Tales #3** — Two enchanting novels of opium by the master, Sax Rohmer. *Dope* and *The Yellow Claw*.
**Tenebrae** — Ernest G. Henham's 1898 horror tale brought back.
**The Singular Problem of the Stygian House-Boat** — Two classic tales by John Kendrick Bangs about the denizens of Hades.
**Tiresias** — Psychotic modern horror novel by Jonathan M. Sweet.
**The One After Snelling** — Kickass modern noir from Richard O'Brien.
**The Sign of the Scorpion** — 1935 Edmund Snell tale of oriental evil.
**The House of the Vampire** — 1907 poetic thriller by George S. Viereck.
**An Angel in the Street** — Modern hardboiled noir by Peter Genovese.
**The Devil's Mistress** — Scottish gothic tale by J. W. Brodie-Innes.
**The Lord of Terror** — 1925 mystery with master-criminal, Fantômas.
**The Lady of the Terraces** — 1925 adventure by E. Charles Vivian.
**My Deadly Angel** — 1955 Cold War drama by John Chelton
**Prose Bowl** — Futuristic satire — Bill Pronzini & Barry N. Malzberg .
**Satan's Den Exposed —** True crime in Truth or Consequences New Mexico — Award-winning journalism by the *Desert Journal*.
**The Amorous Intrigues & Adventures of Aaron Burr** — by Anonymous — Hot historical action.
**I Stole $16,000,000** — A true story by cracksman Herbert E. Wilson.
**The Black Dark Murders** — Vintage 50s college murder yarn by Milt Ozaki, writing as Robert O. Saber.
**Sex Slave** — Potboiler of lust in the days of Cleopatra — Dion Leclerq.
**You'll Die Laughing** — Bruce Elliott's 1945 novel of murder at a practical joker's English countryside manor.
**The Private Journal & Diary of John H. Surratt** — The memoirs of the man who conspired to assassinate President Lincoln.
**Dead Man Talks Too Much** — Hollywood boozer by Weed Dickenson
**Red Light** — History of legal prostitution in Shreveport Louisiana by Eric Brock. Includes wonderful photos of the houses and the ladies.
**A Snark Selection** — Lewis Carroll's *The Hunting of the Snark* with two Snarkian chapters by Harry Stephen Keeler — Illustrated by Gavin L. O'Keefe.
**Ripped from the Headlines!** — The Jack the Ripper story as told in the newspaper articles in the *New York* and *London Times*.
**Geronimo** — S. M. Barrett's 1905 autobiography of a noble American.
**The White Peril in the Far East** — Sidney Lewis Gulick's 1905 indictment of the West and assurance that Japan would never attack the U.S.
**The Compleat Calhoun** — All of Fender Tucker's works: Includes *Totah Six-Pack, Weed, Women and Song* and *Tales from the Tower,* plus a CD of all of his songs.
**Totah Six-Pack** — Just Fender Tucker's six tales about Farmington in one sleek volume.

## RAMBLE HOUSE
Fender Tucker, Prop.
www.ramblehouse.com   fender@ramblehouse.com
228-826-1783   10329 Sheephead Drive, Vancleave MS 39565

Printed in Great Britain
by Amazon.co.uk, Ltd.,
Marston Gate.